Blackrock Island

David Lewis Paget

BARR BOOKS

For all my old Air Force friends
who served and suffered with me
at Wagga, Townsville, Williamstown,
Point Cook and Edinburgh
1966 – 1974

Chapter One

John Varley held onto the phone for a few moments after the caller had hung up, and then replaced it in its cradle with a shaking hand. He looked a little dazed, as if he didn't quite know where he was. He looked aimlessly around the room, then pulled the curtains aside and peered along the street. It was twenty minutes before he heard the expected knock at the door. He got wearily up and out of his chair, and shuffled out of the lounge room to the passageway. His joints had stiffened up in recent years, and he moved slowly.

Between the lounge room and the front door, a thousand thoughts were racing through his mind. He knew what they wanted, and the thought of going through all that again made him feel physically sick. He didn't want any part of it. He saw the outline of a man through the glass in the front door, and suddenly there was a feeling of inevitability about it all, as if events that had happened 34 years before were finally coming to some sort of closure. He opened the door.

'John Varley,' the figure said, tentatively. The man was in full uniform, and he carried a briefcase under his arm, tucked in tight as if he was protecting it.

'That's right. You've come to the right place,' said Varley, standing aside to allow him to enter. He closed the door behind him, and pointed in the direction of the lounge.

'It might be better if we sit at a table. Do you have a table...?' The stranger tailed off, and looked about him.

'In the kitchen. Just go through that door.'

They made their way into the kitchen, and the officer placed his briefcase on the table, opened it, and extracted a handful of documents and a small hand-held tape recorder.

'You don't mind if I tape our conversation?'

Varley shook his head, and took a seat opposite. The pale afternoon sun filtered through the curtains, and Varley stared at them in abstraction. For some unaccountable reason he suddenly thought that it was about time they were taken down and washed. They hadn't been touched since his wife passed away.

'I'm a pretty poor substitute for a housekeeper,' he said, causing the other man to look up, quizzically. Varley avoided looking at him directly, but gazed vacantly around the room as if there was something on his mind.

'Well, let's get to introductions. I'm Squadron Leader Geoff Parker, I know who you are... you can just call me Geoff if that's what you'd prefer.'

Varley focussed his attention on the visitor for the first time, noting the hawk-like nose and the dominant brow.

'I would! The air force cured me of titles and ranks.'

Varley spoke bitterly, like someone who is opening up old wounds.

'Anyway, just how 'official' is this enquiry of yours? I told my story over thirty years ago to the panel they set up at the time. The only result of that was that I was threatened, and told to keep my mouth shut. They threatened me with the Official Secrets Act, seven years jail if I spoke to anyone, or revealed anything of what had taken place. Surely you have access to that report?'

The Squadron Leader looked at him, unsmiling, and shook his head.

'Suppressed,' he said, 'and now lost, it seems. The powers that were, in the '60's, obviously didn't want it to get out.'

Varley relaxed a little.

'So why now? It's old hat, isn't it?'

The Squadron Leader shrugged.

'It's a piece of history that – from the Air Force point of view – is in danger of being lost. You do know that Phil Cusack died last month?'

Varley looked at him through hooded eyes, wary eyes.

Parker thought that they were cold and reptilian, but pushed the thought away. He didn't have to like the man.

'No... No! I didn't know that. I haven't heard from him for a couple of years now. Not that he was ever a friend of mine, you understand. It was only because of the circumstances...'

'...that you were thrown together at all?' the officer cut in. Varley nodded. He found himself staring at those bars on Parker's shoulder. Two and a half bars! Squadron Leader!

'Well, he was an M.T. Fitter and driver. We didn't have much in common.'

'But you *did* keep in touch... over the years! From what I understand, you used to meet once or twice a year.'

Varley nodded, and stared into the middle distance. He was redrawing that anxious face from memory, the almost pleading look that Cusack would get in his eyes at those times when Varley most felt like throwing caution to the winds, and telling it all.

That had happened every time the media came chasing him, offering him pots of money for the story behind the two lost Neptunes. Varley had been tempted, more than tempted as the offers grew in size over the years. He could have done with a nice little lump sum, to cushion his inability to hold onto a job once he'd been discharged. But as the offers came in, so did the visits from the Military Police, warning him of consequences. They'd visited Cusack too. Cusack had been of an extremely nervous disposition. Now he was dead!'

'November 20th,' he said, breaking the silence. 'It was the same every year. That was the date of the flight, you see. The crash actually happened on the 21st, but it was the flight date that we commemorated, because we were both of us last minute additions. They told us on the morning of the 20th to get our gear together, because we would be flying out at three o'clock. It was a shock at the time… Unexpected! The crew list had been up for weeks, and as far as we knew, we'd missed out. Then an Instrument Fitter, Jervies, went down with the flu, and I was seconded to his place. Cusack was pulled in at the last minute because the Wing Commander wanted his own personal driver when we got to Barbers Point, and there wasn't one.'

'Wing Commander Fletcher,' Parker commented, and made a note on his pad. Varley felt his lip curl at the mention of his name, and grunted as if in reply.

'That's right! Wing Commander Fletcher. Arrogant bastard!'

Parker looked up at Varley, and raised an eyebrow.

'I take it that you didn't care for the Wing Commander?'

'That would be an understatement,' Varley replied, and he could almost taste the bitterness he still felt after all these years. He was silent for a moment, then said, 'look… is there any real point to this? You bastards have made me bottle this up for, what… thirty-five years, on pain of imprisonment. Now, all of a sudden, you show up out of the blue, wanting to go over the whole rotten mess once more, dredging up the past. What's occurred in the meantime that's made you change your minds?'

The Squadron Leader put his pen down, and sat back in his chair.

'Politics!' he said. 'Just politics! All the players are off the stage now, except you. You're the only one that was actually there. Cusack's gone, and now I understand that your own health isn't exactly what it was. You're not getting any younger… how old are you now - Sixty?'

'Fifty-nine. I'll be sixty in January… if I make it, that is.'

The Squadron Leader willed him to continue.

'I understand there may be some doubt about your chances!'

Varley touched his throat with the fingers of his right hand. 'I start chemo next week. They say it's about sixty-forty against.' He found it suddenly painful to talk. He could feel the lump in his throat, and it was getting bigger.

'I'm sorry to hear that. But that makes it all the more urgent.' Parker twined his fingers together, and stared down at the table, as if wrestling with some inner problem.

'Look, I'll lay my cards on the table. I've had to fight for this! There were a lot who said 'leave sleeping dogs lie', but I've never believed in that! I'm a historian first, an Air Force Officer second. I think your story needs to be told, and – who knows? They may learn something from it. At the very least you will get the opportunity to set the record straight. Isn't that what you want?'

Varley thought of Cusack, and he thought of Morris. Then a picture of Danny Seaman rose up in his mind, and he just felt angry. But most of all, he thought of Bill O'Connell! He nodded. Oh yes! He wanted to set the record straight, all right.

'How do you know that I'll tell the truth? I might just make up some things, and gloss over others. What's the statute of limitations with things like this? Could I be prosecuted for something that happened 34 years ago?'

'They're not going to do anything to you in your condition. No one's out for vengeance! There's no one left who might have an axe to grind over this! It's just that we need to know... which of course means that we want the truth. I can pretty well guarantee immunity from prosecution, no matter what you did. After all, there's no corroborating evidence. By the time anyone even worked up a case it would be ten years down the track...'

'...and I'd be dead,' said Varley, quietly. 'All the same, give me one good reason why I should. After all, I *know* what happened, and that's good enough for me.'

Parker bit his lip in a ruminative fashion, then sat forward in his seat.

'Because they found the Island!'

Varley's jaw dropped, and he turned white as the blood slowly drained from his face. There was a deathly silence for half a minute, and something akin to fear in Varley's cold, distant eyes. Then his shoulders sagged, and he put his head down on the table. Parker saw an old man, grey, worn out... and defeated.

'There's a crew over there right now, gathering up the remains, bringing what's left back for autopsies. It's pretty obvious how some of them died.'

Varley sat up and fell back in his seat. He bit his lip, and looked searchingly at the Squadron Leader, trying to divine how much the man in front of him really knew.

' I suppose... in that case...I've got nothing to lose, have I? How did they find the Island?'

'An Australian Navy vessel came across it on a mapping survey. Remarkable that no one's come across it before, but there it is. One of the Neptune's is still intact, lying in shallow water, the tail showing at low tide. That's what alerted them. The other is in a dense pine forest on the south side of the island, broken in half, but remarkably well preserved. Still, you knew all that!'

'Yes! I knew! A89-286 and A89-292! Those numbers are burnt onto my memory. 286 is in the bay! That's the one I was on. Cusack was on 292, along with the WAAF, Helen. She could be a pain in the neck... but it was rough on her, too.'

Varley swallowed hard when he thought about Helen. If she hadn't been so cold, so condescending...

'So you're going to tell me what happened... from the

beginning!'

Parker looked at Varley across the kitchen table. Varley was suddenly very tired.

'All right... from the beginning... God help me,' he replied.

He paused, passed his hand over his forehead and mouthed silently, 'God help us all!'

II

Some memories become dim over the years. Others disappear altogether! But clear and bright in John Varley's mind burned the memory of his first sight of the Lockheed Neptunes sitting on the tarmac at 10 Squadron, Garbutt, in July 1968. To Varley, they were a beautiful sight, tall and gaunt with a sting on each tail, like scorpions of the air. There they stood, just waiting for him to join them and become part of their history.

It had taken Varley almost two years to get to that point, his first active posting. After an Instrument Mechanics and then an Instrument Fitters course at the RAAF School of Technical Training, he was about to get his first chance to practice his trade, out in the field. He had stood at the edge of the tarmac and watched other fitters wandering backwards and forwards between aircraft, carrying out basic servicing, replacing parts, and joking with each other as they went about their daily tasks. Varley remembered feeling a swell of pride rising up within him. This was the goal he'd studied so hard for. This was the beginning of the technical career he had dreamed about.

Although he could remember very vividly the aircraft on that day, he had more trouble in remembering the 24-year-old John Varley, as he was then. The aches and pains of age quickly overcome the vigour and freshness of youth, and once that has gone, it's hard to recall ever feeling young. He had been slim, though broad-shouldered, dark haired with a pale complexion. This might have given an impression of weakness, but the set of his jaw, and the furrows in his brow, that continual look of concentration, just made him look perpetually worried when he was young. Other than that, he hadn't been especially good-looking, nothing that attracted the women. Sometimes he'd thought he must be invisible to them, because it wasn't until his early thirties that he had matured enough to present an interesting challenge to the opposite sex.

Varley was a relatively late entrant into the Air Force, after a variety of menial jobs since leaving school at sixteen. He had begun to look ahead to a time when he would be no longer young, no longer able to jump from one job to the next with impunity. He had worked as a storeman, shop assistant, van salesman, cold-room worker and medical orderly. It was this last job at a Repatriation Hospital that had opened his eyes up to the possibility of joining the Air Force and gaining a trade, even at the advanced age of 22. He was too old for an apprenticeship, but it seemed that the Air Force had places for adult trainees, and it didn't take him long to decide that this might just be the last chance for a career. After making initial enquiries he had made the great leap, and signed on in the September of 1966.

It was a long hard slog. After rookies at Edinburgh in South Australia, he was posted to Wagga to determine if he had the ability to be able to undergo trade training. While waiting for his Trainee Mechanics course, he'd spent time in the Airman's Mess, washing pots and pans and putting up with the indignity of being ordered about by every Cook and General Hand on the base. But that was just part of the indoctrination process. As he mopped toilets and cleaned up after everyone else, he held hard to the notion that eventually he would be able to quit Wagga and get out into the real Air Force, the one that had real aircraft sitting out on the runways, with real pilots and real fitters, using their unassuming expertise to keep the planes in the air, protecting the country.

It had finally come to pass. The Neptune ASW (Anti-Submarine Warfare) aircraft were Australia's front line ocean defence, equipped with sonar and Jezebel and Magnetic Anomaly Detection (M.A.D.), not to mention 'Snifter'. It had all been so exciting at the time.

Varley peered across the table at Parker, and shook his head regretfully at the memory. None of that was what the Squadron Leader was there for! He wasn't interested in the naïve dreams of a young fitter. He didn't want to hear about how soon the cold wind of reality had dispatched that naïve idealism, in a world that was divided by rank and privilege. He just wanted to know what had happened to the other eighteen people who had departed with Varley and Cusack on that day in November 1968, in two RAAF Neptunes... never to be heard from again.

The question was, did Varley want to tell him the truth, or would Parker be satisfied with a gloss over the awful facts. Varley wondered if he could even begin to explain how things had fallen apart so quickly, how sane, rational men had shed their civilised veneer in such a short time, had sunk to such violent depths in a world cut off from time itself.

The other question seemed to be – how much did Parker already know? If Varley knew that, then he might be able to sidestep the traps.

Chapter Two

Two 10 Squadron Neptunes took off from RAAF Base Garbutt, Townsville, at 1500 hours on the 20th November 1968, headed for Fiji. The eventual destination was to be Barbers Point, Hawaii, for a two-week junket, supposedly to liaise with units of the USAF there, promoting friendly relations with Australia's allies in the region. In actual fact, for those lucky enough to be on the flight, it was going to be one big holiday.

On the morning of the 20th, Warrant Officer Danny Seaman called LAC Varley into his office, and made him stand at attention for ten minutes before he condescended to turn around and address him. He made a great show of seeing Varley for the first time.

'Oh, there you are, Varley. Do you know why you're here?'

Seaman took a great delight in spinning out the time he had to lord it over those of the lower ranks, and usually managed to turn each interview into a guessing game, which only he knew the answers to.

'No sir!' said Varley. He had good cause to treat Seaman with suspicion, as he had suffered at his hands on more than one occasion.

'No one has said anything to you this morning?'

'No sir! I have no idea.'

'Surely you've noticed something missing in the section this morning. I thought you were more observant, Varley.'

Varley looked out of the door of the office, and scanned the section, as he knew he was meant to do. After looking around for a few moments, he ventured, 'No, sir. I can't see anything missing. Should I, sir?'

'Well, it's as plain as the nose on your face, Varley. I'm

surprised that no one has primed you, before you arrived over here.'

'Nobody said anything, sir.'

'Well I wouldn't be asking you to come over to my office for nothing, would I, Varley?'

The Warrant Officer looked at him expectantly, waiting for a reply.

'No sir! I'm sure you wouldn't.'

By this time John Varley was becoming rather agitated. He could feel his face turning red, and he had great difficulty in suppressing a natural inclination to grab Danny Seaman by the throat and throw him to the floor.

'You don't seem very interested in this, Varley. Is there somewhere else you would rather be?'

Seaman was really beginning to enjoy himself by now. At fifty-three he only had another eighteen months to retirement, and he was happy to spend it conducting these little conundrums to baffle those in his charge.

'No sir! I was asked to report to you, sir, and that's what I'm doing! Sir!'

'Ordered, Varley! You were *ordered* to report to me. No one *asks* in this man's service. That's the point of having a chain of command. Isn't that so, LAC?'

'Yes, Warrant Officer!'

Varley gritted his teeth, trying to stifle the exasperation in his reply.

'So why do you think you were ordered to report to me, Varley?'

'So that you might convey some instruction, sir.'

The Warrant Officer sat back in his seat, and nodded, grimly.

'And yet I can't believe that an instrument fitter, one of the 'elite' of this man's Air Force, doesn't yet have the perspicacity to work out what he would be wanted for – on this day of all days. What day is it, Varley?'

'I believe it's Wednesday, sir.'

'Yes, yes,' said the Warrant Officer, impatiently. 'But what day is it?'

Varley stopped and thought for a moment. He wasn't usually up on dates.

'Is it the 19th November, sir?'

'No... the 20th, Varley! The 20th of November! Does that ring a bell, Varley?'

Seaman began to drum his fingers on the desk. Varley was desperately trying to think of what specific event must have been planned for the day. He'd obviously forgotten, or the old bastard wouldn't be going on about it.

'Errr... was it trade test day, sir?'

He knew he had a trade test coming up, but surely, that wasn't for another two weeks.

'No. What gives you that idea? You know very well that your trade test can't be undertaken until three months after the previous one. And when was your last one, Varley?'

'Errr... beginning of September, sir.'

'Exactly!' said the warrant officer, nodding his head in self-satisfaction. 'Which gives the next date for your trade test as....'

'Early December, sir!'

The sweat was beginning to break out on Varley's brow by this time, and he began to get a pain in the chest.

'I don't know about you, Varley! I thought you were pretty bright, but you made a mess of pulling that drift meter out last week. I don't know if you're up to it.'

Varley forbore to ask what he was not up to, as he knew it would only raise a whole new round of questions that he was unable to answer.

'The screws were rusted in place, sir. I couldn't get them out...'

'*Corroded*, Varley. The screws were *corroded* in position! Don't you know yet that aluminium doesn't rust? I thought you'd covered that as part of your course, LAC.'

Varley took a deep breath.

'We did, sir. I meant corroded... it was just a slip of the tongue, sir.'

Danny nodded with a grim, self-satisfied smile.

'There's many a slip twixt the cup and the lip, LAC. Just remember that! You're going to have to express yourself more carefully.'

They were both silent for a moment. Varley looked helplessly around him as if willing someone to enter the office from the section to let him off the hook.

'Well, against my better judgement, I've decided to let you go anyway. I just hope that you don't let the section down.'

The LAC shook his head as if to clear his brain.

'Let me go, Warrant...?'

'To Hawaii, Varley! Jervies is off with the flu. That's who I said was missing from the section this morning. You didn't pick it up. Anyway, you're taking his place. You'd better go and get your kit together. Take off at 1500.'

The light finally dawned as Varley's mouth fell open in surprise.

'Oh, right... thank you Warrant? I'm on the trip... I see!'

'You'll be flying on 286. You'd better do the pre-flight, and make sure you get it right.'

Seaman waved his hand in dismissal.

Varley took off out of the section, ran down the stairs and across the hangar. He was elated and fuming at the same time. As he got out onto the tarmac he ripped the beret off his head, threw it on the ground and stamped on it. Bill O'Connell was headed the other way with his kit.

'Hey, hey! What's upset you, Varley?'

'The bastard Warrant Officer, what do you think?'

O'Connell burst out laughing.

'Good old Danny! You copped one of his lectures did you? What was it... Instrument Instructions, AAP's or the wrong colour bootlaces?'

'None of the above! The prick wanted me to play guessing games with him about why he'd called me in. I didn't know what the fuck he was talking about.'

O'Connell laughed again.

'Oh, one of those! Well, join the club, mate. He's got nothing better to do with his time than piss people around. He's going to get decked one of these days.'

'He came close today, mate, I'm telling you! Anyway, it was just to tell me I'm on the trip.'

'Good on you, man!' O'Connell seemed genuinely delighted. 'So you'll be sinking some beers in Hawaii with us. What flight are you on?'

'286. I think it's Danny's flight too, worse luck. What are you on?'

'292! - Thank God!' O'Connell chuckled. 'I'm just heading over to stow my kit. I'll catch you later, mate.'

Varley headed for the living area, while O'Connell continued on to the tarmac.

II

Bill O'Connell was one of the older members of Instrument Section. At 42 he had been in the air force only five years, and as a result was still an LAC Fitter. Bill lived off the base with his wife, a nursing sister. Between them they had purchased a big old building and converted it into an aged persons' home. She ran the establishment; he was the odd job man when he was off duty. They planned to have a profitable business going by the time he was ready to retire.

To the other guys he was the jovial sort, the one who very rarely got upset over anything. Of medium height, stocky and darkly Italianate, problems seemed to slide off O'Connell without touching him, and thanks to his advanced age the officers and NCO's treated him with something approaching respect. He was often the mediator in section squabbles, and usually managed to calm frayed tempers.

O'Connell dropped his kit in the hanger, on a trolley provided for the purpose. Then he headed out to 292 where a pilot was running the jet pods up for a red line. He slipped a pair of ear protectors on and skirted around towards the rear of the aircraft to wait until it was over. The slipstream made it impossible to get onboard, as he had discovered previously to his cost. The slipstream from the two Westinghouse J34 Turbojets could bowl you over.

This time he sat down on the grass verge, and waited. An Armament fitter was acting as battery cart/start-up operator, and was concentrating on instructions from the cockpit. It was a couple of minutes before O'Connell noticed that the fitter was trying to attract his attention, and pointing up towards the pilot. The pilot gestured to him to come on board, and dropped the revs so that O'Connell could get around and climb up through the rear hatch. He climbed over the hump and made his way up to the cabin.

It was Flight Lieutenant Peter Dawson in the cockpit, and he pointed to the G2 Compass System. The dial was spinning, a sure sign that the gyro had toppled. O'Connell tapped the glass, then turned it over to DG. That stabilized the spin, and they could hear the gyro motor increasing its revs to 3200 a minute.

'That's bloody strange,' he remarked to the pilot. 'There seems to be a power problem.'

Dawson was concentrating on the engine instruments, and only spared a glance towards him. 'If it's stuffed, change it,' he yelled, over the scream of the jets.

O'Connell nodded, and switched it back to compass. The gyro motor began to hunt, and he could tell it was losing revs. After two minutes it toppled, and began to spin.

'U/S,' he yelled, and Dawson nodded. 'I'll go back to the section and get a serviceable one.'

He was just about to leave when Dawson pointed to the port pod temperature gauge. It was only barely reading 20 degrees, while the other had run up around the 180 degree mark. Bill shook his head, and grimaced at the pilot.

'It could be the gauge, could be a thermocouple. I'll get somebody out here to have a look at it.' Then he swung out of the seat, and headed down towards the rear of the plane.

Dawson was engrossed with his red line, and forgot to drop the revs to let O'Connell out. As he dropped out of the hatch he felt the full weight of the jet stream in his back and started to run. At the forty-yard mark he tripped and came heavily down on his knees. Giving in to the feeling of the moment he just lay flat on his face in the grass, cursing and holding his right knee in agony.

III

Squadron Leader Graham Styles adjusted his tie, and checked his image in the mirror. What stared back at him was a humourless, well shaven face, with cold eyes and a distinct downturn at the edges of the mouth. Styles took himself seriously, very seriously indeed. He would have been happier about the flight to Hawaii if it hadn't been for the fact that the Wing Commander would be coming along for the ride. Styles was used to being the senior officer on these trips, and he didn't take kindly to being displaced along the pecking order. What made it worse was the fact that Fletcher would be sitting in the co-pilot's seat.

Styles knew from his own personal experience that Wing Commander Fletcher hadn't flown, either as a pilot or co-pilot, in a long, long time. That meant that the entire responsibility for 286 was on his shoulders. Fletcher would just be a passenger. It also meant that he would have to sit and listen to the old buffoon's conversation all through the trip, and that didn't sit well either. Styles resented Fletcher, as only the son of a plumber can resent the son of a wartime fighter ace. He was too full of himself and his own opinions, and he insisted on inflicting them on everybody else.

Then there was the question of rank! Graham Styles resented any of his contemporaries who carried a rank greater than his own, but especially Fletcher, because he had a sneaking suspicion that Fletcher had been pushed along by those higher up, because of who he was, rather than what he was. This really rankled.

His own idea was that he should have been made a Wing Commander at least two years before, and he couldn't help harbouring a suspicion that Fletcher had somehow managed to put a stop to his promotion prospects for the immediate future. Why he would do that, Styles could only conjecture.

Perhaps it had something to do with the fact that his wife, who was as stern and unforgiving as he was, had snubbed the Wing Commander's wife on more than one occasion during the arrangements for official receptions, which was the province of the wives. Mrs. Styles refused to be ordered around by a woman 'of loose morals', as she put it. The Wing Commander's wife had been a showgirl before her marriage, and was generally thought to be a bit too flighty to be the wife of such a senior officer. She was blonde and flirty, and had stirred feelings in the other officers that their wives resented.

'That woman's a slut, and she'll be caught out, you mark my words,' confided Amy Styles to her husband. Looking at the square unyielding shape if his wife, Styles thought that it might be rather nice to have sex thrust at one, instead of having to wrestle an embarrassed lump in a dark room every Saturday night. But he kept such thoughts to himself. One must at least maintain an outward display of dignity and decorum.

It was this apparently unbending nature that had made him unpopular with the men in his squadron, but Styles was ambitious, and had no intention of allowing his career to be thwarted by a buffoon, his bimbo, or the men in his charge. In the meantime, he had an aircraft to attend to, and putting on his most dignified face, marched out to make sure the fitters pre-flights were up to scratch.

Chapter Three

LAC Jack Morris sat on the side of his bed, smoking a joint. It was eleven o'clock, he was up on the first floor of his block with the window open, and there was no one else around. He felt he was pretty safe.

Morris was not in the best of moods for flying. His wife had thrown him out the week before, determined to protect their only child from his drug habit. He had a problem with cocaine and speed, not just dope, and on top of that he was a problem drinker. At 28 years of age, life was looking pretty bleak for Jack Morris.

Initially he had been quite looking forward to this trip to Hawaii. It was a bit of a perk, and he had every intention of checking out the call girls in Honolulu if he got half a chance, with no thought about what he might bring home to his wife. He hadn't treated her well during their seven-year marriage, and the daughter she'd had was just a distraction as far as he was concerned. He didn't have much time for kids.

Having to move back into the block on the base was a bit of a humiliation for him. He'd gone around a couple of times to the house, first to coerce, then to rant at his wife over her ultimatum.

'I told you, Jack. Either give up the coke, or get out! You can't say I didn't give you fair warning.'

'You've got no right to turn me out of my own house,' he ranted. 'Since when did you start telling me how to live my life?'

'Since you started treating us with disrespect, Jack. You go out all weekend, hardly ever come home before three or four o'clock on a Sunday morning. How do you think I feel? If I'm going to be stuck in this house on my own, then I might as well live on my own. I don't need you coming back in a bad temper, knocking me around and threatening Denise.'

Jack had adopted a shocked look.

'When did I threaten Denise? I've never threatened Denise! That's a lie! I've never even hit her, or anything.'

'No, Jack, but you came in so drunk or drugged one day, that you fell over her on the step and trod on her hand. You broke a bone in her hand, Jack. For crying out loud, she's only two and a half. Can't you see the damage you're doing to your own daughter?'

'It was an accident! And I wasn't drunk! I was over-tired. I'd been on guard duty all weekend if you remember, and I never got any sleep. It's hard to sleep when you've got that bloody guard dog outside, barking all night.'

Amber crossed her arms and put up a determined front. At five foot eight she was an inch taller than Jack, and now she used her height to gain the psychological high ground.

'No Jack! The social worker warned me about this. You're a typical addict; you're in denial, Jack. Until you accept that you've got a problem, you're never going to get better. Can't you see that?'

Jack had drawn himself up and squared off, pugnaciously. He was dark haired and dark-skinned, with a sullen mouth, never more sullen than now.

'Well, fuck you! You're probably off with some bloke while I'm at work. This is just an excuse, isn't it, to get rid of me. You think there's greener pastures somewhere else. Well I'm telling you… the first time I see you with another guy, I'll break his fucking face.'

'That's typical of you, Jack. You always put your own faults onto other people. You're the one that goes running around all the time. You're the one that's been unfaithful, Jack. Don't you think I don't know about that WAAF? It was all over the base.'

Jack finished the joint then lit a cigarette, and brooded on their conversation. If she was going off with someone else, she'd been pretty cunning about it. She'd never had any strange phone calls; she'd never wanted to go out on her own – not when he was there, anyway. And during the days, when he was at the base, she'd had Denise to look after, which left her very little time for playing up.

But today he had to go to Hawaii, for two weeks! What had seemed like 'boys time out' now felt like an exile. What if she met someone while he was away? He wouldn't be able to do a thing until he got back, and by that time it might be too late.

He scowled, threw his cigarette out of the window and went to his locker. Taking a screwdriver out of his overalls pocket, he prized up the floorboards. There was a packet of white powder underneath, which he pulled out and hid inside a hollowed-out book. This he stashed in his top pocket, then zipped it up. He would take that along on the flight, so that he could have a snort during the trip. It always made him feel on top of the world. As he went to put the boards back, he caught sight of the other object that he always kept hidden beneath his wardrobe. Biting his lip, he looked at it, pulled it out and laid it on his lap. It was an oilcloth, and unwrapping it he stared at the .38 Smith and Wesson that lay in his hand. He picked it up and admired it.

He'd parted with five hundred dollars for that little beauty. It was unlicensed, thus the secrecy. He had intended to join a pistol club, and try his hand at target practice, but for one reason or another he hadn't got around to it. He checked the barrel, and noted that the chambers were full. Suddenly, on a whim, he wrapped it up, back in its oilcloth, and slipped it into the pocket of his overalls. You never knew – Hawaii! There was supposed to be a lot of thugs in Hawaii. He might need it for self-defence if a situation arose. Going back to his hidey-hole he pulled out another dozen bullets, and stuffed them into a sock, putting the sock into his side pocket. Then he lay back on his bed, and waited for lunchtime at the mess.

II

Pilot Officer Jason Mitchell was walking alongside the airmans' block when a cigarette came flying out of an upstairs window, and bounced off the peak of his cap. He looked up in annoyance, took his cap off and dusted the ash off the peak. It was really too much!

For a moment he had a good mind to go into the block and collar the airman that had tossed that cigarette out of the window, maybe even charge him. But he was in a hurry. The Wing Commander had insisted that all the officers attend a briefing before the flight, and that was scheduled for 11.30am. He didn't dare be late.

Mitchell was only twenty-two, and 5' 10" in his socks. But he was painfully thin, so thin that when he turned sideways he almost disappeared. He'd barely had time to finish his 'knife and fork' course at East Sale before he'd been posted to Townsville for training as a Radio Operator. It wasn't what he had dreamed of, but at least it carried a commission, and he could hopefully work his way up.

Initially he had planned to be a pilot, but the math's defeated him. Then he applied for Navigator, only to find that his mathematics were still against him. Radio Operator was about the only flight crew position he could snare. That meant Neptunes, or at the worst Hercules transports. Big noisy things they were, and he was pleasantly surprised to find that the Neptune was quite a civilized aircraft, certainly an improvement on the old lumbering Sunderland Flying boats, or the English versions of sub-hunters, the Shackleton.

Besides the radio he got to operate Jezebel, and work with sonar and M.A.D. It was an interesting vocation. If it weren't for having to put up with the rough and ready lower ranks, the Air Force would have been idyllic. But at least he had enough clout on his shoulder to make them answerable to him.

He'd been brought up in rather a precious atmosphere by a maiden aunt, and had never been allowed to mix in the rough and tumble of other boys. As a result he grew up afraid of the coarse language and hurly-burly of mateship. He kept pretty much to himself, and lived vicariously through his heroes. These were men of taste and distinction, who appeared to be able to pass through this other world without being tainted by the coarse manners of the uneducated masses. He worshipped men like this from afar, and his inclinations were more toward offering himself to them as an acolyte, than to any woman. Women made him anxious, especially self-possessed women. He felt out of his depth with these, and had never had a relationship, even a teenage one.

On his first arrival at the squadron the Wing Commander had taken him aside in the Officer's Mess, and given him a little fatherly advice.

'Don't get too close to the men, Pilot Officer. Always keep your distance. They're in a different class than you altogether, and you must always behave as an officer and a gentleman. You will notice that they swear a lot, have no respect for rank, and will continually try to undermine your authority over them. Remain aloof! They are necessary, of course, to the servicing of the aircraft, and that type of individual seems to excel in the sweaty, oily professions. We can give them full marks for their expertise, of course... But we don't have to socialize with them, if you get my meaning.'

The Wing Commander threw his shoulders back, and shivered momentarily, as if the topic was unpleasant to him. But he continued.

'The only way the system works is if we maintain discipline! Discipline, Pilot Officer Mitchell, or the whole system will collapse. Don't put up with any insubordination. Charge them! That's what the rules are there for, to maintain the chain of command. If you have to communicate with them, do it through their senior NCO's; Warrant Officers and Flight Sergeants. They are principally there to pass your orders down the line to the other ranks.'

Mitchell had taken that advice to heart. If any airman even attempted to speak to him directly, he would turn to the nearest NCO and deliver the reply. Then he would stalk off; ignoring the menials in a way that he considered was expected of him. He managed to put a lot of backs up at 10 Squadron in a very short time. The men called him 'Snitchell', after his habit of turning to the NCO's, and the NCO's called him 'Arsewipe', as they saw him kow-towing to the senior officers.

It was duly noted that he had a tendency to fawn over anyone with more than two bars on his shoulder. There was definitely something unhealthy about the way he seemed to idolize senior officers, and wait for each order with a breathless expectation. In the Officer's Mess it had been said that you wouldn't want to drop your trousers in the same room, or he'd be on his hands and knees before you could turn around. It seemed that no one liked Mitchell over-much.

III

LAC John Varley was in a strange mood. The instrument fitter had recently finished 10 days confined to base for insubordination to Squadron Leader Graham Styles, while on a pre-flight walk-around two weeks before. Styles had always had a contemptuous attitude towards ground crew, and he usually gave them a hard time whenever he had to deal with them direct.

'You haven't pulled the undercarriage pins, LAC,' he snapped. 'When were you going to do that – after I'd taken off?' He was in a sneering mood, and John wasn't in the best of humours himself.

'I'm supposed to do it during the walk-around, sir, not before you get here!'

'Well, bloody do it, man! Don't just stand there! What about the pitot cover?'

'Same with that, sir! We do it on the walk-around.'

'How long do you think I've been flying these things, LAC? Five minutes? The pitot covers and all external pins are always removed before I get here. It saves time.'

'That's not by the book, sir. If you look in the book...'

The Squadron Leader spun around and fronted the LAC.

'Stand to attention when I speak to you, LAC. Don't presume to tell me what the book says – I know the book backwards. I probably wrote the book! I find your attitude sloppy and your manners wanting.'

Varley snapped to attention, and looked more worried than usual.

'I'm sorry, sir, I was just pointing out...'

'You're not paid to point out anything, LAC. What mustering are you?'

'Instruments, sir!'

Styles looked at him contemptuously.

'Oh yes, a clock winder! Wouldn't the other trades have you,' he sneered. 'And while we're on the subject, when did you last have a haircut? I'll be speaking to your section officer about you, LAC Varley.'

Varley had subsequently been charged with insubordination and that good old standby, unairmanlike behaviour. He was given 10 days CB. Varley had no reason to like Squadron Leader Graham Styles.

It wasn't as if this was the first time he'd fallen foul of an officer. While on Guard Duty he'd been reprimanded for not saluting the Wing Commander as he drove in through the gate, even though the Wing Co. was in a private car with no markings, and was dressed in civilian clothes.

'How the fuck was I to know who he was?' he complained later. 'He came boring in at forty miles an hour and nearly clipped the boom. Then he pulls up twenty yards inside the gate and yells out, 'don't you salute your superior officers when they come on base.''

For that minor infringement he had been given five days in the Officers Mess, washing pots and pans. To say that Varley hated officers would be an understatement. It was this previous treatment of him that saw him hatching a plot to get back at them while he was on CB.

As part of his duties as ground crew, he had to drive the oxy trolley around the various aircraft and replenish the oxygen systems. There were six cylinders on the trolley, all painted in their distinctive colours of black and white. It was while on a visit to the dentist that he caught sight of the nitrous oxide bottles. Except for the colour, they could have been oxygen bottles. He suddenly had a vision of the pilots, high on laughing gas, twelve thousand feet over the Pacific Ocean, and the idea gripped his imagination.

A few nights before, he had taken a nocturnal trip around to the rear of Dental Section with a roll of masking tape and two cans of spray paint – one black and one white. Under cover of darkness he had transformed the markings of a cylinder of nitrous oxide to that of oxygen, then driven around in his Utility, picked up the cylinder and taken it to the rear of the hangar that housed the oxy trolley. It took exactly twenty minutes to swap the bottle over, and he stacked the spare oxy cylinder with others in the corner. Then he drove back to his block.

The morning of the flight to Hawaii he found himself on oxy cart duty, and checked the crew listing for each aircraft before driving out there to replenish. A89-292 he filled with ordinary oxygen. But the hated Styles and the Wing Commander would be flying A89-286, and after topping up the primary system with oxygen, he casually changed cylinders, and filled the almost empty secondary system with nitrous oxide. He couldn't help smirking as he did so, imagining the two overcome by a burst of hilarity in the cockpit while trying to control 80,000 pounds of aluminium at 12,000 feet. It was revenge at its sweetest, and nothing that they could sheet back to him. He was just doing his job – not his fault if the cylinders had been wrongly filled!

On the morning of the flight Varley was called in to see his section Warrant Officer, Danny Seaman, and informed that he would be taking the place of LAC Jervies on the Hawaii flight. He would be flying on A89-286. His trick with the oxy bottles had gone completely out of his head, and he received the news with undisguised elation. Except for Seaman's strange way of imparting the news, his mind was full of visions of Hawaii, his first major trip on an air force junket.

By the time he got back to his billet to pack his kit, the immensity of the situation hit him. The nitrous oxide! He'd set it up, and now he was going to be on the flight. He groaned, and kicked the wardrobe a couple of times in disgust. There was no way out of this. He just hoped that there wouldn't be any need to use the back-up oxy system between there and Hawaii. Once there, he might be able to void the system and replenish it with oxygen.

It was not surprising, therefore, that Varley was in an apprehensive frame of mind. When he thought about what could happen up there, he broke out in a sweat. Maybe it hadn't been such a good idea after all.

Chapter Four

Airwoman Helen Currier packed her kit in the women's quarters, making sure to stow a dozen condoms and a full pack of birth control tablets in the bottom of her bag. She was known to be cautious, and felt that she had good reason to be prepared. It was no good relying on her male partners to take preventative measures. Too often in the past, an enjoyable evening had been spoiled by the lack of a condom, or an argument about the pill. So now she took precautions with both.

Twenty-seven years old, with a shapely build, short black hair and a beauty spot on her cheek, she had been in the service for nine years, for each year of which she had been regularly passed over for promotion. Her off-base activities were too well known to her superiors to point to elevation in the service. It didn't seem to worry her. She had only one object in view, and that was to eventually snare an air force officer into marrying her and providing her with a home while she bore children.

In the meantime she played the field, and was remarkably accommodating as long as the partner for the night had at least one broad bar on his shoulder. She drew the line at Pilot Officers! Flying Officers were her baseline, and from there anything up to Group Captain would do, as long as he wasn't over 45. The trouble was that most Group Captains and Wing Commanders were married already, which left Squadron Leaders and Flight Lieutenants as the likely prey.

Helen worked in the Orderly Room as a clerk, which meant that she worked amongst and had dealings with the lower ranks most of the time. She affected an attitude of disdain towards these, as her ambitions were above that station in life. She was attractive to look at, but frigid in attitude when the inevitable overtures from the ranks came her way. She had a way of wrinkling her nose in disgust when the remarks around her became too risqué, and had a stock selection of put-downs when any airman had the audacity to proposition her.

'Not in this lifetime,' was her favourite answer to an invitation out. 'When you graduate from Uni,' was another. 'Maybe, when your mother gets married...' was a crueller one, and 'I might go out with the organ grinder, but never his monkey,' was her most spiteful effort.

A year earlier, she had been carried away by the gentlemanly manners and officer-like conduct of a lowly armament fitter on leave, whom she had met off the base. Gordon Duckett, had managed to overcome her objections to the lower ranks for a while on the basis that he was supposedly studying part time for a degree, so that he could apply for a commission. She had believed him at the time. Gordon was very believable. He was also a con man.

Gordon moved into a flat with her, and they lived together quite happily for a while until one day he found himself 'On Report', after a run-in with a Flight Lieutenant, when a badly secured rocket fell from its wing placement onto the tarmac, and nearly blew them all up. Luckily, it wasn't armed at the time. But for that *faux pas* he had found himself on Wing Commander's Report, was confined to the base for fourteen days, and had his promotion to Corporal suspended for two years.

The grapevine was pretty active at that time, and Helen heard about his punishment on the base. She dimly realized that if he couldn't get a promotion to Corporal, then he certainly wouldn't be offered a commission in the foreseeable future. By the time he'd served his fourteen days, she'd moved out of the flat and back onto the base, refusing to have anything further to do with him.

Gordon was not only heartbroken, but he was bitter with it. He went back to work nursing a grievance against the Air Force that would only compound with time. Helen turned her free-ranging attention to other targets, resolving that *'Officers Only'* would be the byword for the future.

Currently she was enamoured of 31 year-old Flight Lieutenant Eddie Campbell, who was single, and a pilot. He was only of average height, about two inches taller than Helen herself, but he exuded confidence and, to her, was witty and attractive. She had met him while serving drinks at the Officers' Ball, and he had taken her out on a couple of occasions – well away from the camp where they wouldn't be seen. It wouldn't do for an Officer to be seen fraternising with a lowly airwoman. Helen was aware of this, and didn't take offence. If she married an officer she would be required to resign her position anyway, stay at home and attempt to fit in with the other officers wives. The idea of that was repelling, but she was prepared to do it if it meant a comfortable, secure home life.

From the officer's wives that she'd already encountered, she knew that she despised them, the entire breed. They were snobbish and class conscious to a degree far exceeding their husbands. In fact, Helen had often wondered if these women, all civilians, thought that they carried identical bars on their shoulders to that of their husbands, because there was a definite pecking order amongst them.

A Group Captain's wife ruled the roost, and second to her, the Wing Commander's wife. Then the various Squadron Leaders wives, of whom there were many, and these differentiated amongst themselves by the husband's promotion date; those whose husbands were only recently promoted playing second fiddle to those who had been elevated for some years. Beneath these were the wives of Flight Lieutenants, Flying Officers and Pilot Officers. It was a highly organized sub-culture of privilege, and beneath this entire façade was every airman and airwoman of inferior rank. They were all answerable to the wives.

Whenever there was to be a ball, an investiture or a social event amongst the officers, the wives would take over the planning and execution of the reception afterwards. Helen was often seconded to serve in a menial capacity at these events, in full dress uniform. She would become waitress, barmaid, cleaner, lackey – at the beck and call of any officer's wife who deigned to address her. Mostly, she was looked upon with suspicion and hostility by the wives, as a dangerous distraction for bored husbands. The wives regarded airwomen as common sluts, there to service the other ranks and keep to their station – which meant to carry out any duty required by the wife of an officer. Helen decided that if she was to be regarded as a slut, she might as well act like one. But far from servicing the other ranks, her target was every officer in the mess, including the married ones. Each conquest to her was sweet revenge.

The reverse was true with airmen's wives. They were so low on the pecking order that they almost ceased to exist. It was common to post an AC or LAC to a new area, sometimes 2,000 miles away, on a 'B' Grade posting, which meant that the wife was not entitled to accompany him. So, no uplift of furniture or possessions, no Temporary Accommodation Allowance, no Married Quarters and no air tickets for wife or children. Helen had known one of these wives to receive a telegram from the Air Force, after a mix up with her husband's pay, headed – 'Your husbank.' She was determined never to become the wife of a member of the lower ranks.

But now Helen was off to Hawaii, away from the wives and the stultifying attitudes of the base. Two weeks of freedom in

Hawaii, or near freedom, anyway! On top of that, coincidence or not, Helen would be flying on A89-292, the plane to be piloted by none other than Eddie Campbell. At this thought she smiled to herself. It could be an interesting trip.

II

John Varley had no sooner returned to the section with his kit than Sergeant Leacock collared him to work on 292. Leacock was the real power in Instrument Section. While the Warrant Officer sat in his office, waiting for retirement, and concocting ways to unsettle everyone under his charge, Leacock was a dynamo of organisational skills and ability. If there was a job to be done, Leacock had the matter in hand. His forte was the delegation of tasks. Not everyone is capable of delegating. Some NCO's thought that if you wanted a job done properly, you had to do it yourself. Not Leacock!

Sergeant Leacock believed that if you placed great faith in the ability of your men, they would respond by gaining faith in themselves, and do a great job. He was a stickler for accuracy, but tempered this with humour and as a result was a great favourite in the section. His fitters would do anything for him, and he for them. He was a six foot two Aussie of the old school, and had little or no time for overblown egos which he tended to prick like balloons at the first opportunity. Danny was rather afraid of his tongue. Although he outranked him, Leacock was the one man that Danny wouldn't cross.

'Draw a thermocouple and a temp. gauge from the store, and meet me at 292. I'll go and rustle up a sumpy to take the cowling off, then you can replace the thermocouple. O'Connell's already out there changing the G2. Go on, get a move on!'

It was already 1230 hours, and once the G2 had been run up they would have to do a compass swing. It was cutting it fine for a 1500 take-off.

Varley took off to the store on the trot, drew the components and was out on the tarmac as Corporal Bailey was removing the cowling. Bailey was on the trip too, so he didn't want to hang around.

'I'll come back when you're through and replace the cowling. I've still got to get my own stuff together.'

'It might not be here,' said Leacock. 'We might be out there, on a swing. You'll see us anyway. We'll take the cowling with us on the tow cart.'

It took only twelve minutes to change over the thermocouple, and another fifteen to fit the gauge, as Varley had to wait until Bill O'Connell was out of the way. Then Bill came back to run up the gyro, while the Sergeant down below arranged for a tow out to the field. The plane was towed while O'Connell checked the instruments.

'I really stuffed my knee up before – arse over in the slipstream,' Bill muttered to Varley as he worked. 'I had to go and strap it up. Don't say anything, or they might take me off the flight.'

'Don't worry, I won't say a word,' said Varley. He knew how much O'Connell was looking forward to the trip.

'If we're going to check the temp gauge, we'll have to get another red line done. Where we're going to find the time for that, I'm buggered if I know,' said O'Connell. He looked at Varley, as if for suggestions.

'Don't worry about it. They should be all right – they've been checked in the section. If you're worried about it, ask Leacock.'

'Yeah, right,' said Bill. 'He's the sergeant. Let him worry about it.'

They did the compass swing in record time, Bill guiding the driver around to the four points of the compass, while Varley adjusted the flux meter.

'She's all go,' he said, on the final reading. Bill gave him the thumbs up, then they had to wait while Bailey replaced the cowling. The plane was then towed back to the line and hooked up to a battery cart.

'I'll do the pre-flight on this one, you go and do 286! It's...' O'Connell consulted his watch, '...a quarter to two. Let's hope nothing else is unserviceable, or we'll never get away from here.'

Varley climbed in the rear hatch of 286 and made his way over the hump towards the cabin. There was a sparky sitting in the co-pilot's seat with the instrument panel out.

'What the hell...' said Varley. 'What are you doing with the panel out?'

There was a strict protocol in place regarding the demarcation lines between trades, and removing a panel was not an electrician's prerogative.

'Your Sergeant said it was all right! There's a crook loom to replace, just a small one.'

'Well, how long's that going to take. I have to do a pre-flight.'

'Another five minutes and I'll be done. Don't worry, I'm on this flight too.'

Varley went back into the body of the aircraft and sat down in the Navigator's seat to wait. By this time all the kit bags were being assembled at two points on the tarmac, ready to load onboard. 292 trundled past the nose of 286, behind the tow cart, and through the front canopy Varley could see the tanker approaching from the other end of the tarmac to refuel both planes. Shortly it would pump 33,000 pounds of AVGAS into the tanks, and they'd be ready to go.

Ian Johnson, the sparky, wandered out of the cockpit and gave Varley the nod.

'You can run her up now. Just wait until I reconnect the battery cart.'

On power-on, the gyros started up, and Varley did a full pre-flight check on all instruments. Everything seemed okay. Then he stuck a mask on his face and checked the oxygen. He took a few deep breaths, just to make sure it was flowing on demand, and a few more to give him a bit of a kick. Then he turned it off. Wandering back into the hangar he signed the pre-flight and noticed that of the other trades, only the gunnies hadn't signed their pre-flight. Still, that wasn't his concern. Bill O'Connell came limping into the hangar to sign off 292, looking as if he were in some pain.

'It'll be all right soon. I bruised the knee when I fell. Bloody painful! Are you coming over to join the others in despatch?'

Varley nodded, and they wandered over there together.

III

Danny Seaman was filling the position of Flight Engineer on 286. He wasn't especially qualified, but with Peter Leacock for back up, he knew he could just delegate if things went wrong. He gathered the lower ranks together and gave them a last minute brief.

'Now listen to me for a minute. Quiet in the back! We will be departing in just over thirty minutes. The two aircraft will be flying in tandem, about half a mile apart. The first stop, tonight, will be at Nadi in Fiji. On landing the trades will carry out both after-flights, and report any unserviceable items. We have a full complement of spares between the two aircraft, so as long as we don't get two duds of any one item, we should be well covered.

The aircraft will be refuelled on arrival, then made secure for the night. Two members will guard the aircraft overnight, taking it in turns, an hour about. They will be armed with SLR's. On being relieved they will then hand over their arms to their reliefs, and go on to dinner at the place assigned. If any member,' here he raised his voice as if in warning; 'I repeat, if *any* member is found asleep on guard duty, they will be charged with dereliction of duty. Take note; you *will* be charged!'

The Warrant Officer looked around him to make sure the message had sunk in. Sergeant Leacock was busy talking in low tones to the Electrical Fitter, Ian Johnson, at the rear. Seaman pursed his lips in displeasure.

'I take it that you know all this already, Corporal. You don't need to be briefed!'

Johnson looked uncomfortable. He didn't work with Seaman, and was unaware of his sarcastic tongue.

'Sorry Warrant Officer! I was just explaining...'

'I can see what you were doing, Corporal. Just pay attention when I'm speaking. You never know, the information might come in handy.'

'My fault, Warrant,' said Leacock. 'I was just finding out about the new loom that was fitted to 292.'

'I didn't ask for your input, Sergeant. Just pay attention!'

Leacock scowled at him, and Danny turned back to the others.

'You will be staying overnight at the old Colonial Hotel. It isn't the Hilton, so don't get your hopes up.' There was a general chuckle among the crew.

'Will the officers be staying there, Warrant?' said O'Connell, with a straight face.

'You should know better than that, O'Connell. No, the Officers will take their rest at the Domayne, alongside the miniature golf course for those that are interested.' Another ripple of good-humoured laughter ran through the group. Even Danny Seaman wasn't above sniping at the officers.

'After breakfast you will proceed to the airport where you will carry out any repairs that need to be done, and pre-flight the aircraft. The departure time is open, and will be up to the Group Captain. He may decide to leave late afternoon and incorporate a Navex into the trip, which will mean that we'll arrive and depart Canton Island under cover of darkness. There's nothing at Canton, except refuelling.'

'How far is that leg, Warrant – from Nadi to Canton?'

'As far as I know, four hours flying time; about twelve hundred miles.'

'Thirteen fifty,' said Leacock, from the rear. He'd been there before. Danny stopped for a moment, not happy at being interrupted.

'The sergeant says thirteen hundred and fifty miles. So about four-and-a-half hours! Is that correct, sergeant?' Seaman enquired, with a vein of sarcasm in his voice. He hated being corrected at the best of times.

'It depends on whether they sit on patrol speed, or get up to height and use the jet pods,' said Leacock. 'You can usually count on 250 miles an hour on a trip. Flat out they can do 390.'

'Anyway,' said Seaman, discounting anything that anyone else had to say. The final leg is about 2,000 miles. About eight hours flying! So if we leave Canton the same night, you can expect it to be daylight by the time we get to Barber's Point. Any further questions?'

'Yeah, what is this Canton Island, Warrant?'

'Ask Sergeant Leacock. He's been there a few times.'

They all turned to Leacock.

'It's a coral atoll, only three and a half square miles in area. It's part of the Phoenix Group, but that doesn't say much because it's the largest island of the group. There's a runway along the north shore, and a refuelling facility. And that's about it! If we have to sleep there, it'll be under the stars, boys, so be prepared. Make sure you've got your sleeping bags.'

'How do you know we'll be able to find the bloody thing, Sarge – it sounds like a pisshole in the snow,' remarked Phil Cusack, who had arrived just in time for the briefing.

'A pimple on an elephant, actually,' said Leacock. 'And in answer to your question – ever heard of a Navigator, lad?'

They all laughed, and made their way out to the two Neptunes that were to carry them over five thousand miles into the North Pacific.

Chapter Five

When the officers came wandering out in their flying suits, they were almost jovial. They'd had a good briefing with the Wing Commander, who would be accompanying them in the co-pilot's seat of 286. The lead pilot would be Squadron Leader Styles, as he had the most hours up, and the most experience flying Neptunes. The pilot and co-pilot of 292 were Flight Lt. Eddie Campbell, and Flight Lt. Peter Dawson. They were to follow 286 at a distance of a mile or so, 'and not go gadding about the South Pacific on their own', the Wing Commander had joked.

'I don't want to get halfway to Fiji and have to come back looking for you. So just keep us in your sights and we won't go wrong.'

The officers had all duly laughed, but Eddie Campbell and Peter Dawson had caught each other's eye, and their look was smouldering.

'I doubt if the old boy would be capable of finding his own car in a car park, let alone fly a Neptune. He's been flying a desk for too long in base squadron,' whispered Campbell, and Dawson smirked.

'I think we'll take it easy in Fiji tomorrow, fellows. No need for us to burst an artery,' said the Wing Commander, pointedly, 'not when we've got the 'erks' along to do that for us. If we wander out for, say, 1600 hours, we should be able to incorporate a Navigation Exercise on the second leg.'

He turned to Flying Officer Adrian McLeish, and said, pointedly:

'I suppose you will be able to find Canton Atoll in the dark, McLeish, because if you can't, you'd better tell us now.'

The group roared the expected response, and McLeish coloured somewhat.

'Aye, sirr! I ken I'll find it, the noo!'

'Well, for god sake man, make sure you find it in English. We don't want to land and find all the refuelling instructions in Celtic.'

'Gaelic, sirr -,' McLeish growled under his breath. The others curled up at his expense, but for some reason 'Scotty' McLeish didn't think it so hilarious. He was sick to death of the smart alecs taking the micky out of his accent.

As they left he brushed past Eddie Campbell who was still sniggering at his discomfiture.

'And who're you to laugh, laddie? Wi' a name like Campbell you're as Scots as I am. Though, I forgot, your lot betrayed us to the Sassenachs, isn't that reet? Took the thirty pieces of silver and sold your ain down the river.'

McLeish scowled at him and walked on. Behind him he heard Flt. Lt. Campbell's mocking tones:

'An' who're you to laugh - Sirrr! Dinna ferget the Siirrrr, laddie.' He and Dawson chuckled at the retreating figure, and followed him out to 292.

By the time everyone was aboard the two aircraft, there were twenty people all told, stowed in various spare seats and along the fuselage on the floor. There was also a mound of kit bags by the hump, and behind them trunks full of spares. There wasn't a lot of room to move. The passengers were still trying to get comfortable when 286 rolled onto the airstrip and revved the two Wright Cyclone 18 cylinder engines, slicing the four bladed props noisily through the afternoon air. Once they applied pitch, there was a kick like a mule in the rear, and the Neptune roared off down the strip towards Magnetic Island, closely followed by 292. Once airborne they climbed steadily, left the Island behind and headed out over the Great Barrier Reef.

Up at the back of 286 sat Jack Morris, his back against the M.A.D. compartment, and sitting on a couple of kit bags that he had grabbed for the purpose. One of them was his own. In his pocket he could feel the hard lump of the Smith and Wesson, still wrapped in the oilcloth in his pocket. In the top pocket of his overalls, and protected by a zip, was his book, containing the stash of white powder that he intended to use over the next twenty-four hours. That should help to make the trip more bearable.

Sitting further forward, in one of the radio operator's seats, was John Varley. He had his head stuck in a book that he had brought along for the purpose, but was finding it hard to concentrate as his mind raced around the problem of the nitrous oxide. He knew it was commonly known as laughing gas, but he didn't really know what prolonged exposure to it would do, and if the pilots didn't have the sense to shut it off they could all be in real trouble.

During his meanderings he even considered coming clean, confessing all and wearing it. But it would almost certainly be seen as a criminal offence, and he could very well be charged with sabotage, even attempted murder if they wanted to be nasty about it. There was nothing about the way he perceived the air force to work that would make him believe they would go easy on him. They punished for the slightest infringement, and it was possible that after being charged by a military court, he might even be charged again in a civilian court. He could go to jail – not once, but twice for the same offence. He dismissed the idea of owning up as pure stupidity, and attempted to concentrate on his book.

Gordon Duckett sat down in the observer's position in the nose cone, with only the Perspex cover between him and the elements. It was comfortable enough, but he was beginning to realize that if anything happened, the escape route was so small that he'd be lucky if he could squeeze out in time. In the meantime he got a birds eye look at the ocean, and sat thinking about Helen Currier in the plane following. He'd heard about her rendezvous with Flight Lieutenant Campbell, and was eaten up with jealousy. The difference a couple of lousy bars on the shoulder made! He was as good as them, he thought, and he was determined to prove it one day. But he had to prove it to Helen, and that might be more difficult. In the meantime he nursed an unhealthy grievance against Eddie Campbell, and resolved that he wasn't going to get away with latching on to his woman.

Warrant Officer Seaman sat in a camp chair behind the co-pilot's seat, feeling rather out of place in an environment that was strangely alien to him. He was a little like a leprechaun with his wizened face and his bow legs, and the fact that he stood only five feet six in his stockinged feet was probably the reason he was so aggressive. The old story about snappy little dogs held. He was used to running an Instrument Section, not flying, and his honorary position as Flight Engineer on this trip had him a little worried. Leacock was back in the body of the plane, so if something went seriously wrong, and Danny couldn't fix it, it would be a serious loss of face to have to call his Sergeant in. He just hoped that the flight would proceed without incident.

The Wing Commander was humming a little ditty from the 1940's through the microphone, and it was reverberating in the pilot's headset. Styles flashed a couple of annoyed glances at his superior, hoping that he would take the hint. But the Wing Co. was sitting back enjoying the view, already in holiday mode. There was nothing for him to do. The pilot could take care of most of it, so he sat back and hummed.

'Prepare to climb to 11,000 feet,' Styles rasped through the headset, and caught the reply from 292, 'Roger', before setting a steady rate of climb on the gauge, and watching the artificial horizon begin to move. He'd hoped that the interruption might have shut the Wing Commander up, but it had no effect. He still hummed through the headset.

After about five minutes a voice came through from 292.

'Who's the dork humming on the R/T. Is that one of the 'erks?'

It was an annoyed Eddie Campbell not realizing that, in that one brief query, he had set his promotion prospects back by three years.

Styles looked at Fletcher, and the Wing Commander looked startled for a moment. Then he composed himself, sat back in his seat and ceased humming for the remainder of the trip.

II

Just over a mile further back, 292 was climbing slowly behind the lead aircraft, and Campbell and Dawson were carrying on a private conversation in the cockpit, the intercom switched off.

'This is going to be fun,' said Campbell, sarcastically, 'playing follow my leader. Did you bring any cards with you, Dawson?'

Peter Dawson grinned, and shook his head.

'We might as well have attached a tow-rope, and just let them tow us over there. Then at least we could have taken it in turns to get some sleep,' he replied.

'That's what happens when you get gaga senior officers, left over from WW2, running amok in the modern Air Force. They should chain him to his desk! The silly old bugger's only going along for the ride, anyway. He shouldn't be in the co-pilot's seat. He should be back with the Radio Ops.'

'Are you going to tell him that?' said Dawson, tongue in cheek.

'Yeah, and collect my pension when I get back,' said Campbell, sarcastically. 'But I mean it – anyone from a Wing Commander up should be banned from flying duties. They're invariably past it. The Air Force is for Flight Louies and the occasional Squadron Leader, but even they can be a pain in the arse. Look at Styles!'

'Well, the erks certainly hate him,' said Dawson. 'He's always throwing his weight around, charging them for one thing or another. I don't know what his problem is – maybe his wife won't come across anymore.'

'Have you seen his wife,' said Campbell, a malicious grin on his face. 'She's got a face like a half-chewed mango. I don't think you'd want that one to come across!'

'In fact you wouldn't want to come across her in a dark alley,' Dawson laughed.

'I'm telling you, I wouldn't want to come across her with yours, let alone mine.' They grinned at each other, and laughed at their own jokes.

The altimeter was reading 10,800 feet, so Campbell started to level her out on the autopilot.

'We'd better put the oxy on. If we're going to stay at this height, we'll need it. How's the cabin pressure – holding up?'

'No problems so far.'

'All the same, better be safe than sorry.'

He switched on the R/T to the crew.

'All personnel, please apply oxygen masks. We're approaching 11,000 feet. Oxygen until further notice.'

Everyone found an oxygen mask stowed near them, and put it on. That pretty well curtailed the conversation for the time being.

Further back in the fuselage Bill O'Connell and Phil Cusack draped themselves either side of the main spar, otherwise known as 'the hump', and played gin rummy with the cards that Bill had thoughtfully brought along. The ground crew was used to passing the time this way, in between pre-flights and after-flight servicings. There was sometimes a long time between flights.

Cusack was a slightly built, red-headed lad who looked younger than his 22 years. He was freckle-faced, with a cheeky disposition, who was always getting himself into strife over one thing or another. He had a strange, maladjusted sense of humour that did not always go down well among the more sober elements of the crew. But he was a motor transport fitter and driver, so he wasn't often to be seen on the tarmac.

Flight Sergeant Barry Mackintosh was curled up in the observers position, and feeling the cold. He'd missed the announcement about the oxygen, and was in a shallow sleep. He'd had a few too many late nights during the previous week, and needed to get a solid ten hours in to catch up. That wasn't possible now, unless he slept on the flight. As the air got thinner, his breathing began to increase in tempo, and he was soon out cold. Luckily for him, the aircraft was pressurized.

Helen Currier waited until the flight path levelled out, then made her way forward to the cockpit. Eddie Campbell had proffered the invitation when he had seen her the day before. She had never been inside an aircraft, so it was a novel experience for her. When she entered, Dawson looked around and raised an eyebrow. Then he looked searchingly at Campbell.

'It's okay, Pete, I told Airwoman Currier that I'd show her around the cockpit.'

Campbell eased himself out of his seat, and joined her in the rear of the compartment.

'How are you finding it, so far?'

Helen smiled, and nervously ran her fingers through her black, wavy hair.

'It's great. I thought I might get airsick, and when we took off it was a bit freaky, but I've been fine. I'm surprised how smooth it is.'

Campbell laughed.

'Don't take that for granted. If we hit turbulence, we'll get thrown around all over the shop. We're just cruising along at the moment at about 240 knots, playing follow my leader.' He pointed out through the windscreen to A89-286 about a mile and a half ahead of them. 'The Wing Co. wants to lead us all the way, so it's a bit of a bore as far as we're concerned. We forgot to bring the monkey along, so we have to sit it out up here until we get to Nadi.'

Helen laughed.

'I don't know about that. There are a couple of monkeys playing cards over that big hump in the back.'

'You mean the main spar. That's the best place for them, keeps them occupied.'

'I just wish I didn't have to sit near them.'

She made a show of shivering, as if to show her contempt of the other ranks. This wasn't lost on Campbell.

'Unfortunately there's not a lot of space to spread out in the old Neppy, not with a full load, like this. What about down in the observer's position, in the nose? Is there anyone down there?'

'I don't know, but it sounds all right. Maybe I should go down there?'

'I'll check it out for you,' said Campbell.

He turned to Dawson and whispered something to him. Dawson nodded. Then the pilot and WAAF left the cockpit and he made his way down towards the lower compartment. It was a hands and knees job, but he got down to the crawlway and saw that there was someone already in the seat.

Campbell could only see the back of his head, but there was something unnatural about the angle of it. He reached over, and shook the figure by his shoulder. There was no response, and he was incredibly cold.

The pilot scrambled back up to the deck, brushed past Helen and collared Johnson, the sparky, and Kevin Bailey, an Engine Fitter.

'There's a guy down in the observer's seat, I think he's unconscious,' he shouted over the engine noise. 'Go down and drag him out.'

It took over ten minutes to get the flight sergeant out of his seat and up onto the deck.

'Oxygen!' yelled Johnson, and an oxy mask was pulled out and applied to Barry Mackintosh's face. It took three or four minutes, then he began to come around, though he remained very pale.

'It looked like oxygen depletion,' Campbell said to Helen Currier. 'I don't think it would be a good idea for you to go down there. He's incredibly cold, and I don't think you're really dressed for that,' he said, looking at her standard issue skirt and top.

'Maybe you're right,' she said. 'I suppose I shall just have to put up with the 'erks'.'

She moved in towards Campbell as if to kiss him, but he looked nervously around at the others, who might have been watching them, and managed to slide back into the cockpit without any further contact. Helen looked disappointed, and turned back to reclaim her seat along the fuselage.

Chapter Six

The landing at Nadi went without incident. By the time the two aircraft had pulled up at the end of the runway and taxied over to the refueling area, everyone was on their feet, just waiting to get out and stretch their legs. They swung out and down through the rear hatch, spilling out of the planes and either exercising out in the open, or flopping down onto the grass and lying inert. It was a relief to get out into the fresh air, even though it was now getting dark. It was humid and warm, quite different to Townsville's dry warm climate. A few minutes out in their overalls and boots, and the fitters began to sweat.

'Here, it's bloody hot, isn't it,' said Varley to Gordon Duckett. Gordon was indulging in violent exercise, swinging his arms to relieve his backache. That observer's seat was more cramped than he'd imagined.

'I don't care. I like the heat! It was bloody cold in that nose cone, I kid you not.'

Varley spotted Bill O'Connell over by 292, and wandered over.

'How'd you go,' he said. 'Was it as boring on your flight as it was on ours?'

O'Connell laughed.

'You should have brought a pack of cards. We've had a great time playing gin rummy all the way over.'

'I just read my book,' said Varley.

'We did get one bit of excitement, though. The Flight Sergeant over there, Barry Mackintosh – he's a framey. He was down in the observer's seat and didn't put the oxy on at 11,000 feet, and passed out. If Flight Lieutenant Campbell hadn't gone down there to check, he might not be walking around right now.'

Mackintosh was sitting on the grass, his head between his knees looking particularly sorry for himself. Danny Seaman suddenly noticed them chatting, and wandered over, a quizzical look on his face.

'Have you two resigned from this Air Force and joined the tourists? Aren't you supposed to be doing after-flights?'

Varley and O'Connell looked at each other.

'Yes, Warrant!' They split up and headed for their own aircraft. Danny stared after them in aggravation.

The various trades completed their servicings, then the fuelling crew knocked up the old Fijian tanker driver, who was having a late siesta. He came grumbling out of his office and drove the tanker over, and the crews refuelled first 292, and then 286.

The officers had long gone by this, and they'd taken Helen Currier with them. It seemed that she wasn't going to have to put up with the 'erks' after all. They'd gone off in a small mini-bus that had been arranged to take them out to their lodgings at the Domayne, and that was the last the fitters would see of them until they reassembled at the aircraft the following day.

Another mini-bus was waiting to take the ground crew to the old Colonial Hotel. They arrived in time for a late meal, then sat out on the balconies and had a couple of Fijian ales. Everyone was in good spirits except for Jack Morris, who sat brooding alone on the state of his marriage, and wondering whether his wife, Amber, was already seeing someone else.

At the thought of another man sleeping with his wife, Jack's mind went black. He would kill him, he thought, at the very least, and then probably kill her too. The voice of reason tried to interject, warning of the consequences of following that path, but Jack was in no mood to listen to that inner voice. He sat and nursed a bottle of Jim Beam, throwing it back hit after hit, until his eyes glazed.

He thought of his wife's long legs and taut body, her firm breasts and tight buttocks. Amber kept herself in good shape, and there was really no reason for him to want to go off and have flings with other women, other than that he bored quickly, and saw affairs as conquests over the weaker sex. But he couldn't bear the thought of losing Amber. She was his property, his woman! The delights of her body were reserved for him alone. It was as if another man would defile his shrine, alienate him from his own property. The green eye of jealousy burned brightly in his mind.

At eleven o'clock that night, a jeep rolled up, driven by Sergeant Leacock. The distinctive insignia of the Fijian Military was painted on the door. Leacock jumped out and took with him a pad, clamped at the top with a bulldog clip.

'LAC's Morris and Duckett,' he yelled up at the balcony. 'You two are on the next guard. Put on gaiters and white webbing belt and meet me down here in five minutes time. Don't forget your hats!'

On the way out to the airport the two fitters were largely silent. Two hours of wandering around, guarding two aircraft at midnight was no-one's idea of a good time.

'You'll be relieving Cusack and Grainger. They've been on since 2130 hours. You will take over from 2330 until 0130. Still time to have a couple of drinks once you get back. As long as you're up by 0730 in time for breakfast, and fighting fit. No hangovers tomorrow, or they'll have your guts for garters.'

Leacock looked pointedly at Morris.

'What are you looking at me for, Sarge,' Morris said, aggrieved.

'Let's just say that your reputation precedes you, Morris. Your

Flight Sergeant has been pretty vocal about your habits around the Sergeants Mess.'

'Well, he had no fucking right,' scowled Morris. 'I don't go talking about him!'

'That is: 'He had no fucking right, *Sergeant!*'' said Leacock, with a barely suppressed grin. 'And whether you like it or not, if you roll into Airframe Section drunk on more than one occasion, then people will talk! It's only human nature.'

Morris scowled again, and looked away.

'That's what I bloody hate about this Air Force. No one minds their own business! I've got problems at home... the wife chucked me out. I think she's seeing some other bloke,' he muttered, in a vain attempt to gain sympathy.

Leacock glanced at him laconically, but didn't reply. He never got involved in domestics.

'What are we supposed to do here, Sarge? Just wander about, looking stupid!'

'You're a framey, aren't you,' Leacock said, sarcastically. 'Just do what comes naturally!'

Even Morris grinned at that. The trades loved taking the piss out of each other in those days.

The Neptunes stood gaunt against the moonlit sky as the jeep pulled in beside 286. Cusack and Grainger detached themselves from the shadows beside 292, and wandered over.

'Thank fuck for that,' said Grainger. 'We thought you were never coming.'

They handed over their SLR's to the new guards, and jumped into the jeep. Leacock turned to them before taking off.

'Anything these guys should know about?'

'Quiet as a graveyard, Sarge! A couple of natives came over an hour ago to have a look at the planes, but we told them to piss off!' said Grainger.

'I hope you told them to piss off nicely,' said Leacock with a hint of sarcasm. 'We don't want to start an international incident in Fiji.'

'He p.pointed his gun at them, and they p.p.pissed off quick,' Cusack stammered, grinning. Leacock slapped his forehead with the palm of his hand.

'God! I hope they don't complain to the Wing Commander. If you two have any trouble,' he said to Morris and Duckett, 'one of you just go over there and say, *nicely* – 'I'm sorry, but this area is out of bounds to all civilian and military personnel!' – and if that doesn't do the trick, *then* point your guns at them!'

'Okay Sarge,' they replied, as the other three drove away.

Morris and Duckett were left in the dark, clutching their rifles. Duckett said:

'I don't know about you, but I'm not going to wander about here all night. I'm going to climb into 292 and get my head down for an hour. Cover for me, and I'll cover for you during the second hour. Deal?'

'Yeah, okay,' muttered Morris.

He began to wander between the two aircraft at a slow pace, while Duckett disappeared up inside the rear hatch of 292. He took his SLR with him. Morris waited for a few minutes, until any sounds of Duckett making himself comfortable had died down, then skirted the aircraft and went to the edge of the apron where he sat himself down on the grass. There wasn't a movement anywhere.

With the area clear, Morris pulled his book from his top pocket, and extracted the small package of white powder. He then produced a plastic straw from his pocket that he had taken from the mess, and took a snort of pure cocaine. He shuddered uncontrollably as it hit home, then settled back to feel the sense of well-being flood through his system. Slipping the book with its valuable contents back into his pocket, he suddenly leapt to his feet and snatched up his rifle, filled with an overwhelming sense of power.

Within two minutes he felt there was nothing he couldn't do. He felt physically powerful, and mentally godlike. He was the arbiter of his own destiny, and stuff everybody else!

He began to march up and down, his rifle at the slope, his boots making a regular clatter on the bitumen. He swung his right arm proudly, and kept his back straight. In his mind's eye he was back on the bullring at Edinburgh, for the parade at the end of his rookies training. He was so overwhelmed by the effects of the drug that he forgot about his present surroundings, and began to bark orders at himself.

'Squad… a-bout turn! Quick march! Left, right left…'

Presently he was interrupted by Duckett, who had dropped out of the rear hatch of 292 to see what all the commotion was about.

'What the bloody hell…. Morris! What are you doing, it's nearly fucking midnight?' he called out to Morris's retreating figure. Morris suddenly spun around and pulled the rifle down from the slope, adopted the firing position and yelled:

'Put your hands up you bastard! Hands up now or I shoot!'

Duckett froze. The guy was stark raving mad. Morris began to wave his rifle at him like a maniac, and for a moment there he thought he was really going to get shot.

'Hang on, hang on – it's me, Duckett! Fuckin' hell, man, what are you on? You'd better sort yourself out before the others get back or you'll be in the brig, man.'

'I don't give a fuck for those bastards,' snarled Morris. 'I don't give a shit for this Air Force! Bring 'em on; bring 'em all on. I'll sort the bastards out! No-one's going to tell me what to do – fuck 'em! I'll shoot the bastards!'

Duckett realized that whatever Morris was on, he was presently deranged and possibly dangerous. He was staggering about now, like a man who was drunk.

'Look mate,' he ventured from a distance, 'you're over-tired! It's been a long day. I think you'd better get some sleep while I keep watch. You'll be all right once you've had a sleep.'

Morris began to laugh.

'Sleep! That's a good one. Sleep! I couldn't sleep now if I tried. Some guy's fuckin' my wife, and you want me to sleep? I'm gonna get the bastard, you see if I don't. I bet it's one of the blokes in the section. Yeah, that's what it is! I should've thought of that before. One of the guys in the section! Could even be that bloody sergeant of yours, Leacock. Could be him! Could be bloody Varley. How do I know what's going on when I'm on guard duty? Right now, even now! She could be fuckin' half the section, and I'd never get to know unless somebody told me.'

He was rambling, and Duckett felt his mouth go dry in apprehension. What was he supposed to do with this incoherent mess of paranoia? He couldn't overcome him without using his own gun, and then they both might get shot. He waited for the rambling to die down, clinging onto the side of 292 in the darkness. Finally, Morris staggered muttering off the tarmac, dropped his rifle and wandered off into the darkness through the grass.

Duckett let a minute or so go by then ventured over to pick up Morris's SLR. There was no sign of Morris now. He removed the clip, and operated the bolt action, ejecting a bullet from the spout. For chrisesake, he could have been shot! He didn't know there was a bullet up the spout. Shoving the clip in his pocket, and picking up the stray bullet, he threw the SLR up through the rear hatch of 286 and wandered around the aircraft, trying to see where Morris had disappeared to. He was nowhere to be seen.

Duckett had his own grievances with the Air Force, though he didn't necessarily want to get another member into trouble. He knew the sort of pressures that could make a man snap, and in Morris he thought he recognized a man close to a nervous breakdown.

He thought back to his own brushes with authority, remembering the Wing Commander's Report that had effectively halted his promotional prospects for two years, and stuffed his chances with Helen Currier. Now she was off with that Eddie Campbell, two bars and a pilot. He knew he had no chance with competition like that. But there was more than one way to skin a cat.

With Morris off wandering about in the darkness, another twenty minutes found Duckett staring up into the front wheel well of 292, at the orange tag hanging off the front undercarriage pin. Moodily, he seized the tag and yanked the pin out. He stood and looked at it, and an idea began to form in his mind. Going up into the aircraft, he went to the toolbox and pulled out some bolt cutters, then he neatly sheared the pin in half. Putting the bolt cutters back, he dropped out of the hatch and walked back to the wheel well, inserting the sheared pin in place, minus the tag. Anyone who did a walk around on that would presume the pin had been removed, and leave it in place. You couldn't actually see it, once it had been rammed home. Duckett smiled grimly to himself. Serve the bastard right. Campbell wouldn't be able to get the nose wheel up. Panic panic! He grinned, took the remainder of the pin and tag out along the skirt and buried it in the loose soil. This was going to be interesting.

Morris reappeared ten minutes before the sergeant returned, moaning that he was suffering from food poisoning, and that he had thrown up out in a field somewhere. He seemed quite recovered from his brainstorm so Duckett resolved to say nothing to Leacock. There would be no point in stirring the pot after what he had done to jolly things up.

'Look here, Morris. I won't say anything, but you haven't got food poisoning. You were on some sort of drug, man, and I don't give a shit what it was or where you got it... But I'll tell you this! If you take anything like that again while I'm around, I'll kick your fucking arse. You scared the shit out of me.'

Morris looked at him aggressively, then dropped his eyes, somewhat cowed.

'Look mate, I'm sorry if I went off a bit. It's my missus...'

'I don't care if your missus is screwing the whole of R.A.A.F. Base Garbutt, man. You came within an inch of shooting me with that SLR. There was a bullet up the spout.'

Duckett reached in his pocket and produced the clip and the spare bullet. 'You'd better reload it for the next guard, or they'll wonder what's going on. You're bloody lucky I'm not reporting this, because you'd be spending Hawaii in irons, mate.'

Leacock picked them up five minutes later, and dropped Kevin Bailey and Bill O'Connell off for the next shift. Back at the Hotel, both Duckett and Morris went straight to bed.

Chapter Seven

Helen Currier had been dreading going to the Colonial with the other ranks. It would mean that she would run into Gordon, and there would probably be a scene. She was determined to avoid that at all costs. She caught Eddie Campbell's eye as they disembarked at Nadi, and he wandered over to her briefly on the tarmac.

'Is there any chance of going with you, sir? I don't feel like braving a night of fending off airmen.'

Campbell looked at her in sympathy, and patted her arm.

'No, heaven forbid! I'll have a word with the Wing Commander and see if we can take you along with our party.'

Campbell had to wait while some of the kit was unloaded, and Fletcher was safely away from the others by the minibus.

'Excuse me, sir,' he said, in a lowered tone. 'The WAAF is understandably worried about having to spend the night at the Colonial. She thinks the men might… well, you know, try it on, sir.'

Barton Fletcher raised one eyebrow, and glanced over at the airwoman where she stood apprehensively near 292. It was the first time it had really registered that there was a woman on this flight. Now that he looked, he saw – not just an airwoman – but a shapely beauty, craving protection from the men-beasts that made up the lower ranks. He cleared his throat.

'Ahemm! Yes, well – understandable that! Only natural that the young lady would look to the officers to do the right thing, Campbell! Thanks for bringing it to my attention. I'll speak to the young lady myself.'

He made to wander over to 292, and Campbell started to go with him. But Fletcher waved him back. Even though Fletcher was forty-four years old, with a tendency to carry extra baggage around the jowls, he nevertheless thought of himself as a modern Lothario and didn't need a Flight Lieutenant to act as chaperon. He straightened his cap, and the first thing that registered with Helen was the scrambled egg all over the peak. She felt an anticipatory shiver pass through her as the great man approached.

'I understand you're a little apprehensive, young lady, about accompanying *'the men'* to the Colonial Hotel.' He always inserted parentheses around *'the men'* in his allusions to them. His meaning was always thus plain for all.

'I'm a little worried, yes,' Helen replied, in the best helpless-little-girl voice she could muster. She mentally slipped Eddie Campbell into her pending tray, and concentrated her attention on the real thing, a Wing Commander.

'Have no fear young lady, it will not be necessary for you to share the hardships of the menials. I shall personally attend to your welfare. I extend an invitation to join the officers and myself at the Domayne, where you may feel quite secure.'

Helen simpered at him, and fluttered her eyelashes. She knew what signals to give out to make the maximum impact, and invariably hit the mark. Fletcher took her by the arm and led her over to the minibus, personally escorting her on board.

Campbell stared after him, feeling justifiably annoyed. It seemed that it wasn't all right for junior officers to fraternise with airwomen from the lower ranks, but it was quite all right for a Wing Commander. That bastard could get away with anything.

At the Domayne, Fletcher made sure that Helen sat at his elbow, but far from affording her preferential treatment he suggested that she might like to pour the officers wine. In one split second she was back in a menial capacity, serving as a waitress. She was understandably annoyed! Campbell grinned at her as she filled his glass, as if to say 'that will teach you. The pecking order is alive and well!'

'I'll see *you* later,' she whispered, not in a tone that anticipated a pleasant interlude.

When she sat down again, she felt all eyes on her as the only woman at the table. Some of the stares were distinctly hostile. Squadron Leader Styles had no truck with the lower ranks, male or female. He felt Helen's presence as an intrusion. It would never have been allowed in the Officers' Mess!

Pilot Officer Jason Mitchell was torn between wanting to appear well on both sides. He had problems with good looking young women, even if they were from the ranks, but he was desperate to hide that fact in this company, and so looked to the others for clues about how to conduct himself.

Flying Officer Adrian McLeish sat further down the table, scowling at the assembly of officers. If the truth were known, he didn't like any of them. With his broad Scottish accent he had been the butt of their jokes for too long. He didn't have any especial friends, not in this company, anyway. But unlike the others, he was not prejudiced against the other ranks, and often exchanged a few words or a joke with the fitters working on his aircraft. As a result he was quite popular amongst the men, who referred to him as Scotty amongst themselves.

Flight Lieutenant Ron Gray was the 26 year-old Navigator on 292. He sat on the other side of Helen to the Wing Co., and suffered in silence as her perfume assaulted his nostrils, turning his thoughts to things other than flying. He felt her thigh pressed firmly up against his left leg, and this was affecting his nervous system in peculiar ways. He wasn't above flirting with the WAAF's when the others weren't around, and he was also quite willing to take it further. But the politics at that table were too intense, and he confined himself to erotic thoughts, and the roast pork on the plate in front of him.

Pilot Officer Steve Bishop was a young and brash 22 year-old Radio Operator, like Mitchell. He was on 292, and had been furtively watching Helen all during the flight. She was a few years older than he was, but he thought her extremely attractive, and when he found himself sitting opposite her at the table, he felt it incumbent on him to attempt conversation.

'Where do you hail from, Helen?' he opened, taking a sip of wine.

'I'm from Dandenong originally,' she replied, realizing that it would be churlish to ignore him. He was only a Pilot Officer, and was thus beneath her sights in the officer brigade.

'Oh, that's interesting. I'm from Essendon. We're both Vics.'

'Kick a Vic,' muttered Campbell, further down the table. He was from Adelaide, and a fervent Aussie Rules fan. Dawson and McLeish overheard the remark, and grinned.

'What was that?' demanded the Wing Co. He didn't like to be left out of the conversation.

'I was just making a comment on the relative merits of South Australian and Victorian Football, sir. The mention of Essendon brought it to mind.'

'I see, a football fan, are you Campbell?'

There was a general mumble of approval around the table, and Helen found herself suddenly ignored.

'Port Adelaide would kick Essendon's butt,' said Dawson, goading Bishop.

'Oh, I don't think so, sir. Essendon, Collingwood, Carlton – any of those would make Port Adelaide look second rate.'

'Sturt would destroy Collingwood,' remarked Campbell. 'So would Norwood.'

'You're not serious, sir. Everyone knows…'

'Everyone knows it's a pansy's game,' muttered McLeish, bringing a hush on the conversation.

'What was that you said, McLeish?' said Campbell, disbelievingly. 'A pansy's game?'

'Aye! Aerial ping-pong! If you want a real game of footbau', watch soccer! That's the only real footbau', mon.'

There was a roar of dissent as the Rules supporters took him on.

'I suppose that's all you can get in Scotland, laddie,' Campbell remarked, grinning. 'And even that would be second rate. England pretty well dominates over there, doesn't it?'

McLeish looked at him in contempt.

'Have ye never heard o' the Wee Blue Devils, mon? They kicked England's arse.'

'Well, it doesn't really affect us over here, does it. When in Australia, do as the Aussies do, McLeish,' said Dawson.

'What? Lean on your shovel,' cracked McLeish. 'Wait for the Gas Company to fill in a trench and bitumenise it, so you can go and dig it up again to lay phone cables?'

Dawson laughed.

'You've got us there! Then they wait for the Phone Company to fill it in so the sewage mob can come along and dig it up again to lay pipes. True, all true! But at least we've got full employment,' he laughed.

'I don't think it's good form to make fun of Australia's institutions,' said the Wing Commander, pompously. He glared at Campbell as he said it, still smarting from the comment he'd heard over the R/T regarding his humming.

'Agreed, sir,' said Dawson. 'And Australian Rules Football *is* an Australian Institution.'

'That's not the sort of Institution I was referring to,' said Fletcher, waspishly, who had been thinking more of the

Postmaster General's Department. His remark had the effect of cutting all conversation dead, and they all turned to concentrate on the food in front of them. After a few moments he turned to Helen.

'Now what was that you were saying, my dear? About Dandenong.'

Helen looked uncomfortable. All eyes were on her now, and she felt totally out of place.

'I... I just said that that was where I came from,' she stammered, 'that's all.'

'And what did your father do,' the Wing Co. enquired, politely. He was just making conversation to fill the gap in the general hush brought about by his embarrassing put-down.

'He was with the Victorian Railways,' she replied, self-consciously. Then she saw the amused look on the face of the others, and the embarrassment of the Wing Commander. She added, quickly: 'The Commissioner – he was the Commissioner of Victorian Rail.'

The amused faces straightened, glanced at one another, and one or two grimaced at the *fau pas*. That was different!

'They thought you meant he was a conductor, lassie,' grinned McLeish.

'Just what do you mean by that, Flying Officer,' snapped Squadron Leader Styles. He wasn't finding the conversation amusing at all.

'Jest that for the stuffed shirts amang us, there's a big difference between a conductor and a Commissioner. No offence meant, lassie.'

'Well, I find your remarks offensive for a start, McLeish,' said Styles.

'Yo' wud,' said McLeish, forgetting himself.

'What was that you said, Flying Officer McLeish?' said

Styles, astonished.

McLeish put down his knife and fork on his plate, and sat back. His black eyes turned defiantly towards the squadron leader.

'I said, you would, sirrr,' he replied, aggressively. 'After au', ye seem to find everything offensive.... Sirrr!'

There was a deathly silence around the table. They all knew that McLeish had overstepped the mark. Now Styles had to save face.

'I would appreciate it if you would come to see me after the meal is over, McLeish. Then, depending on whether you apologize or not will depend whether or not I place you on Wing Commander's Report.' He nodded deferentially at Fletcher, who sat back impassively.

McLeish picked up his glass, and downed his drink. Then he turned to face Styles, his face thunderous.

'Apologize is it? Tae a Sassenach! *Oh Scots wha hae wi' Wallace bled...!* I dinna think so! *A king can mak' a belted knight, a marquis, duke and a' that, but he canna mak' an honest man – a man's a man, for a' that!* Tek that fer yer answer... Sirrr!' McLeish got to his feet and stormed out of the room, leaving Styles gaping, and red in the face.

'What the hell was that all about,' chuckled Dawson.

'I think he was making a point about rank,' muttered Campbell, quietly. 'I don't think he's too fond of it.'

'I shall expect you to take McLeish in hand for that,' Styles spluttered to the Wing Commander.

Fletcher shrugged his shoulders, and looked resigned.

'I'll have a word, of course. But I'm damned if I understood a word of what he was saying, Styles.' Fletcher turned to Helen and gave her an embarrassed smile. 'Even the officers argue at times, my dear.' He did his best to look long suffering and misunderstood, and Helen's heart went out to him. She was a sucker for ploys, too.

The rest of the meal was spent in desultory conversation, with long silences in-between. Afterwards, Helen was shown to a room next to the Wing Commander's, at the end of a corridor. For anyone to get in or out, they would have to pass Fletcher's room, and he sat for most of the evening with his door open. At eleven o'clock his door closed, and Eddie Campbell took his chance. He tiptoed past the closed door and rapped quietly on Helen's. There was a long silence. He rapped again.

The door suddenly opened and Campbell stood back in surprise. The navigator Ron Gray stood in the doorway, his coat over his shoulder.

'Hi Eddie. I'm just leaving. Did you want to see Helen?' he grinned. He left the door open and walked away up the corridor as Campbell entered the room.

Helen was lying in bed, looking rather flushed. Her hair was in disarray, and the bed was a mess. Campbell just stood there, his mouth open in shock.

'Did he...' he began. 'Did you...'

Helen looked at him slumberously from underneath sensuous eyelashes. Then she poked a long shapely leg out from underneath the covers, and waved it at him.

'Any more for any more,' she giggled. 'You're welcome to join in if you like.'

Campbell took a step backwards, towards the door. He looked at her in horror.

'You're not serious... are you?' he said.

She replied with a shrug of her shoulders, and a bemused smile.

'I'll be in it if you will,' she said.

Campbell turned and stalked out, pulling the door to behind

him.

At midnight, her door opened and Helen checked briefly along the passageway before venturing out in her dressing gown. She walked along to the room next door and tapped quietly. The door opened, and she was ushered inside. No one could say the Wing Commander wasn't a bit of a lad at heart.

Chapter Eight

At take-off the following afternoon, the crews were as follows;

A89-286 Lockheed Neptune P2V7

Pilot – Squadron Leader Graham Styles, age 34
Co-Pilot – Wing Commander Barton Fletcher, 44
Navigator – Flying Officer Adrian McLeish, 25
Radio Operator – Pilot Officer Jason Mitchell, 22
Flight Engineer – Warrant Officer Danny Seaman
                                 (Instruments), age 53
Load Master – Sgt Peter Leacock (Instruments), 38
Instrument Fitter – LAC John Varley, 24
Armament Fitter - LAC Gordon Duckett, 28
Airframe Fitter – LAC Jack Morris, 28

A89-292 Lockheed Neptune P2V7

Pilot – Flight Lieutenant Eddie Campbell, 31
Co-Pilot – Flight Lieutenant Peter Dawson, 30
Navigator – Flight Lieutenant Ron Gray, 26
Radio Operator – Pilot Officer Steve Bishop, 22
Flight Engineer – Flight Sgt Barry Mackintosh, 38
Engine Fitter – Corporal Kevin Bailey, 29
Electrical Fitter – Corporal Ian Johnson, 26
Instrument Fitter – LAC Bill O'Connell, 42

Motor Transport Fitter – LAC Phil Cusack, 22
Radio Tech – LAC Don Grainger, 23
Clerical – Airwoman Helen Currier, 27

As predicted, the officers didn't arrive in their minibus until after 1600 hours. They'd had a pleasant morning playing miniature golf, sleeping in, taking a leisurely breakfast, and in some instances such as Helen Currier's, enjoying even more exotic pursuits. Two other officers had a rather large smile on their faces by midday, the Navigator Adrian McLeish, and Flight Lieutenant Peter Dawson, the latter proving that there is no honour among friends. Eddie Campbell, on the contrary, looked quite bilious.

Then the group had enjoyed a late lunch of three courses, alcohol excluded. Some of them had even managed to grab a nap after that, and as a result they were all rather full of spirits when they arrived at the airstrip.

The lower ranks, on the other hand, had been unceremoniously rousted out of bed at 0710 by Warrant Officer Seaman, had partaken of an adequate though unexceptional breakfast, then were taken out to the airstrip and dumped at their aircraft by 0815. To say that they were not impressed would have been an understatement. There was a lot of grumbling about the necessity for all this rush when the officers wouldn't be arriving yet for hours.

'Don't you worry about the officers; you worry about you! You have a job to do, and so do they, and your job is more important. They only fly the things; your job is to keep them in the air,' snapped Danny Seaman, as contrary as ever.

'Yeah, but they get paid more than us,' muttered Bill O'Connell, feeling out of sorts as his knee had played up all night. He had a nasty bruise on the kneecap, and it was showing no signs of going down.

'And they get to play miniature golf,' grumbled John Varley, as he wandered off to do an instrument check on 286.

If there had been some shelter near the aircraft, it wouldn't have been so bad. But as the sun rose in the sky and the humidity took hold, the men were looking for any bit of shade they could find. By lunchtime, when a jeep brought them out a hamper of pre-packed sandwiches for their midday meal, the talk was almost mutinous.

'What is this crap?' snapped Ian Johnson, the sparky corporal. He opened up one of the sandwiches, held it up for all to see, then slapped it together again and flung it on the ground. 'Peanut Paste! What the fuck – do they think we're Charlie Brown or something?'

'Now now, Corporal! You're supposed to lead by example,' Danny Seaman interjected. He would have said more, but as Johnson was an Electrical Fitter, Danny didn't have the same hold over him that he had over the instrument guys. If there was a discipline problem, it was usually referred back through the section commander.

'I fuckin' hate peanut paste,' said Jack Morris in disgust, 'and I'm not going to eat that crap.'

Sergeant Leacock wandered over and took a bite out of one, then unceremoniously spat it out. He held the remains up and looked at it in disgust.

'Quite right, men! This is an insult!' He wandered over to speak to Seaman. 'They're right, Warrant Officer. You can't expect the men to eat this pap. They need a decent feed! With your permission I'll drive in to town and see what I can rustle up.'

Danny looked at Peter Leacock with distaste. This was one Sergeant who was always a thorn in his side, but he had the backing of the troops. If the truth were told, Danny was a little afraid of Leacock, because he had a habit of calling a spade a bloody shovel, and he wasn't afraid to answer back. He and the Warrant Officer had locked horns on a number of occasions, and Danny had been forced to back down more than once.

Danny's natural inclination would have been to tell the men to lump it, and then he could have enjoyed the simmering discontent he had caused. It always gave him great joy to thwart people's natural desires on the basis of 'you can't always have what you want in this life.' He had been in at the close of the Second World War, and remembered the many restrictions that had been in place under wartime conditions. He had also served in Korea, and had lived with very primitive arrangements, on extremely primitive airfields. He considered the current lot were pampered and spoiled, and that it was his job to teach them to suffer. But this time, he caught the glint of determination in the Sergeant's eye.

'Oh, I suppose so. If this namby-pamby lot can't put up with a bit of hardship every now and then,' he sneered; but Leacock cut him off.

'It's not a question of that, Warrant Officer. It's a question of respect! It's not wartime now, and you can bet your boots that the officers aren't dining on peanut butter. If that's the case, there's no reason why we should.'

'Point taken, Sergeant,' said Danny dismissively, then turned away in disgust. The fitters closest gave out a cheer.

'Good on you, Sergeant!'

Danny rounded on them as Leacock jumped into the jeep.

'Well what are you standing around for? While he's gone you can make yourselves useful around the aircraft. Finish off your pre-flights if you haven't already, and get the paperwork up to scratch. We might as well be ready when they get here.'

Leacock came back just on an hour later with five loaves of fresh bread, butter, half a roast pig, six roast chickens, and two huge snapper baked in alfoil. On top of that he'd managed a bucket of coleslaw, and a pound of potato bake. To drink he'd managed six litres of soft drink, and three litres of milk.

'It's party time, boys. Come and get it,' he yelled, triumphantly. 'We can even have a coffee afterwards.'

The fitters descended on the food and demolished it in twenty minutes flat. Even Danny was impressed.

'How on earth did you manage that, Sergeant?' he exclaimed, slicing off some pork.

Peter tapped the side of his nose.

'Trade secret, Warrant! Don't forget, I've been here before. I just called in a few favours,' he grinned.

By the time the officers got there, the ground crew were flat out on the ground, napping in whatever shade they had managed to find. When the Wing Commander got off the bus and took in the scene, he didn't look too pleased.

'Warrant Officer,' he snapped, as Danny Seaman approached. 'Call your men to order. What are they all lying around for?'

For some reason, Danny was suddenly incensed. They'd been waiting there all day while the officers sunned themselves and enjoyed the high life. Knowing his own invulnerability, he suddenly decided to speak out. He pointedly looked around him at the men lying in the shade, looked the Wing Commander in the eye and said, 'It looks as if they're all practicing to be officers, doesn't it, Sir?'

Fletcher's jaw dropped, and his face turned to thunder.

'How dare you speak to your Commanding Officer in such a disrespectful way, Warrant Officer! I'm absolutely appalled!'

Danny turned to Fletcher and curled his lip.

'I think twenty four years of service in this man's Air Force, and the fact that I hold a Warrant from Her Majesty the Queen, gives me the right to speak out when I sense that these men are being held in contempt, Sir!'

'Oh, you do, do you? And how's that, Warrant,' said Fletcher, taken aback.

'These men have been here for almost eight hours, sir. They have serviced the aircraft, completed any and all maintenance required, and have then had to sit out here in intolerable conditions for hours, with no shade except that provided by the aircraft. The food sent out for their midday meal consisted of peanut paste sandwiches, with nothing to drink. But, no doubt, your experience at the Domayne was just as daunting - Sir!'

Fletcher took a step back and swallowed once or twice.

'Well yes, I concede that, Warrant Officer. I do concede that you have a point. It was rather thoughtless of me to overlook those facts.'

'Thank you sir! I'm sure it won't happen again!'

Danny turned on his heel and stalked off, feeling rather proud of himself. He approached Peter Leacock who was now standing underneath the port wing of 286.

'Get the men together, Sergeant. It looks like we'll be moving off shortly.'

Peter Leacock looked at Danny with one eyebrow raised, and a wry smile on his face. He'd heard the whole thing. Suddenly he snapped to attention and saluted.

'The men would like to thank you, Warrant Officer.' In a lower voice he said, 'for myself... I don't believe it, but... well said, sir!'

Danny almost blushed. He was unused to praise of any kind.

'All right, all right! Get the battery carts hooked up.'

Squadron Leader Styles, having heard his superior bested by a mere Warrant Officer, put on his grittiest look, stalked over to

286 and began his walk-around. Don Grainger was the duty crew, and walked around with him.

'Have all the pins been removed, LAC?'

'Yes sir, we've done all that. Everything's been checked out.'

'The flaps are down. Why have the flaps been left down?' Styles was looking for any excuse to start an argument.

'I don't know, sir. I'm a Radio Tech, that's outside my sphere.'

'You're duty crew, aren't you, LAC?'

'Yes sir, I am. But…'

'No buts, LAC! You should be familiar with every aspect of the pre-flight. If something looks wrong, you should find out why.'

'Yes sir.'

'Who would have put the flaps down?'

'Possibly the framey, sir! Maybe they were…'

'Framey? Use the correct term when you're addressing an Officer.'

'Airframe Fitter, sir! I should imagine…'

'You're not paid to imagine, LAC Grainger. You're paid to know! Report to me at Barbers Point. You'll be doing some extra duties, to help you remember your responsibilities.'

Styles stalked off and boarded the plane, leaving Grainger fuming. Grainger was a Radio Technician, and quite unused to being treated so peremptorily. The Radio Techs were usually held in high regard as the real brains of the outfit.

'What's up his arse,' Grainger snarled at Bill O'Connell, who was on the battery cart.

'Two and a half stripes, what do you think,' Bill snorted. 'Don't take it to heart – he's the same with everyone!'

Nothing an officer could say would ever phase O'Connell. There again, he had never found himself to be the target of their ire. He was forty-two, affable and apparently competent, and this made him bullet-proof, where the younger guys often seemed to lack confidence.

Within ten minutes everyone had boarded, and both aircraft were idling on the tarmac. Fletcher had issued strict instructions that 292 was to follow two miles behind, and be ready for violent changes of direction as they began their Navex.

'We'll be operating in conditions of radio silence, as if we were at war,' he warned. 'So I don't want to hear any little chats going on over the ether. Flying Officer McLeish will be navigating, and as this is part of his ongoing training, I don't want him getting any outside help.'

'What if we lose sight of you in the dark, sir?' Eddie Campbell was a little perturbed about the hard and fast nature of the rules.

'Just follow our navigation lights and you can't go wrong, Flight Lieutenant. Your navigator's up to speed – he should be able to counterplot the course by following the readings on the DG. There will be six legs of approximately equal flying time, so by the time we come to the end of the fifth leg he should be able to plot the final leg on his own.'

'I must admit, I don't like it, sir.'

Fletcher looked at Campbell, and stuck out his jaw.

'What don't you like, Campbell?'

'I don't like the idea of radio silence, sir. And I think that my navigator should be furnished with the co-ordinates of the Navex before we take off. It's a big ocean, sir.'

'Oh ye of little faith!' Fletcher replied. The other officers grinned. 'You must have done this trip ten times, Campbell. You should be able to fly it blindfold. Anyway, that's my final word. I will, however, relent, and give you the first co-ordinate. We'll be heading 55 degrees on Directional Gyro for the first leg. Line your G2 up on the runway, then switch over to DG before take-off. Then we'll be on the same heading. Just keep your eyes on the drift meter – that will be your only correction, and you will correct for drift on the half-hour, each half-hour, starting at...' he looked at his watch, '1715.'

'That will make about three-quarters of an hour before the first correction, sir,' said Ron Gray, frowning.

'That's correct, Gray. Any more questions?'

There was a feeling of apprehension aboard A89-292 as they sat at the end of the runway, waiting for the lead aircraft to take off.

'He's a fucking idiot,' swore Campbell, under his breath

'He's got no right to place twenty lives in jeopardy,' said Dawson. 'But what can you do?'

Campbell lined up the G2 and switched to DG.

'Tell Gray I've got 15 degrees on DG,' Campbell told Dawson. Dawson switched through on the internal R/T and passed on the message. Then pitch was applied, and they were racing along the runway at ninety miles an hour.

Chapter Nine

Campbell was in the air and climbing, before Dawson pointed out the red light.

'What the blazes is that?' he said to the co-pilot.

'Looks like the undercarriage hasn't come up! Hang on – it's just the nose wheel. Why would the nose wheel stay down? Call up the Flight Engineer.'

Dawson put a call through the R/T to the navigator, who spun around in his seat and tapped on Barry Mackintosh's shoulder across the aisle.

'They want you up front,' he yelled, gesturing towards the cockpit.

Flight Sergeant Mackintosh made his way unsteadily up to the front of the aircraft. Dawson half-turned in his seat, and pointed to the red light.

'The nose wheel's still down, Flight Sergeant! Can you check it out please?'

Mackintosh looked bemused. He leaned forward and operated the retraction handle a couple of times, and there was a distant thump from underneath.

'We've tried that, Flight,' said Campbell, annoyed. If he was only going to play with the handle, what was the use of having him along?

'There's no access to it from inside the aircraft, sir. You'll have to land.'

Campbell turned and spluttered in his seat.

'Land? We can't land! We have to follow them.' He indicated the silhouette of 286, now just a small outline in the distance. They must have been four miles ahead by this time, and the distance was increasing.

'Get on the radio, sir, and tell them to abort. It's probably only a minor problem.'

'We can't,' Dawson snapped. 'We're on radio silence! Even if we turned ours on, theirs would be off.'

'But I don't understand....' The Flight Sergeant looked confused.

'Wing Commander's orders,' said Campbell. 'Our illustrious superior has deemed radio as superfluous to our requirements. We're on a Navex, and we're not allowed to communicate by radio.'

'But that's bloody...'

'I know... Ridiculous! You don't have to tell us, Flight Sergeant. The only thing we can do is try and catch up with them, and show them the wheel's down. Then we can turn around and come back.'

'It's causing a lot of drag, Eddie. I don't know whether we'd be able to overhaul them,' said Dawson, grimly.

Campbell looked at the airspeed indicator, and noted that they were down to 210 mph.

'We should be sitting on 240 with these settings,' he yelled. 'You'd better calculate how much extra fuel we're going to use up following those idiots. Did you hear me, Flight Sergeant?'

Mackintosh nodded, and disappeared out of the cockpit. Two or three minutes later he poked his head back in.

'We'll lose about an hour's flying time over the trip – not enough to worry us, sir.'

'Well, that's something at least,' said Campbell. He turned to Dawson. 'Decision time – do we keep going, or risk the ire of the Wing Commander and turn back?'

Dawson looked glum.

'If we turn back and lose touch, we'll get it in the neck for not following orders, especially if it's only a minor problem. If the whole undercarriage was down, I think we'd have to turn back. But as things stand, we'd better push on.'

Campbell nodded.

'I think you're right. They'd never let us live it down if we lost them. I'll open her up a bit and see if we can't narrow the distance.'

He slid the central control forward a couple of notches. The airspeed indicator began to move up, slowly at first, then it peaked at 265.

'Dare I push it up any further?'

It was a rhetorical question, and Dawson knew it. They couldn't afford to waste fuel. At 265 they might conceivably gain on the other aircraft at about 25 miles an hour, which meant that in ten minutes they should be fairly well up close. But that was only if 286 was travelling at 240, and there was no guarantee of that.

As it happened, the Wing Co. had planned the six legs to be flown at various speeds, though he hadn't passed this information on to the following aircraft. No doubt he had reasoned that they would just match the speed of the aircraft ahead of them, speed up when they increased speed, and slow down when they slowed down. It just happened that the first leg was to be flown at 275 mph, so instead of 292 gradually closing the distance, it wasn't long before Campbell realized that they were falling behind.

'Blast the man,' he swore into his mouthpiece.

'You'd better notch her up a bit,' said Dawson, as if in reply.

Campbell pushed it up to 285, until they began to feel a bit of vibration. 'Do you think that's the nose wheel, causing that?' he said to Dawson.

Dawson nodded.

'It's bound to cause a bit of instability. It's sticking out like a sore thumb. You'd better drop back a touch.'

Campbell notched it back to 280, at which point the vibration ceased.

'It looks like we're stuck at this speed, come what may,' he said. 'Navigator,' he said over the R/T, 'you'd better plot us an alternate route to Canton, just in case we lose sight of the lead aircraft. The nose wheel is stuck down, and we can't go back. Plot your course so that if at any moment we need to peel off and head for Canton Atoll, you've got your co-ordinates ready and an E.T.A.'

'Roger, Eddie,' Ron Gray replied, and swore under his breath. Trust something to go wrong now. He mentally called Fletcher all the fatheads in creation, and returned to his plotter. He would have to make some pretty complicated calculations.

Bill O'Connell and Phil Cusack played their game of cards over the main spar, and looked nervously at each other when they felt the vibration. But it only lasted for two minutes, and they continued to deal, unaware of the drama that had been going on in the cockpit. Don Grainger was lying up the back, his eyes closed, still annoyed at the thought of the extra duty he was going to cop in Hawaii. Steve Bishop, the radio operator was sitting at his station, his radio turned off, listening to the interchange in the cockpit over the R/T. He was only 22, and he was worried. He looked at the others around him, oblivious to the problem, and envied them. He didn't need this.

II

Helen Currier had borrowed a flying suit, and was seated down in the Observer's position behind the perspex nose cone. It was cold, but she was wrapped up enough not to feel it. She was wondering about her standing with Eddie Campbell, after allowing herself to be seduced by more than one officer at the first stop. It wasn't guilt she felt, more the annoyance of being found out. To Helen, sex was the natural centre-point of her life, and she wasn't that fussy about who she did it with as long as there was a bar on the shoulder. It had just been unfortunate that Eddie had turned up before Ron Gray had managed to get away free.

The truth was that she had waited in her room for two hours for Eddie to appear, not realizing that the reason he didn't was that the Wing Commander's door had been left open, and he would see anyone who walked by. By the time Ron Gray plucked up the courage to slip past, unseen, as it happened, Helen had given up on Eddie Campbell, thinking that he wasn't sufficiently enamoured of her to risk a brief sorty in her room. So when Flight Lieutenant Gray poked his head in, she accepted him as a welcome diversion.

Eddie's appearance as Ron was leaving was just unfortunate. She was embarrassed, and tried to make light of it, just compounding the problem as it turned out. The next morning, Campbell had avoided her at breakfast, and when she approached him out on the putting green, where she was playing in a foursome, partnering the Wing Commander, he pointedly turned his back and snubbed her. So much for him, she thought. But despite herself, she couldn't get him out of her mind, and she spent most of the flight cursing her bad luck.

After Eddie had taken off in a huff the previous night, she had been lying in bed, feeling sorry for herself, when there was a tap at the door. She immediately thought that Eddie had come back, and opened the door, smiling. But it was Barton Fletcher standing there, a sheepish grin on his face.

'I know it's rather late, my dear, but I have a rather smashing bottle of champagne in my room, and I need help to drink it. If you would consider...'

Helen smiled sweetly.

'Of course, I'd love to, sir. I'd better tidy myself up first, though.' She made a point of pulling her gown around herself at the breast.

'Say twelve o'clock then,' he whispered. 'Midnight! Don't knock, just come in.' He turned to go back to his room, then turned back and leaned towards her, confidentially.

'Err. If you just check the passage first, you understand. Wouldn't want the others to see you... they might come to the wrong conclusion.'

'To the right conclusion,' she thought the next day. 'God! He was a bull! She'd played her little girl part, and had negligently allowed her gown to fall away and reveal her legs while she hugged herself and sucked on a finger. It never failed to turn them on.

When that funny little Scotsman had turned up after breakfast, with Campbell nowhere to be seen, she had succumbed again, and his mate Dawson had fallen in with her before lunch. She'd been a busy girl.

Helen excused herself these excesses on the grounds that she was a nymphomaniac. She would have made an interesting case study for a psycho-analyst in actual fact, because just as she found it impossible to refuse an officer, so on the other hand, she now found it impossible to accept an 'other ranks.' Her distaste for them was obsessive. And yet there hadn't been any major problems during the six months she spent with Gordon Duckett. That even puzzled her! Perhaps it was because she had slept with him before realizing that he was 'one of them'. Then of course, he had fooled her into thinking that a commission was imminent in his case, and it just went on from there. But never again!

'Oxygen masks on until further orders,' came over the R/T, and she pulled the mask down and pulled it over her face. They were uncomfortable things, but necessary at this altitude, she understood that. As she breathed, she became somewhat light-headed, and sat back to enjoy the experience. It was almost as good as a drug. She had no idea that pure oxygen could make you feel like that.

III

In 286, Squadron Leader Styles was enduring a monologue through the R/T delivered by the Wing Commander, on the positive training potential of this type of Navex.

'Navigators should be able to operate under all kinds of conditions, Styles. I should be able to throw a few loops in here or there, and if they're up to the mark, it shouldn't phase them at all. Take this chappie, McLeish. Seems to have a bit of a chip on his shoulder, but he knows his job all right. On the other hand, I was surprised that Ron Gray - and his pilot I might add - made such a fuss about the radio blackout. After all, he doesn't need the radio to navigate, he just needs his charts and his plotter... just about does it for him. Throw in the readings from the drift meter and – Tally Ho! What's so hard about that?'

'Yes sir,' Styles replied. Privately, he just wished the old windbag would shut up. He could do with a bit of space right now, after that humiliation over the evening meal. How dare McLeish speak to a superior officer like that? A damned Flying Officer, for god's sake! And the Wing Commander had been as good as useless.

'I don't know how some of these fellows would have fared in the old days,' mused Fletcher. 'Flying by the seat of your pants, thirty or forty years ago. I mean, go back to the first war, and my father was up there in one of those little bi-planes with a Browning pistol, taking pot-shots at Gerry as he flew by. *That* was flying,' he went on. 'No radio's in those days, just your instincts, and pure flying ability. And if you wanted to get home, you just followed the railway lines,' he chuckled.

Styles forbore to point out that there were no railway lines to follow in the middle of the Pacific, and silently questioned whether Fletcher had ever been a worthwhile pilot. He was such a blowhard!

From what he'd heard, Fletcher had been pushed along because Daddy was a World War I Ace, with 39 kills to his credit. Old man Fletcher had lied about his age in order to fly in 1916, and was only 17 when the war ended in 1918. He'd served again in the second war, signing up again at the age of 38, and had been flying in Lancasters until the end of the conflict. Barton Fletcher had been an unexpected addition to the Fletcher family, arriving within a year of his father marrying in 1923. There was never any question about what his career would be, whereas Styles had been the poor son of a jobbing plumber, and had to struggle for everything he'd achieved.

The head of his course at No.1 Flying Training School, Point Cook, he had enjoyed rapid promotion up to Squadron Leader, which he had managed by the age of 26. But his rather arrogant attitude to the men, and his predisposition to distance himself from other officers - an attempt to overcome his poorer origins some thought - halted his promotion at that point. He had been a Squadron Leader now for eight years, and felt that he was well overdue for his Wing Commanders. Others obviously felt differently.

Even after the oxygen went on in 286, Fletcher continued to chatter. They were cruising at 11,500 feet, heading into a darkening sky. At the 45 minute mark, the navigator relayed 'turrn 45 degrees to porrt, to a setting of 10 degrees. Please confirrm.'

Styles rotated a dial on the autopilot, and the aircraft began to turn. After thirty seconds he straightened her up.

'Heading 10 degrees, confirmed! How's our drift?' Styles enquired, coldly.

'Fifteen feet per second, west-sou-west, sirr. Aboot 10 knots per 'oor. But it hasn't affected us that much yet – it will be a wee bit more noticeable on this leg.'

Styles didn't bother to thank McLeish for the information. It was all he could do to talk to him, but nevertheless, the Scot was nothing if not professional in his job.

By the end of the following hour, the skies were almost dark, though a full moon reflected off the tops of low lying, cumulus clouds, making it appear lighter than it was. They made their second turn after 50 minutes, to a corrected heading of 340 degrees by DG. Fletcher had finally lapsed into silence. He appeared to be looking out of the side windscreen, but Styles suspected that he had fallen asleep. Not that it mattered. He had full control of the aircraft, the Wing Commander was really only along for the ride. The drone of the engines was hypnotic if you didn't keep your mind occupied, but Styles was not one to succumb to that.

He brooded on his lack of recent promotion, and tried to work out what *fau pas* he might have committed that had held him back. He was 34 years old, and as his target rank was Air Commodore, time was of the essence. If he didn't get his Wing Commander's in the next couple of years, he'd be lucky to make Group Captain before 48. With retirement at 55, he wouldn't have enough time left to make the higher grades, and his pension scheme would be blown to bits. He wondered if it would be worth asking the Wing Commander what his immediate chances were, though that might not be such a good idea. It wasn't good form to appear over anxious about promotion. You were supposed to be patient, and wait on the good offices of the powers that be. The trouble was that if promotion stopped at this level, he might well find himself being advised to look around for another career within the next four or five years. These things had been known to happen.

He was still brooding on the problem when the next change of heading came through, an hour later. He turned her 30 degrees to starboard, with a two-degree correction for drift, and set the autopilot on a course of 12 degrees. Ten minutes later, the oxygen ran out.

Chapter Ten

In 286, Gordon Duckett sat back in his seat and waited for the fireworks to begin. There was no way that nose wheel was going to retract on take-off in 292, which meant that they'd have to go back to Nadi to fix it. When they found the sheared pin blocking the works, they would just think that it had somehow sheared off before take-off, leaving part of the pin in place. It would mean an hour of stuffing around, and probably another night at Nadi. Duckett's satisfaction would be in putting the wind up Campbell.

Gordon took it for granted that the two aircraft were in radio contact with each other, so when 286 hadn't made any attempt to turn around after ten minutes flying time, he began to get worried. What had gone wrong? There was no way he could see to the rear of the aircraft, so he didn't even know if 292 was following. Maybe they'd been told to turn back, fix the U/S then make their own way to Canton Atoll. But somehow he didn't think so. The atmosphere on 286 was too even, too normal. Surely there would have been a flurry of activity for a minute or so, while they made their minds up about what course to pursue?

He looked up and down the aircraft, hoping that there would be some sign that could relieve his mind. Nothing! Seaman was up in the cockpit, Varley was reading a book, Jack Morris was up the back somewhere, sprawled out on a couple of kit bags. Leacock was playing pocket chess with the Radio Operator, Jason Mitchell. Leacock didn't care for Mitchell, nor Mitchell for Leacock, but in the event any chess player was better than no chess player. The navigator was busily poring over his charts, and watching the plotter trace out their course.

Gordon looked back at the sergeant and the Radio Operator.

The Radio was turned off. It took a few moments to register. Then he leant over and attracted Leacock's attention.

'Excuse me Sarge. Why is the Radio off?'

Leacock looked at the Radio, then turned back to Duckett.

'Radio silence! No radio contact between here and Canton – Wing Co.'s orders.' Then he went back to his game.

Duckett felt his heart drop into his stomach. Suddenly he had a foreboding of disaster, and became distinctly uncomfortable. Helen Currier was in that plane! He went white at the thought, then mentally kicked himself. Stupid! Now there was nothing he could do except hope for the best; hope that 292 arrived safely at Canton Atoll.

Varley was suffering too. From the time they had to apply oxygen at 11,000 feet, he kept the mask only loosely over his face, alert to any change in smell or taste that might occur. If they had to change to the back-up supply, he didn't know what he was going to do. He couldn't very well dive into the cockpit and rip the masks off the pilot and co-pilot. He would be arrested on the spot. Everyone on that aircraft would be affected, knocked out! Then if they kept breathing it, they could all end up dead. He could end up being the only person still conscious on the flight, and they were in the middle of the Pacific Ocean, god knew where, and he'd never flown a plane in his life!

Varley was an Instrument Fitter. He knew all about instrumentation, what each gauge was for, how the autopilot worked, and how to repair a navigator's plotter. But about landing an aircraft he knew nothing. About navigation, reading charts... Nothing!

The further into the flight they got, the more agitated he became. At the end of the second leg, he felt he had to tell someone. He looked around him, beads of sweat now breaking out on his brow, and saw Duckett sitting further along the fuselage, more or less on his own. Taking a deep breath, he made a decision. Duckett was an Armament Fitter, but he seemed a decent type. Maybe he wouldn't put him in... maybe, between them, they could create a diversion, make the pilot take the plane down to a lower altitude and turn off the oxygen. He got up and went to sit by Duckett.

'Hey, Gordon, I've got something to tell you. But first of all, you've got no reason to love the Air Force, have you? I mean, I've seen some of the trouble you've been in over the time.'

Gordon looked at him, warily. How did he know? How could he know? Varley had been at the Colonial when he'd cut that pin. Morris had gone bush, or had he?

'You're not going to tell anyone, are you,' said Duckett, suddenly fearful of the consequences. 'Who fucking told you – Morris?'

'Told me what?' said Varley, confused.

'About that fucking pin. It was just a bloody joke. I thought I'd stick it up that arsehole Campbell, for going off with Helen. It can't do anything – they'll still be able to land.'

Varley sat back with a start, and looked at Duckett in a new light.

'You left an undercarriage safety pin in place! What? Deliberately! How come it wasn't picked up on the walk-round,' he whispered.

'Are you going to put me in?' said Duckett, afraid now.

'Don't be silly, mate. We fitters have got to stick together. Fuck the officers!'

Gordon's face relaxed into a grin.

'Thank god you said that, mate. I've been crapping myself since we took off from Nadi. I thought we'd get a recall and have to land again, but it seems we're travelling under radio silence, so 292 wouldn't have been able to report it anyway.

They've either peeled off and gone back to Nadi, or they're following us with the nose wheel down. I wasn't going to tell anyone, but I'm glad now. It takes a bit of the weight off my shoulders. Do you think they'll be all right?'

'No reason to think otherwise. These thing's could fly halfway round the world with the undercarriage down. It would just produce a lot of extra drag. The fuel bill will be sky high.'

They grinned at each other. Now it was like a harmless conspiracy, a joke for the boys. Varley suddenly remembered his mission.

'Yeah, no worries! But I've got a confession to make as well... same conditions!'

'You mean, would I put you in?' said Gordon. 'Of course not!'

'Well listen, because this is serious. I may need your help on this one. I filled the back-up oxy system with nitrous oxide...'

Gordon looked blank.

'You know, nitrous oxide... laughing gas!'

Gordon's jaw dropped, then he began to laugh.

'You fuckin' mad bastard,' he grinned. 'And I thought I was stupid! So we're all going to be pissing ourselves laughing when they change over?'

Varley shook his head fiercely, and tried to get Gordon to concentrate.

'No mate, no! That's only an interim stage. If the pilots take more than a few breaths, it will knock them out. Then if they keep breathing it while unconscious, it will probably kill them. It could kill everyone on this plane!'

Gordon suddenly stopped laughing, and ripped his oxy mask away from his face.

'Fucken hell!... Fucken hell! What are you going to do?'

'That's what I wanted to talk to you about!'

At that moment the plane went into a turn, setting up the fourth leg of the Navex. Morris had staggered down from the rear of the plane, and was trying to get past them when the turn was made. He lost his balance and grabbed Varley by the shoulder to steady himself. If either Varley or Duckett had bothered to look, they would have noticed that his pupils were dilated, and that he was totally out of it. But they were too caught up in the immensity of their own dilemmas.

'We've somehow got to get the pilot to take this thing down to five thousand feet, where we won't need oxygen. But I've got no idea how to do that. What would make them drop to five thousand feet?' said Varley.

'How the fuck would I know – I'm just a gunny! You're the instrument guy. What about if the Nav Plotter fucked up. If it was daylight they might go down to see if they could spot this island by sight.'

'Good thought,' said Varley, musingly. 'The only trouble is there's about eight hours to daylight. Anything could happen in that time.'

'You might just have to go and rip their masks off. You could always say you smelled something funny, then you noticed everyone was passing out around you.'

Varley looked at Gordon, and nodded.

'Think I'd get away with that?'

'You could say you have an acute sense of smell, and something just wasn't right. If you like, I could say that I smelt it too, and we both ripped our masks off at the same time.'

'Would you do that?' said Varley, hopefully. 'That might be the answer!'

'Well, you cover my arse, and I'll cover yours,' said Gordon, shrugging.

'It's a deal!'

They both sat back and simultaneously breathed a sigh of relief.

II

Up in the cockpit of 286, Styles peered through the perspex at flashes in the distance. They were heading into an electrical storm. He cleared his throat through the R/T to try and wake the Wing Commander up. There was no response. He leant over and gave him a shake. Fletcher came to with a series of spluttering sounds, as if he were surfacing in his bath.

'Oh, what's up, oh, dear me! Must have dropped off. Sorry about that, Squadron Leader.'

'Looks like an electrical storm ahead, sir. Do you want to take evasive action?'

Fletcher peered out through the Perspex, and saw a few small flashes some miles away.

'Oh! I see. Well, what do you think, Styles? Are we above it?'

'Hard to tell, sir! It looks like cumulonimbus cloud. We might be able to ride over the top of it without much trouble. There again, it could be sitting up around twenty thousand feet, in which case we'd be in the thick of it, and the turbulence will be pretty severe.'

Fletcher, who'd never been through an electrical storm in his life, shrugged his shoulders.

'What the hell, eh? We'll just go through it. At the worst we'll get a bit of shaking around. Not much chance of a lightning strike, is there?'

Styles thought to himself 'you're telling the story, Wingco!' He stole a glance at the man next to him. It might just do the old blowhard good to go through a storm, even through a lightning strike. It might make him a little more cautious in the future.

'If that's what you want, sir!'

Fletcher waved his hand at it, as if to dismiss the storm as of no consequence.

'Keep going. We don't want to upset our navigator too much on this leg, do we.' He chuckled. 'He might start spitting that Gaelic at us again, and we won't know where we are.'

The first of the turbulence hit just as the oxygen supply ran out. Styles reached behind him to automatically switch over to the back-up supply, then concentrated on the storm. Neither of them noticed the subtle change in the oxygen, or if they did, they probably thought the smell came from the first oxy in the new tank.

Styles was staring straight ahead when he felt a strangeness in his head, like a blanket being pulled over his brain. For the next twenty seconds, he and the Wing Commander kept breathing pure nitrous oxide.

At that moment, Jack Morris clattered into the cockpit, waving a gun and yelling 'turn around you bastards. You've got to turn around.' Then he loosed a shot into the instrument panel, and Styles threw his hands up and inadvertently knocked the mask away from his face. In the co-pilot's seat, the Wing Commander stared straight ahead until his eyes rolled up into his head and he sagged forwards.

Styles was totally disoriented. It was as if the world had suddenly collapsed around him, releasing this madman into his line of vision, and the Squadron Leader was suddenly incapable of reacting, responding or making any decision whatsoever. Unknown to him, those extra few seconds of breathing pure 100% nitrous oxide had depressed his nervous system, and had begun to act on his brain, brain stem and spinal cord, and had created a minor lesion in his brain. If he hadn't knocked the mask off when he did, he would have been dead within another thirty seconds.

Back in the aircraft, Varley and Duckett had leapt up at the sound of the shot, then run along the aircraft tearing off oxygen masks. Varley got to Leacock first, but somehow they missed Jason Mitchell. He was found dead five minutes later, lying across the bench having just placed a rook in position to checkmate Leacock's King. Danny Seaman woke up on the floor, his mask hanging above him and Ron Gray was all right as his was half off to start with, and at the first sign of a strange smell he'd pushed it aside.

In the confusion, no-one thought to ask Duckett or Varley what they were doing. All anyone could hear was Morris ranting in the cockpit, waving his gun and demanding that they turn around. Styles was trying to get his head back together, but was slightly brain-damaged, and incapable of following any instruction. The Wing Commander appeared to be dead.

Morris staggered back into the fuselage and fired a shot at the navigator, which missed, but destroyed the plotter. Then in his deranged state he told Leacock, Varley and Duckett to hit the deck, while he went back and put a bullet through the radio.

'What the fuck are you doing, Morris,' yelled Varley from the floor, protecting his head with his hands. 'Have you gone fucking raving mad… you'll kill us all!'

'I don't care! I don't fucking care,' ranted Morris, turning to Varley. He pointed his gun, then thought better of it. Danny Seaman still lay dazed on the floor behind him, and Morris kicked his arm out of the way.

'You, Duckett, Varley, get into the cockpit. This fuck doesn't seem to understand what I want. Tell him to turn the fucking plane around.'

Varley was in the cockpit first. One look at the slumped body of the Wing Commander, and the glazed, confused eyes of the Squadron Leader told him they were in real trouble.

'Tell him to turn the plane around, back to Townsville. I've got to see my wife!'

Varley turned around.

'He's dead… the Wing Commander's dead! Can't you see?'

Morris looked at the body of the co-pilot, and took a pace back.

'Well get him out of there. One of you can go co-pilot. You Varley! You're fucking instruments. You can fly it!'

'No, I can't, Morris. I can't fly.'

While Morris waved his gun about in his dementia, Duckett and Varley heaved Fletcher's body out of the seat and laid him on his back on the floor. Styles was still sitting in his seat, but was agitated now, looking first at them and then at the controls, and then at Morris in quick succession, as if he didn't know what to concentrate on first. Varley climbed into the co-pilot's seat, and looked at Styles.

'Calm down, sir. You're going to have to tell me what to do.'

Styles looked at him uncomprehending, trying to battle back through the fog that had taken over his thought processes. He seemed incapable of getting a grasp on anything.

'Take deep breaths, sir. Breathe deep. That's it.'

'You fucking take his place, Duckett,' said Morris, pointing the gun at Duckett's head. Duckett hurried to obey, and half dragged the Squadron Leader out of his seat. Morris knocked Styles to the floor, and as he did so he spun around and the gun went off again, this time placing a bullet clean through the G2 compass gyro.

Back in the fuselage, Peter Leacock had managed to crawl up to the rear of the plane and get his hands on the gun locker. He twisted a screwdriver in the padlock and took out one of the SLR's they'd brought along to guard the aircraft. He slipped a clip into place and operated the bolt action once, then crawled back towards the main spar. Keeping low, he rested the rifle on the spar and aimed it up towards the cockpit, then waited.

Danny Seaman had also made his way back, still fuzzy but appreciating the great danger they were in. He saw Leacock with the rifle and obligingly got down and out of the way. He was trying to attract the attention of the Navigator to keep down and give the Sergeant a clear shot. McLeish got the message, and dropped to the floor.

As Duckett dropped into the pilot's seat, Morris got hold of Styles by the collar and began to drag him back into the fuselage.

'As for you, you bastard! You're going to get yours. Who's fucking top dog now, hey… Sir!' He was ranting like one quite demented.

Morris raised the gun and put it to the back of Styles head. There was an explosion further along the plane, and the back of Morris's head blew out, splattering brains and blood all over the perspex and the instrument panel. He toppled slowly backwards and fell onto the body of the Wing Commander.

Peter Leacock jumped up and vaulted over the wing spar, taking the SLR with him. Danny scrambled to his feet, and the two of them made their way to the cockpit.

'Thank God for you, Sergeant,' Danny swore.

In the seats, Varley and Duckett were nursing their eardrums. The bullet from the SLR had passed clean through Morris's head and out through the perspex canopy, causing an explosive decompression that had affected their ears. The wind was whistling around the hole in the screen, while the blood on the panel had run through and shorted out some of the instruments. Leacock stood in the doorway, and shook his head at the mess.

'Have you ever seen anything fucking like this,' he yelled. 'Are you okay, you two?'

Varley turned in his seat and nodded, holding his ears. Duckett sat with his hands in the air for some reason known only to himself. When he realized the SLR wasn't pointed at him, he gave in to the stress of the moment, and burst into tears.

'Get him out of there, Sergeant,' Danny Seaman said from somewhere behind. He was helping the squadron leader to his feet, and trying to calm him down.

'Are you going to be all right, sir?'

Styles looked at Danny, staggered back against the doorway, then shook himself violently as if to shake off the deadly torpor that had overcome him.

'Yes Warrant Officer, yes! I'm all right. What in god's name has happened here?'

'An LAC went berserk, sir, with a gun. He was going to shoot you!'

'But what about the Wing Commander. Is he dead? What happened to the Wing Commander?' They were all gasping for breath at this stage.

'I have no idea,' shouted Danny over the din. 'But we need to get down to a lower altitude sir. It's too hard to breathe up here, and the aircraft has decompressed.'

Styles nodded in understanding. Duckett had made way for him, and Styles climbed back into his seat. He immediately put 286 into a shallow dive.

Adrian McLeish stuck his head into the cabin and addressed the pilot.

'I have'na' got no plotter, and that wee loon has taken out the radio. We canna even send oot a Mayday.'

'Do you have any idea where we are, McLeish?'

'Och aye! I have the co-ordinates for up t' twenty minutes ago, but we've lost oor compass.' He pointed to the G2, smashed beyond repair in the panel.'

'We'll have to hope 292 is behind us, and realizes we're in some sort of trouble. I'll take it down to 5,000 feet then do a 360 degree turn, see if we can sight the others.'

'Right you are, sirr!'

Styles went to put the oxy mask back on, but Varley in the co-pilot's seat gestured violently.

'I think it's contaminated, sir! Don't use the oxygen!'

He shot a panicking glance at Leacock behind him, and at the Warrant Officer. Surely they must know now? Leacock looked at Varley thoughtfully, but kept his ideas to himself.

'Somebody's going to answer for this,' swore Danny Seaman, looking black. 'By God, someone's going to answer!'

Chapter Eleven

Eddie Campbell noted the navigation lights ahead of him turning into the fourth leg, and snapped at Dawson, 'here he goes again!' Then to the Navigator over the R/T, 'Wake up Ron, we're playing games again. Mark here, and I'll give you the new heading when we straighten up.'

Ron Gray marked his chart by the plotting head, and sat in readiness. They were two miles behind 286, and it was becoming a bit of a strain charting the course.

'New heading 12 degrees, speed 260 mph. Time 1952 hours.'

Gray made the appropriate notations.

'How many more friggin' headings is he going to torture us with,' he muttered through the headset. Dawson laughed.

'Don't worry, Ron boy. We'll get our own back – we'll spike his drinks in Honolulu!'

Campbell smiled at the exchange, but it was a grim smile. He was on edge, and getting very tired.

'Is that an electrical storm ahead? Look – flashes, about five miles ahead. It bloody is! What's the old trout leading us into now?'

'Oh, for chrisesake,' muttered Dawson. 'I went through one of those over New Guinea last year. It just about knocked us out of the sky. You'd better hang on, fellows! Alert the ground crew, Ron.'

Gray turned and spoke briefly to Barry Mackintosh, who nodded, and made his way along the fuselage. Bill O'Connell and Phil Cusack were still playing cards, but at a word from Mackintosh they packed them up, and got ready to weather some turbulence. The Flight Sergeant alerted Don Grainger up the back, then made his way back across the main spar looking for Helen Currier.

'Have you seen the airwoman,' he asked the sparky, Ian Johnson. Johnson indicated that she was down in the observer's position, and Bailey offered to go down and get her out.

'She can stay there if she likes, but she'd better strap in,' said Mackintosh. 'It could get a little rough down there.'

Bailey squeezed himself down the crawlway and tapped Helen on the shoulder. It made her jump.

'We're running into a storm. If you're going to stay down here, you'd better buckle up. There could be some turbulence.'

Helen looked concerned.

'Is it safe down here?'

'As safe as anywhere. It might get a bit spectacular, you're in the box seat.'

Helen nodded, and smiled, nervously.

'I think I'll stay here.' She pulled the straps over her shoulders and buckled up.

Back in the cockpit, Campbell was watching the aircraft ahead with a puzzled look on his face.

'Am I imagining things, or are they starting to pitch and yaw? Maybe they just hit some turbulence.'

'I didn't see anything,' said Dawson. 'Mind you, I wasn't really watching that closely.'

Two minutes later, 286 went into a shallow dive, and continued to lose height.

'What the bloody hell,' muttered Campbell. 'He's going down – look – he's definitely losing height.'

'Thanks for telling us, Wing Commander' Dawson remarked. 'It looks like he's going down to a lower level. What would he be doing that for, with a storm up ahead.'

'I know, you'd think he'd try to stay on top of it, wouldn't you? Maybe he wants to experience being in the eye of a storm.'

'If that's the case, he's raving mad,' said Dawson. 'Are we going to follow them down?'

'What choice have we got,' said Campbell, bitterly. 'I tell you what, I've got a good mind to put in an official complaint about this trip. It's the most unprofessional exercise I've ever taken part in. Talk about frustrating!'

Eddie knocked off the autopilot and pushed the joystick forward, putting 292 into a shallow dive behind 286. They followed it down to 5,000 feet, then leveled out along with the aircraft in front. At this height, the turbulence was quite violent, the aircraft shuddering along the whole of its length.

'I don't like this one bit,' said Campbell, now rather white in the face. His lips were pinched and bloodless, and although he was fighting to control himself, even he looked scared. Lightning was flashing brightly in front of them, and every so often they felt the rumble of thunder assault the perspex canopy, making it shake. 'I'm going to close up the gap... stuff this!' He pushed the central control forward and ignited the Westinghouse turbojets, which kicked in and catapulted them back into their seats. The airspeed indicator rapidly climbed up to 325 mph, and they began to gain on 286 rapidly.

'Do you think that's wise,' yelled Dawson, trying to make himself heard over the din. 'They really chew up the fuel!'

'We've got to get past the bastards, let them see our nose wheel is stuck down. I should have done it hours ago.'

There were howls and protests from the rear of the aircraft, from some of the crew who had been unceremoniously thrown to the floor when the jets cut in. Now, in addition to turbulence, there was a regular vibration through the mainplane.

'Fuckin' thanks very much,' yelled Cusack, who had been thrown into the main spar.

'Bloody terrific,' said Bailey, who was picking himself up off the floor.

Within minutes they were overhauling the lead aircraft, sitting two hundred yards behind and slightly to starboard. Campbell intended to cruise past the starboard side of 286 so they could spot his predicament. Just as he was making his run, however, 286 banked off to port, and started to turn in a wide circle through the storm.

'Not another heading change! Hang on, everybody! Navigator – mark this position and time at, let's see – 1956 hours.'

'Confirmed,' came the reply through the headset.

The rain suddenly came down like a sheet, restricting their view to only an occasional glimpse of a red navigation light ahead. Campbell was trying to follow as best he could, though as he had started off slightly to starboard of the aircraft in front he was more or less exactly behind them, and unable to be seen by the crew of the lead aircraft.

He switched off the jet pods and tried to adjust to the speed of the lead aircraft.

'We're too close, too close,' yelled Dawson. 'Pull back, or we'll be grinding their coffee!'

Eddie blanched, and dropped his airspeed to 260. In brief glimpses they watched the red port navigation light start to pull away, still sweeping around in a steady curve.

'What the fuck's he playing at,' yelled Campbell, the nervous tension getting to him. 'We've just about done 180 degrees. Is this some stupid, fucking game he's come up with?'

A huge flash of lightning lit up the aircraft in front, and almost blinded the pilots of 292. They automatically threw their hands up to shield their eyes, and cursed.

'God almighty,' yelled Dawson. 'That just about burnt my eyeballs out!'

The roll of thunder hit them then, like an atomic blast, shaking the canopy as if it would burst. Visibility was almost non-existent. The navigation light of 286 ahead continued to turn, and Campbell continued to follow it. Then the hail hit them.

Like a machine-gun burst on the perspex canopy, hail suddenly took the place of the rain that had been reducing visibility, and began to build up on the screen. Campbell switched on the screen wipers.

'De-icers on,' snapped Campbell, and Dawson threw a switch. 'Ten minutes of this and we'll be flying blind,' he yelled over the din.

The sky above them was glowing with a weird light, and the cumulonimbus formation of the cloud cover could be clearly seen between bursts of hail.

'How high do you think that cloud cover is sitting?' the pilot yelled at Dawson.

'About 16,000 feet. We could get above this!'

'Not while we've got to follow this prick through his mad dream. I feel like punching him out.'

'Get in line,' cracked Dawson with a wry smile.

The cockpit suddenly lit up with a blinding flash, accompanied by a sound like an explosion. The lights went out on the panel.

'Oh, Christ! We've been hit,' yelled Dawson.

Campbell looked out of the side screen to check if the engines were all right. There seemed to be no problem there, but power to certain instruments and to the panel lights had dropped out. A minute later the DG and artificial horizon began to spin uselessly on their gymbals.

'We've lost the G2... and the AH. Call the instrument guy. Check for damage control.'

Back in the fuselage Bill O'Connell and Ian Johnson were making their way to the cockpit. They briefly looked at each other in the gloom.

'We're fucked,' said Johnson, biting his lip. O'Connell shook his head, gloomily.

Down in the observer's seat, Helen Currier was desperately trying to undo the straps so she could get out of there. Seconds before the lightning had hit her hair had stood up on end, a result of the intense static electricity in the area. Then the lightning had hit, and for a moment she thought that the perspex canopy between her and the ocean had blown apart, leaving her open to the elements. She had screamed and put her hands over her head to protect herself, but there was no sudden wind, just a huge sound like an explosion before the lights went out. Once the straps were off, she climbed around the seat and scrabbled her way, half blinded, up the crawlway into the relative safety of the fuselage, sobbing in blind panic.

'We've lost power to the gyro's,' Campbell yelled at O'Connell. Bill looked at Ian Johnson.

'That's your department, Sparky,' he said. Johnson nodded.

'Could just be fuses in the main bus,' he said. 'I'll check it out.'

Bill looked over the instruments. The only gauges still working were those that worked off static and pressure, and the thermocouples. So the altimeter, rate of climb, and airspeed indicators were okay, as were the oil temperature gauges. The fuel gauges also were registering for some strange reason, though all the gyros were down. The drift computer was out, and the lat-long indicator. The Navigator's Plotter had ceased to function, and a quick check of the radio showed that it was out also.

Campbell had his hands full trying to follow 286 around the loop.

'When's this prick going to straighten up,' he said,

exasperated. 'We've almost gone 360 degrees.'

As he spoke, the aircraft in front went into a shallow dive once more, and Campbell followed.

'If they keep going down at this rate, we'll be able to go for a midnight swim,' Dawson muttered.

'I don't suppose they've been hit by lightning too,' said Campbell. 'Surely, that would be too much of a coincidence.'

'I didn't see it – but there again, after that flash, who could see anything?'

The hail gave way to rain once more and cleared the ice off the screen. A89-286 was still locked into a turning circle, and still descending.

'3,000 feet,' said Campbell, 'and still falling.'

At 2,000 feet the lead aircraft leveled out, then straightened its course on a new heading. The only problem was that neither Campbell nor Dawson knew what the new heading was.

There was a small magnetic compass at the top of the panel, not much good for anything but giving a general direction.

'According to that, we're heading approximately northwest. After all the jerking about we've been doing to the east, I would suppose that's about right.'

Johnson shoved his head back into the cockpit.

'Excuse me, sir. The main fuse box is burnt out. Not just the fuses, but a lot of the wiring behind it. It's a major overhaul job, sir.'

'So we're flying by the skin of our teeth,' Dawson muttered.

Campbell just looked around and nodded. Johnson could see the strain in his face, and glanced knowingly at Bill O'Connell.

'Where's this Canton Atoll then, Sir?'

Bill looked at the DG spinning uselessly behind the glass. Dawson looked up at him from his seat and said, 'Where would you like it to be, LAC? Your guess is as good as ours!'

'It's like that, is it, sir?' said Bill, grimly. Then he turned to go back into the fuselage.

II

After the dive to 5,000 feet Styles didn't trust himself to be able to hold on to the aircraft, which was being buffeted by sudden winds, so he engaged the autopilot and set it to describe a lazy circle to port. The turbulence was extreme now, and regular shudders ran through the mainplane, keeping everyone on the edge of their seats.

'Keep an eye out for 292 as we turn, and keep an eye on me. I've got a splitting headache, and I don't know whether or not I'm going to pass out.'

Varley looked across from the co-pilot's seat, feeling totally helpless. If Styles went, they'd had it. He was the only one who could land this thing.

A flash of lightning lit up the cockpit and made everyone jump. Then the thunder hit, and the whole plane rumbled with it. The hail was just as unexpected. It rattled on the screen, and gathered in a cone around the bullet hole, temporarily blocking it off. It was so cold that Varley's teeth were chattering.

Danny Seaman and Peter Leacock were leaning forward, trying to look back along the aircraft to see if they could spot 292. Visibility in that direction was almost nil, but at one point Leacock pulled closer to the screen.

'I thought I saw their port navigation light. If so, they're only about fifty yards behind us. What are they playing at?'

'They're supposed to be two miles behind,' said Styles. 'Maybe they're in trouble themselves.'

'Forget about 292,' said Danny. 'They're quite capable of looking after themselves. If they *are* behind us, and anything happens, they will be able to send out a Mayday. If not, then no doubt they will be able to give an approximation of our position the last time they saw us.'

'Are we going to crash,' said Leacock. 'If so, I'd better organize a raft.'

'Have we got any?' said the Warrant Officer. 'How many men can they hold?'

'We should have two four men rafts stowed at the rear,' said the sergeant.

'That's if the duty crew have done their job properly,' said Styles, dryly. His attitude towards the ground crew was always negative.

'I'll have you know, sir, that it was a member of the ground crew, Sergeant Leacock here, that saved your life not so long ago... Sir!' Danny was not in the mood for aggravation.

Styles looked around at the Warrant Officer, and scowled.

'And it was a member of your ground crew, Warrant Officer, that ran amok with a handgun. I'd like an explanation of that before too much longer.'

'Well you're going to have to wait, Squadron Leader, until a more auspicious moment,' said Danny, off-handedly. 'Your job is to get us to Canton Atoll in one piece, Sir!'

Styles turned in his seat, enraged.

'Don't you dare presume to tell me my job, Warrant! I'm well aware of my duties and responsibilities, unlike some!'

'Meaning...' said Danny, staring him down.

'Meaning that there's going to be an official enquiry into these events, and there will be a few courts martial for the members involved.'

Peter Leacock looked contemptuously down on Styles from his position behind his seat, and said to Danny: 'We don't need to put up with this, Warrant Officer. No doubt the Squadron

Leader's got a direct line to God, because he's got it all signed and sealed before the plane's even landed.'

Both Leacock and Seaman left the cockpit, and retired to a position at the front of the fuselage. Leacock then approached the navigator, McLeish, who was poring over a chart with a pair of dividers. The smashed plotter lay uselessly beside him.

'Can you plot us through to Canton Atoll, sir?'

'That indeed is the question, Serrgeant. On the original Navex we had another two legs to fly. I'm jest trying to work oot a shortcut, skipping the fifth heading. But the G2 is oot – I dinna see how we're going to find it. It's a vast ocean, Sergeant!'

There was a flash and a sound like an explosion on the starboard side, and the Wright Cyclone Radial began to sound a new note. It began feathering, then within a minute cut out altogether.

'Fire!' someone yelled from the cockpit.

It was Varley, peering out towards the starboard engine. There were flames and smoke streaming from under the cowling, and Varley was panicking.

Styles shut the fuel off to the engine and listened to it come to a halt. Twenty seconds later, Varley said, 'I can't see any flames now, sir. It seems to have gone out.'

Styles looked at him in undisguised hostility, as if to say 'what would you know?'

The aircraft began to pitch and yaw alarmingly, and Styles reached over to start the pods.

'I'm going down to five hundred feet to have a look around,' Styles snapped through the headset. 'Did you get that, navigator? We're headed approximately northwest.'

'Aye sir,' came the reply.

Styles nudged the nose down and everyone tried to equalize the pressure in their ears. It was a painful process. Shortly they heard the jet pods begin their whine, and the aircraft steadied.

The rain still streamed across the perspex screen, but the moon suddenly peeped out from behind the cloud cover and lit up their path. Varley looked down to an endless sea, its rippled surface stretching away to infinity, and his heart dropped into his stomach. There was no way they were going to survive this, no way at all!

Chapter Twelve

When the starboard engine of 286 caught fire, Eddie Campbell's jaw fell open in disbelief.

'I'll be stuffed! They really are in trouble,' he said. 'They've feathered the starboard engine. What the hell's going on! Ask the sparky if there's any way he can patch power through to the radio, will you Mackintosh,' he said. 'We need to see if they're on the air.'

Johnson stuck his head back into the cockpit.

'I told you, the wiring behind the main bus has burnt out. The loom runs inside the skin of the aircraft. I'd have to pull half the plane apart.'

'Well pull the fucking thing apart!' yelled Campbell, losing patience. 'What's the good of you guys if you can't use a bit of creativity? This is serious!'

'The name's Johnson, not Jesus Christ,' the Corporal shot back.

'Is that so? Well, Corporal – if we don't do something soon, you might find yourself walking on water!'

Johnson stormed off to have another look at the main bus, muttering as he went.

A slipstream appeared from the rear of 286 as it went into a shallow dive, and Campbell cursed again.

'They've fired the pods. It looks as if they're going down to have a look around.'

Dawson looked over, and nodded.

'I think we could both be in the shit! If they go in, we haven't got a hope in hell. Looking for Canton without a G2 would be like looking for an Englishman in an Irish bar.'

'I'd laugh if it wasn't so serious,' yelled Campbell in reply.

'We've got to get that power back on.'

There was a commotion in the rear of the cockpit, and Campbell looked around to see Flight Sergeant Mackintosh trying to prevent Helen Currier from entering. She had been crying.

'Eddie, tell him to let me in. I just want to talk to you.'

Campbell nodded to Mackintosh, who stood back and let her go. Her eyes were puffy with crying, and her hair was in disarray. She flung herself on him and wound her arms around his throat.

'Are we going to die... are we going to die, sir? I was down in the observer's seat, and when that lightning hit us it was like seeing God!'

'No, Helen. We've lost some power, but not our engines. We're okay! For god's sake control yourself, or you'll have everyone in hysterics.' He tried to unwind her arms from his shoulders.

'I'm sorry, sir. I just can't help it. I'm so scared! I thought this was just going to be a routine flight.'

'Didn't we all,' said Dawson.

'I think it would be better if you went back to your seat and strapped yourself in. We're not out of the storm yet.'

'But Eddie, I...'

Campbell turned in his seat and literally threw Helen off him.

'Airwoman Currier! I'm ordering you back to your seat! Can't you see we've got our hands full with an emergency here?'

Helen looked crushed, and her face puckered and collapsed. Flight Sergeant Mackintosh took her by the arm and firmly led her to a seat further down the fuselage. Back in the cockpit, Dawson shot Campbell a quizzical glance.

'Didn't get your end in, Eddie? That's a pity – everyone else did.' He grinned.

'I'm well aware of that! Thanks for nothing,' Campbell replied, not without a little bitterness. He had liked Helen.

The lead aircraft levelled out at 500 feet, and Campbell brought 292 hard up behind. There was nothing but ocean down there.

'I'm going alongside,' said Campbell, and pushed the control forward. This time he made ground and in three minutes had drawn abreast of 286, about 60 yards away on his port side. He peered through the side screen, and found it hard to believe what he saw.

'Hey, there's a mess all over the screen... a hell of a mess. It looks like blood, for Chrisesake. And there's a crack, no, a bloody great hole in the windshield. Have a look, Dawson, what do you think?'

The co-pilot stood up and leant across the centre console. There was enough of a glow from the moon to show that there was something very wrong in 286.

'What is it - a birdstrike!' said Dawson.

'Not at this bloody altitude,' Campbell replied. 'Besides, that blood or whatever it is, is on the inside.'

At that moment, Varley shoved his face up against the screen, and stared at 292 for the first time. His jaw dropped as he saw the exposed nose wheel.

'Is that a fitter in the co-pilot's seat?' said Campbell, in the other plane. 'Where the hell is the Wing Commander? Putting a fitter in the box seat? Never! It doesn't happen.'

He made interrogatory gestures to Varley in the other plane. Then he tapped the bars on his shoulder, as if to say 'where's the Wing Commander.'

Varley half stood in his seat, and drew his finger across his throat. Then he did it again, unless there was any doubt about his meaning.

'God, he's bloody dead,' said Campbell, aghast. 'I'm sure that's what he means. The Wing Commander's dead!'

'Surely not! Maybe he had a heart attack,' said Dawson, panicking.

'Not with all that blood all over the screen! It is blood, you know. Every now and then you get a flash, and it's red.'

'And they've got one engine out. God, we're in deep trouble.'

Suddenly Styles face appeared in the screen, where he leaned across Varley to see 292. He pointed to their nose wheel, as if they didn't know it was down. Campbell pointed downwards, and nodded his head, vigorously. Then he placed his palms upwards, to indicate that they couldn't do anything about it. Styles indicated that he understood.

With further sign language, they both managed to convey the fact that both radios were out, and Campbell held up a sign saying 'G2 OUT.' A few moments later, Varley held up a sign saying 'G2 OUT.' Both pilots sat back and took stock.

Slowly, 292 moved away, and took up a position abreast of 286 but 100 yards away, and Styles began to scan the horizon for salvation.

II

Styles called Danny Seaman into the cockpit. He turned, and nodded towards the bodies of Morris and Fletcher on the floor.

'Don't you think it's about time they were moved?'

The Warrant Officer stuck his head out and called Peter Leacock and Gordon Duckett.

'Get those two out of here, will you? You'll have to stow them down by the main spar. Try and keep them out of the way.'

Morris was a mess. Half of the back of his head was missing, and the floor was awash with his blood. Before they moved him

Duckett was sent off to find a plastic bag to cover his head and face, so they wouldn't spread the mess all through the aircraft. They had to half drag and half carry the body along the narrow aisle, and finally stowed him under a workstation. Then they went back for the Wing Commander.

The moment Leacock tried to lift Fletcher by the shoulders, the body let out a groan. He dropped it again, and jumped back.

'Bloody hell, that gave me a start!' he said.

Duckett grabbed the legs and once again, Peter bent to lift Fletcher by the shoulders. This time Fletcher opened his eyes.

'What… what… what… 'he stuttered, and was promptly dropped again.

'God almighty, he's alive,' said Leacock.

Fletcher lay staring at the roof of the cockpit, his mouth moving and attempting to make sounds. Styles looked around and stared in amazement.

'I could have sworn he was dead. He must have just passed out. I couldn't rouse him, I know that.'

With difficulty, the Wing Commander was manoeuvred into the fuselage, and strapped into a seat. He was breathing heavily, and didn't appear to be in charge of his faculties.

'Just you watch him,' the Sergeant said to Duckett. 'He's in your care. Make sure he doesn't harm himself.'

Danny Seaman watched the proceedings from a distance. He beckoned Leacock over.

'What do you think – stroke?' he said.

'I don't know, Warrant. He looks pretty awful, his colouring's all grey. Maybe he had some sort of a fit. I heard Varley say something about the oxygen being contaminated. Maybe we should ask him what he meant.'

Danny nodded, and approached Varley in the co-pilot's seat from behind.

'LAC, we need to know what you meant about the oxy being 'contaminated'. What did you mean by that?'

Varley's mouth went dry, and he swallowed hard.

'I don't know sir, but I noticed a chronic smell and taste all of a sudden... Duckett noticed it too! We pulled our masks off because it was so chronic. Then we noticed everyone else flaking out. You fell off your seat, sir, and the mask was wrenched off your face when you hit the floor. I saw Sergeant Leacock fall forward, so I jumped over and pulled his mask off. Then we were going to go up to the cockpit, but Morris was firing shots and ranting by then, so we ended up on the floor.'

'And what happened to the Pilot Officer?'

'We must have missed him, sir, in the mad panic when that gun went off. I'm sorry sir. We should have been more alert.'

'Hmmm!' Danny stared at Varley as if unconvinced. 'I want you to take a whiff of that oxygen – don't breathe it in, just take a whiff – and tell me what you think it is.'

Varley eyed the mask off uncertainly. Then he put it up to his face and turned the supply on. He took a whiff of the gas, pulled a face and coughed.

'God – that's awful! It reminds me of the dentist when I was a kid, sir!'

'You mean laughing gas, Varley?'

'Yeah, that's what it smells like. Laughing gas, sir!'

Danny went back out to Leacock.

'Varley reckons it smells like laughing gas, Sergeant. What are the chances of a cylinder getting mixed up on the oxy trolley?'

Leacock shook his head, emphatically.

'No chance! Come on, Warrant, you know very well that the oxy cylinders are colour coded, black and white. You'd have to be colour blind – or stupid!'

'Or just plain bloody evil,' muttered the Warrant Officer. 'It looks like a clear case of sabotage to me.'

'I wouldn't go that far, sir. That's a bit heavy.'

'We have a pilot officer dead, Sergeant, and a Wing Commander *non compos mentis. That's* what I'd call a bit heavy!'

Danny brooded for a moment or so, then began to speak in more of a whisper, so they wouldn't be overheard by the others.

'What about the nose wheel on 292? Coincidence? Someone has obviously done something to the hydraulics on 292 to make sure that nose wheel won't retract. Maybe they've just left an undercarriage pin in place. If so, why wasn't it picked up on the walk-round? The tags on those pins are a foot long and bright orange. You can't miss them – you know that! I think someone set out to sabotage this flight, and they've done a pretty good job, so far. What's more, it's a member of the ground crew. Do you remember who was on oxy replenishment over the past few days?'

Leacock thought back, frowning.

'It could have been anyone, Warrant. There's been a bit of night flying, so it could have been someone on duty crew. The oxy cart isn't something that is restricted to one mustering. They share those sorts of duties on the line. One day it's an instrument fitter, the next it might be a sumpie. It just depends who's available.'

'I'll tell you what I think,' said Danny, quietly. 'I think it's someone on one of these two aircraft. The nose wheel problem on 292 wasn't evident before Nadi, so it must be someone with us, on the crew.'

'Now that's a bit hasty, Warrant. It might be a genuine U/S. We won't know until the framies' pull it down and have a look. It could be a blocked hydraulics line.'

'Highly unlikely, Sergeant! Highly unlikely! No, I think we've got a problem fitter on board, and I'm a bit worried about what he might do next.'

'What about Morris?' Leacock expostulated. 'If you're looking for a problem fitter, there's your man! He obviously had head problems... he brought a gun on board.'

'I've already thought about that. But he just wanted to turn around and go back to Townsville to see his wife. To do that, the aircraft needs to be in working order. No, there's more to it than that. Morris was just a flake.'

Leacock shrugged.

'Well we won't find out unless we get to Canton in one piece, will we Warrant?'

III

Flying Officer McLeish made his way to the cockpit, and stood staring moodily ahead at the sea below.

'How are you going with our course, McLeish?' said Styles. 'Are we on course for Canton or not?'

'It's almost impossible to tell, sirr! With all the junketing around we did, and without a G2 to guide us, it's almost impossible to chart a course... within a couple of hundred miles, anyway. But there are literally hundreds of islands out here. I'm surprised that we haven't seen any yet. I think the best thing we can do is hold on this heading, and hope we come across Guam, or one of the Marshall Islands. The yanks have got a few airstrips in the region, if we can only find one.'

'Our fuel isn't going to hold out forever, Flying Officer. I suggest you get back to your charts and *do* something!'

'A chart isn'a going to save us the noo! Your eyes might though.'

He stood back, frowning at the continuing expanse of ocean passing beneath them, lit by a full moon. The storm was well behind them now, and they flew steadily at five hundred feet above the rippling waters. Suddenly he began to quote:

'Alone, alone, all, all alone,
Alone on a wide, wide sea!
And never a saint took pity on
My soul in agony.'

McLeish then fell silent, slipped out of the cockpit and returned to his seat.

'What the blazes was that all about,' snapped Styles, exasperated.

'I think he was quoting from '*The Rime of the Ancient Mariner*',' said Varley. He saw Styles uncomprehending look, and added, 'Samuel Taylor Coleridge, sir.'

'I see! A poetry buff! What's an erk like you reading poetry for, LAC.'

'It's a passion of mine,' said Varley. Then in a bitter aside, 'we're not all grease and gaiters, sir.'

Styles went to reply, then thought better of it. Down on his port side, in the distance, was a dark shape that attracted his attention. It was some miles away yet, but he studied it with an overwhelming sense of relief. There was an island down there. No doubt about it! But what island? And was there an airstrip?

Chapter Thirteen

'Hey, look at that,' said Campbell, gesturing through the windscreen to port. Dawson strained his eyes in that direction. He saw nothing at first, then the distant outline of a dark speck in the endless ocean.

'Is that an island?' he said. Campbell looked at him, and nodded, smiling for the first time since leaving Nadi. 'It sure is! …That it is, my boy!'

'I don't suppose it's *'the'* island – Canton Atoll!'

'No,' said Campbell, shaking his head. 'I don't suppose it is. But it's an island, and as we only have half an hour's fuel left, any port in a storm, eh?'

'Half an hour?' Dawson frowned, and checked the gauges. 'Firing those pods must have used up more than we thought.'

'Piss-farting halfway around the Pacific used up more than we thought. If we ever get back to civilization, I will definitely be making a case for Wing Commanders to butt out of Navex's. Flying a chair in base squadron for five years doesn't exactly put you at the cutting edge of decision making.'

'I don't understand. We should have another three hours fuel, at least. Surely the drag on the nose wheel couldn't have made that much difference.'

'Well, you're wrong! What with one thing and another, we've managed to burn up almost 30,000 pounds of AVGAS. You can thank our glorious leader for his expert planning for that.'

Dawson wiped his forehead with the back of his hand. He looked distinctly upset.

'What if there's no airstrip?'

'Then we'll have to land on the beach, or at least find a flat area without too many trees in the way.'

'Wouldn't it be better to ditch it in the sea?'

Campbell looked at him in mock horror.

'What – dump a couple of million dollars worth of our employer's aircraft into the Pacific? Not on your life! Besides, I have a great fear of drowning. The other thing of course is that with the nose wheel down, what do you think would happen when it contacted the water?'

'I have no idea… and neither do you,' Dawson retorted.

'We'd bloody cartwheel, my friend! Head over heels! Arse over head! Would you like to end up upside down in the drink?'

'Of course not, but I don't feel like wearing a tree, either.'

They were prophetic words.

The island was a lot closer by this time. They were approaching it from the southeast. As they got closer, 286 banked off to port and headed down towards it, and Campbell followed suit, travelling slightly behind and to the starboard of the other plane. As they approached, the altimeter read 200 feet. The first glimpse close-up was of a black escarpment rearing up for a hundred feet or more, and extending along the south and southwest side of the island. As they followed it along, they noticed a wide bay with a sandy bottom, and a fifty-yard break through the cliffs leading up from the beach to higher ground. It had obviously been cut out by the action of water, and a brook of fresh water was seen still running along the centre of this. There was vegetation along the top of the cliffs, some palm trees, and other tropical plants growing in profusion.

Campbell followed 286 at a distance, noting that the only significant beach was the one fronting the bay. At other places along the seafront, the cliffs went straight down into the water, and were battered by a heavy swell.

The two Neptunes flew on, banked to starboard around the southwestern corner and here the cliffs were small in size, tapering off along the western side of the island into a low-lying marshy mangrove, with both trees and bushes growing up out of the surrounding water.

Continuing on, the northern part of the island was taken up almost entirely with the crater of an active volcano, plumes of smoke floating up from its depths and dissipating into the atmosphere. It wasn't hard to see where those black cliffs had come from. The volcano seemed to be angled to spill any eruption towards the south. On the southeastern side, the area was heavily forested, mainly with pine trees, and there seemed little hope as far as finding a flat area for landing.

'How big do you reckon it is,' said Campbell, moodily.

'About six miles by... I'd say four,' said Dawson.

In 286 Styles was looking out desperately for an airstrip. McLeish stood behind him, looking down at the forbidding cliffs and the lack of a dry, flat stretch to put it down.

'Do ye' think it's inhabited?' said McLeish.

'Does it look inhabited? Of course not,' snapped Styles. 'There are no buildings, huts or signs of human activity. There must be hundreds of islands like this. Not exactly the greatest place to be stranded.'

'Do ye' intend to put her down here, sirr?'

'I have no choice, McLeish. You can't supply me with a course, and even if you could, I couldn't fly to it.' Styles sounded resigned. He thought for a moment, then continued.

'On top of that, I'm down to one engine, and those jet pods are gobbling up fuel at an incredible rate. We could go on and look for another island, but we might fall short, then we wouldn't stand any chance at all.'

'What will ye' do, then,' said McLeish. 'I don't see any obvious landing place.'

'We'll put down in the sea. If I take her out a couple of miles and head in towards that break in the cliffs on the South side, I might be able to run her up onto the beach. That's the only thing I can do.'

Leacock had entered the cockpit and stood beside McLeish, staring out at the island as they continued to fly around it.

'What about 292? Do you think they're going to go in as well?'

'That will be up to Flight Lieutenant Campbell. Only he knows the state of his aircraft, though I'm given to understand that his compass system is out as well, and no doubt his fuel is also running low. He'll have to pick his own landing ground.'

'But their nose wheel's down. They couldn't put down in the drink, anyway. It would be disastrous,' said Leacock.

'I'm sure the Flight Lieutenant is aware of that fact. He might as well drop the rest of his undercarriage and try to land on that long beach on the other side.'

Leacock shook his head.

'That's just a marsh, he'd dig in, nose first. God knows what would happen.'

Styles looked around and glowered at the Sergeant. He hated being challenged, especially by an NCO.

'That's not my problem, Sergeant. I've got enough problems of my own. Campbell will have to shift for himself.'

'If you'd stood up to the Wing Commander when you had the chance, we wouldn't be in this mess... Sir!'

'You're getting very close to insubordination, Sergeant. I suggest you hold your tongue!'

'Or you'll what, Squadron Leader... charge me? Don't stand on your bars with me!' Leacock's voice was laden with sarcasm. 'You fly boys think you're so terrific! The only problem is that every time you stand on ceremony, common sense flies out the window. Whose stupid idea was it to travel in radio silence?'

'By God, Sergeant. Another word, and I'll have you placed under arrest.'

'That's your answer to everything, isn't it? Shut it up, charge it, arrest it! Heaven forbid that the truth may assign any blame to you! It must be great to be congenitally without fault. It was your place to query the Wing Commander's Navex. He obviously got his sums wrong – look at your fuel gauges!'

'By God, I won't listen to this any longer. Warrant Officer,' he yelled. 'Get this man out of my cockpit!'

Varley sat and listened to all this, and became increasingly nervous. McLeish had slipped away in the meantime, not wanting to become involved. He knew that his outburst at Nadi had already fitted him for the high jump when they got back. He gave the nod to Danny Seaman on the way out, and Danny arrived on the end of the exchange.

Styles twisted in his seat and bawled at Danny, 'Remove this man or I will!'

'You and whose Air Force, Squadron Leader?' said Leacock.

Danny grabbed Leacock by the arm and tried to tug him away.

'Come on Sergeant. Don't make it any worse!'

'Worse! How much worse can it get? Thanks to these incompetents we're about to ditch two perfectly good aircraft into the middle of the Pacific. On top of that, we probably won't survive!'

Styles threw the aircraft into autopilot, and struggled to get out of his seat to front the Sergeant. Danny dragged Leacock backwards, towards the entrance, and Styles tried to throw a punch. Varley, left in the co-pilot's seat, panicked.

'Who the fuck's flying this thing,' he yelled.

Everyone came to their senses at the same moment. Leacock left the cockpit, helped by a firm push by the Warrant Officer. Styles turned back and occupied his seat, and Varley tried to clamber out of his.

'Stay where you are, LAC. I'll deal with this when we're safely on the deck. I'll need you to help pull back on the stick when we hit.'

He put the aircraft into a turn to port and headed out to sea, opposite the bay that he'd decided would be the final resting-place of A89-286. At four miles out he turned her in towards the island. Varley noticed that the pilot's hands were shaking.

'Everyone – Crash Stations!' Leacock yelled down the length of the aircraft, then sat down with his back to the bulkhead. Danny joined him. The others strapped in, and everyone hung on for dear life.

At two miles out Styles dropped to fifty feet above the moonlit water and feathered the port engine. Going in on just the jet pods, Varley watched in horror the tall black cliffs approaching at 190 miles an hour. At a little over half a mile Styles dropped it onto its belly, and there was a horrendous crunch as the props hit. Then they appeared to bounce, just once, like a flat stone skimmed across a lake. The second hit threw the nose down and sent a tidal wave up which blew in the windscreen. It also took off the Perspex nose cone underneath, sending a flood of water up through the observer's position, along the crawlway and into the body of the plane. Before it came to a halt, Styles threw the retraction lever to drop the undercarriage, and with the last dying pounds of hydraulic pressure, the great wheels went down.

Water was pouring into the cockpit, and the electrics behind the panel were going off like fireworks. Varley threw off his straps and struggled out of his seat. At the last surge, Styles had been thrown forward, hit his head, and was out cold. Varley had to reach over and free him, half dragging him out of the seat before the rising water picked them both up, and in a reflux action, sucked them out through the gaping hole where the windscreen had been.

Back in the fuselage, Leacock released the star port in the centre of the fuselage roof. The navigator lay on the floor, a large gash in his forehead, and blood spurting from the wound. He was dazed, and seemed incapable of getting on to his feet. Leacock threw the port open, and helped Danny Seaman climb up and through, and then with Gordon Duckett's help, lifted and shoved Adrian McLeish out through the port.

Up to their waists in water, they then seized a confused Wing Commander and pushed him out to the others. By the time Duckett and Leacock crawled out to sit on top of the fuselage, the aircraft was full of water and sinking rapidly. They were about fifty yards off the beach, and the nose of the aircraft had already disappeared. Before they knew it they were all washed off the top of the fuselage as it sank, and found themselves struggling towards the shore.

There was total confusion in the water. Leacock had the Wing Commander in hand, and ahead of them Varley was trying to cope with the Squadron Leader, who was just struggling back to consciousness. He suddenly seemed to appreciate the indignity of his position, and pushed Varley away angrily, before striking out for the shore himself.

They were in the shallows and dragging themselves up onto the beach before Leacock looked back to see McLeish floating face down in the water.

'Hey Duckett, Varley, the Flying Officer's in trouble out there,' he yelled. He himself was exhausted, trying to keep Fletcher's head above water.

Varley and Duckett stripped off their overalls and boots, and swam out to get McLeish. But it was too late! The Scotsman was dead by the time they got him to the beach.

Overhead, 292 circled slowly over the scene, and watched as the aircraft hit the water, throwing up a huge tidal wave that dissipated on the beach. The survivors swam and crawled through the shallows, finally collapsing exhausted on to the white sand.

'How many got out?' said Dawson.

'I can see five, no six! And there's a body floating in the water. Look, they're going out to pull it in.'

'Who is it? Can you see?'

'No. I could see the Wing Commander lying on the beach, but I thought he was already dead. Maybe he is, maybe it's just his body. He's not moving. I can see Styles, he's pacing up and down for some reason, away from the others.'

The aircraft continued to turn and they drifted out of view.

'That bloody crash looked horrific,' said Dawson, shakily.

'Well at least, most of them got out. If Styles can survive, I reckon I can,' said Eddie.

'Yeah, but is the fitter that was in the co-pilot's seat down on the beach?'

'How the hell would I know. They all look the same to me in their bloody overalls,' said Campbell. He suddenly burst out laughing, totally inappropriately.

'You'll just have to take your chances, Pete.'

'In that case, I should have a say in where we go in,' said Dawson.

Campbell suddenly became serious.

'You can make a suggestion, but as pilot I make the final decision.' He looked meaningfully at Dawson, and grimaced, as if to say *'good try.'*

'I think we should put her belly down in the swamp, over on the other side. No undercarriage!'

'Well that's bloody stupid! The nose wheel's down, whether you like it or not. We could very well end up with the strut being rammed up through the floor of the cockpit.'

'Well what's your suggestion?'

'I'm leaning towards coming down in that pine forest. No – hear me out,' said Campbell, seeing the look of horror on Dawson's face. 'If we let her down gently in the treetops, with the nose pulled right up, the trees might act as a brake. We'd take the tops off, of course, and as we drop further down, and the trunks get thicker, they'll probably take the wings off. But I think it would be preferable to cartwheeling across the water, or digging into a swamp... or getting hoist on that strut for that matter. What do you think?'

'I think you're bloody mad,' Dawson replied, 'and I don't want a bar of it.'

'There's not a hard, or flat, or dry area on the whole island. If we land in that mangrove area, we don't know what we might be getting into. It might be quicksand. We might not be able to make our way through it.'

'What if we burst into flames? We might get incinerated in a forest fire.'

'It doesn't seem to matter what we do, Peter, the risks are going to be high. But we're just about out of fuel, so there's not much to burn.'

292 swept around once more over the bay, and they looked down at 286 in the water.

'Look, the tail is exposed, above the waterline. It must only be about twenty feet deep. I wonder if the undercarriage is down – can you see?'

'I think it's down. The fuselage doesn't look as if it's sitting flat on the bottom. We'll be able to tell once the water clears again.'

Campbell checked the fuel gauges.

'We're not going to have time for that. I'm going to have to put her down. Are you with me?'

'I haven't got much bloody choice, have I? What do you intend doing?' said Dawson.

'We'll come in, pretty much as normal, drop the flaps about five degrees and pull right back on the stick. That should give us nose up with a bit of lift. Then we'll just throttle back, and pray.' Campbell looked at Dawson, and cracked a smile. 'Come on, mate, let's get it over.'

Dawson swallowed, and they turned 292 out to sea, heading southeast. Three miles out they made a final turn and headed back in towards the most heavily forested part of the island. When the Neptune came in over the first scattered trees they pulled the nose up and throttled back, and suddenly they were staring up at the night sky, and watching the treetops rise above them on each side as they went down in a bedlam of grating, grinding and ear-splitting explosions that convinced them, finally and totally, that they were all about to die.

Chapter Fourteen

A few seconds in a life or death situation can seem like a million years! To Campbell and Dawson, watching that awful descent and experiencing the initial contact with the pines at first hand, everything seemed to happen in slow motion. Campbell caught sight of a bright constellation of stars in a suddenly cloudless sky, gritted his teeth and wondered if there was life after death.

Dawson felt his gorge rise and threw up all over himself. One point seven seconds later, a wayward branch from a falling pine tree shattered the perspex in front of him and speared into his open mouth, taking his head with it as it continued through the bulkhead into the fuselage. Dawson's headless body threw up once more through his neck before they finally came to a halt, then sat patiently in his seat like a small child waiting to be cleaned up after an accident with its porridge. Don Grainger, the Radio Tech, flew like a missile, horizontally, the length of the fuselage, through the cockpit and out through the perspex windscreen, disappearing into the trees some seventy-five yards ahead of the wreckage.

There was a grinding crash as the starboard wing severed itself from the mainframe, to end up suspended thirty feet above the ground, cradled in the bough of a tree. The fuselage skewed sideways and broke in half, just behind the main spar, precipitating Barry Mackintosh and Ron Gray out into the mercy of the woods at just over seventy miles an hour.

The engine fitter, Kevin Bailey, was standing up front by the bulkhead when a toolbox sailed towards him at approximately the same speed, smashing his ribcage into his spine. This had the effect of propelling his heart and lungs sideways out into his overalls, as he belched a shower of blood all over Helen Currier in a fine spray.

Within thirty seconds of the plane coming to a standstill, Bill O'Connell was outside and spinning around in circles yelling, 'God!... God!... God!... God!' as if he could will the deity to come to their aid.

There was no fire! What AVGAS there was had spilt along the wake of the plane, and glistened on the stunted remains of trees that seconds before had been tall, proud and alive. It looked like a scene from Paschendaele or the Somme. The only sound was a high pitched keening that was eventually revealed to be Helen Currier, terrified out of her mind and covered in Bailey's blood.

Gradually there was movement amongst the wreckage. Flight Lieutenant Campbell climbed out over the wrecked nose and fell against a tree, gasping and sobbing uncontrollably at the shock of seeing Dawson's headless body. Pilot Officer Steve Bishop collapsed outside the aircraft, his left arm shattered, and blood weeping from a cut on his forehead. Ian Johnson, the sparky, was shocked, but unhurt. He seemed least affected of them all, but wandered around in a daze for ten minutes until he could convince himself that he was actually still alive.

Phil Cusack had been huddled in a pile of kitbags, and was only badly bruised on the legs and face. He took it on himself to slap Helen's face, breaking her hysteria, and dragging her out of the wreckage just in case it decided to go up in flames.

After about twenty minutes, the survivors were gathered around a tree some thirty yards from the wreckage, taking stock of themselves and working out who hadn't survived.

Campbell took charge, once he had composed himself.

'Right. We've got to sort ourselves out. Let's do this in a military fashion, men. We're the lucky ones. Now... dead! Who's dead?'

'Kevin Bailey bought it, sir. He's up by the bulkhead.'

'The Navigator, sir! Flight Lieutenant Gray! And Flight Sergeant Mackintosh! Their bodies are over there somewhere,' said O'Connell, pointing through the trees to the starboard side of the wreck.

'Don Grainger's not here,' said Cusack. 'Did anyone see…?'

'He went through the windscreen,' said Campbell. 'He's dead! So's Flight Lieutenant Dawson. He's still in the seat. We're going to have to bury these men… I know it's bloody awful, and it's the last thing you want to do right now. But I think we'd better get it over and done with before we try to make contact with the survivors of 286.'

'I don't think that's a good idea, sir,' said Johnson.

Campbell looked up, and fixed the electrician with a penetrating stare.

'And why's that, Corporal?'

'When the rescue team gets here, they'll want to fly the bodies back to Australia, sir.'

Campbell frowned. He knew the electrician was right.

'Well, we can't have them putrefying all over the place. And I don't think any of us are in good enough condition to carry them down to the beach. So what do you suggest?'

'Sleeping bags, sir!' said Bill O'Connell. 'We've all got a sleeping bag with our kit. What if we put the bodies into sleeping bags and stow them in the front end of the fuselage. Then when the others get here, they can come and pick them up themselves.'

'It will stop any animals getting at them, sir,' Cusack added.

Campbell looked around him for agreement. They all concurred.

'Okay, that's what we'll do. We'll need… what? Five! Five sleeping bags! You look them out will you LAC O'Connell.'

Cusack went with him, and they began to throw kit bags out of the fuselage so they could be sorted and claimed.

Johnson sorted out some kit from Grainger's bag, tore a shirt into strips and bound Pilot Officer Bishop's arm up. He made a creditable sling, and relieved the pain somewhat, though Bishop almost passed out while he was doing it.

'Are you all right, Bishop. Just how bad is it?' Campbell enquired of him.

'I'll get by, sir. But I don't think it's going to heal properly. I'll probably have to have it broken again and re-fixed back at base.'

'Well just hang in there, Pilot Officer. You know the drill.' Then he whispered, 'don't let the men see you're in pain. Grit your teeth – you're an officer!'

Helen Currier was sitting on the ground, still in shock. There was nothing to clean the blood off with, and she seemed both fascinated and horrified at the same time. She couldn't stop looking at her hands. Ian Johnson knelt down beside her.

'When we get down to the beach, you'll be able to wash that off in the sea, Helen,' he said, kindly. 'Just hang in there.'

Helen glared at him as if he was an intruder in her thoughts.

'Get away from me! Leave me alone. Don't you dare touch me!'

Johnson looked at her in disdain.

'Well, fuck you! Sort your own problems out, you bitch!'

Suddenly she screamed, and he jumped up and backed off. Campbell came running over to where she was sitting.

'What's going on, Corporal? What have you done?'

'I haven't bloody done anything. I just came over to see how she was, offer a bit of support, and she bloody insulted me. She's mad, the bitch!'

'That will be quite enough of that, Corporal. Control your

tongue! The airwoman's in shock, that's all!'

Johnson stalked off and went back to the others. Helen burst into tears.

'Keep them away from me, Eddie. There's blood, blood all over me. It's that Corporal's blood... an *engine fitter*,' she said, wrinkling her face in disgust. 'I feel dirty.'

Campbell looked around at the others, to see if she'd been heard. Then he knelt beside her, and spoke in low tones.

'You can't say things like that, Helen. That's terrible! Corporal Bailey was a first rate tradesman. He was a man, for god's sake – and he's dead!'

Helen looked at him, confused.

'But he wasn't an officer, Eddie. He threw up his blood all over me. It was disgusting!'

'I'd advise you to keep quiet, Helen, or you'll upset a lot of people. You don't want to upset everyone at the moment, do you,' he said, meaningfully.

She hung her head and shrugged her shoulders, but said nothing further.

It took an hour and a half to collect the bodies, and put them in sleeping bags. Grainger was in two pieces, his right arm had been severed in its flight, and was found ten yards away from the rest of the body. Dawson's head was in pieces, and Campbell made Cusack go in search of it and put it together with the body into a bag. Afterwards, Cusack threw up.

It was the same with O'Connell and Johnson. They felt vaguely resentful that Campbell opted out of the collection, and Helen of course, did nothing. Steve Bishop couldn't help, with his smashed arm, so it was down to the erks.

'Bloody typical,' said O'Connell. 'The officers sit on their arses while the men do all the dirty work.'

'I just want to get down to the beach,' said Cusack, 'jump in the sea and clean myself off. I've got all this dried blood all over me, and it's putrid.'

'Well, you're not an orphan. As long as they don't expect us to carry that bitch down to the beach, I don't care,' said Johnson.

Campbell walked over in time to catch Johnson's remark.

'I'm losing patience with you, Corporal. The airwoman is in shock. Where's your compassion?'

'I don't have to put up with her tantrums,' Johnson scowled. 'We're all in bloody shock!'

'We're all in shock... Sir!' said Campbell, a mean note entering his voice. "Don't let's forget that we are still members of the Royal Australian Air Force, Corporal!'

Johnson looked at him in disbelief.

'Oh, yes sir, three bags full, sir!' he muttered, as he turned away.

'If you take that tone with me, Corporal, you will find yourself on the wrong end of a charge. Don't push me!'

Johnson scowled, but said nothing.

Campbell watched them load the last of the sleeping bags with their grisly contents into the fuselage, then helped Pilot Officer Steve Bishop to his feet.

'Right men! LAC O'Connell, I want you to help Pilot Officer Bishop as we make our way to the beach. He might need support. You'll have to carry his kit for him, anyway. If you can't carry his and your own, you'll have to come back for yours tomorrow. Corporal Johnson and LAC Cusack, I want you to bring two kit bags each. You can bring mine, Cusack, and Johnson can carry Miss Currier's. I will be helping Miss Currier through the undergrowth and down through the cliffs. She's the most susceptible at the moment.'

'The most fuckable,' Cusack whispered to O'Connell. Bill smirked in reply. Johnson looked absolutely ropeable.

'I thought women were supposed to be our equals these days,' he remarked, sourly.

'Just do it, Johnson,' Campbell snapped. He turned back to Helen, helped her to her feet, and they set off, picking their way through the trees. The others following, laden like pack-horses, and muttering their discontent.

II

Down on the beach, the survivors watched 292 circle above them a couple of times, and then head off towards the southeast. They could still see it as it turned, and made its run back in towards the island, but lost sight of it as it went behind the cliffs. They waited for half a minute, thinking it might reappear. But then in the distance they heard the crash, which rumbled on for twenty seconds or so, and then went silent.

They all looked at each other, but no one wanted to be the first to speak. Finally Varley broke the spell.

'I wonder how many survived,' he said.

'It's not your place to wonder, LAC. We'll find out in due course,' snapped Squadron Leader Styles.

'No, it's not your place to wonder, LAC,' said Sergeant Leacock, sarcastically. 'Why should you worry whether your mates are dead or not?'

'Sergeant!' Danny Seaman barked out, warningly. He shook his head and gave him a look that said 'don't ask for trouble.' Styles turned to face Leacock, and thrust his chin in the air.

'Don't worry, Warrant Officer. I have a feeling that the Sergeant will be talking himself out of his pension before too long. Just give him enough rope.'

'I doubt if Department of Air will cancel my pension on the word of a Squadron Leader,' Leacock remarked, dismissively.

Styles took two paces towards him, going red in the face. Then he stopped, and addressed the Warrant Officer.

'I've had enough of this insubordination. You will place the Sergeant under arrest until the rescue party arrives, Warrant. That's an order!'

'Now hang on, sir,' said Danny, alarmed at the turn of events. 'We're all pretty well shell-shocked here. Maybe we should just give ourselves time to calm down and get back to normal. I'm sure the Sergeant didn't mean to be offensive... *did you Sergeant?*'

Leacock just scowled, turned his back on Styles, and folded his arms in resolve.

'I'll accept no less than a direct apology, Warrant Officer!'

Leacock turned back to Styles and sneered, 'Oh! I'm so sorry that you're an inconsiderate, incompetent pig, Squadron Leader, and that you have the leadership qualities of a donkey! I'm also sorry that you have been the cause of the deaths of at least two good men, and God knows how many on 292. Yes, I'm certainly sorry about that... Sir!'

Styles flew at him and went for his throat. The Sergeant grabbed Styles by the collar and picked him up with one hand. The Squadron leader was struggling to breathe, and threw a punch that hit Leacock on top of his head. This just seemed to enrage him. He pushed Styles away, then flattened him with an upper cut to the jaw. The Sergeant stood threateningly over his superior officer, who was lying flat on his back on the sand, bleeding from the side of his mouth. He looked down at him angrily, and shook his finger, warningly.

'You ever fucking lay a hand on me again, you arrogant cunt, and I will not only drop you, I'll drown you, you bastard!'

Danny stood back, shaking his head and looking undecided about his course of action. He was only eighteen months from his pension, and didn't want to blow it at this stage of the game.

'You give me no choice, Sergeant Leacock,' he said, a tremor in his voice. 'You'd better consider yourself under open arrest until a court martial can be convened.'

Leacock rounded on Seaman.

'You weak little man,' he sneered. 'Worried about your pension, Warrant Officer? Just like you to take the side of the pigs!'

'You would be well advised, Sergeant, to hold your tongue. You're supposed to be leading by example. If you allow this to go any further, I'll be in no position to help you.'

'You never helped anyone in your life, Warrant Officer,' Leacock said, shaking his head. 'Why should I expect you to begin now?'

He wandered off along the beach, and the others stared after him, not knowing what to do for the best. Danny helped Styles to his feet, but the Squadron Leader short-temperedly pushed him away, and re-arranged his clothing.

'I will have that man dishonourably discharged, Warrant Officer, if it's the last thing I do. You have been a witness to these events, and you *will* be called to testify. You'd better make your mind up whose side you're on, Warrant, because any man here that refuses to obey a direct order from me, while we're on this island, will join him in the dock.'

Danny stood to attention.

'I'd like to point out, sir, that you are not the Commanding Officer here. The Wing Commander is. I shall most certainly follow the orders of the senior Commanding Officer.'

'Wing Commander Fletcher, is *non compos mentis,* Warrant. He's no longer capable of command.' He looked at Fletcher lying motionless on the beach. 'There's no guarantee that he will even survive. I think he's brain damaged, and we have no access to medical help. As such, I am within my rights to declare myself the most senior, able officer on this island. I am therefore in command.'

'Whatever you say, sir,' sighed the Warrant Officer, and sat down on the beach.

Chapter Fifteen

The survivors from 292 staggered down onto the beach at about four in the morning. Gordon Duckett and Varley were still awake, and walked up through the cutting to meet them. The others were asleep on the beach. It was a balmy night, the temperature in the low to mid twenties, so it wasn't at all uncomfortable.

Sergeant Leacock had found himself a niche further along the beach, at the base of the cliff, and was asleep there. Styles slept sitting up. He'd wandered over to the cliff face on the opposite side of the cutting, and sat propped up against that. He'd armed himself with a piece of driftwood, and hugged it close to his body. He wasn't going to let the Sergeant get the better of him again.

The crew from 292 was exhausted when they appeared, following along the line of the brook that flowed down into the bay. Helen Currier was whimpering and clinging onto the Flight Lieutenant, and the first thing she did was head into the water. She went in fully clothed, and was soon surrounded by a spreading red stain as the blood dissolved from her skin and clothing. She stayed in there for a good twenty minutes, paying particular attention to her hair. One by one the others joined her, though being careful to keep their distance. Only Pilot Officer Bishop stayed on the beach. His arm was giving him hell, and he almost passed out with the pain.

Campbell ultimately went in with Helen, and they talked in low tones in the half-light, away from the prying ears of the others. This was duly noted by the men, and a number of unkind remarks were bandied about between them.

'There you are, Varley. It's one rule for the men, and another for the officers. There weren't supposed to be any animals on this flight, and yet the Flight Lieutenant's brought his pussy along.'

'His bitch, don't you mean?' said Johnson, swimming past them.

'Are you insinuating she's a dog, Johnson?' laughed O'Connell, splashing in the water.

'I don't know about that, but she's a bitch all right,' he replied.

Duckett made as if to say something, then changed his mind. They saw Campbell watching them from a distance, and changed the subject.

'It's a pity about Don Grainger. He wasn't a bad lad. And Bailey, though I didn't know much about him. He seemed nice enough.'

'Let's face it… it could have been any of us,' said Phil Cusack. 'We're lucky to be here.'

O'Connell looked up at the towering cliffs, their brooding immensity.

'I just wonder where *'here'* is? I wonder what the name of this island is. Does anyone know?'

Johnson pulled a face, and stared in the same direction.

'Going by the look of those cliffs – it's a sort of black rock, isn't it. I've never seen anything quite like it.'

'Blackrock Island! I like that,' said O'Connell. 'It's a bit 'Treasure Islandish, isn't it?'

'Did you see the volcano on the other side, while we were flying over it? It looked active to me. There were whisps of smoke coming up from the core. I hope the bloody thing doesn't go up.'

'Well, there's a clue. A volcanic island! Who knows anything about where all the volcanic activity is in the pacific?'

The others shook their heads. No one, it seemed, was full bottle on volcanoes.

'Well a few days here on a beautiful tropical island won't go amiss, as long as the rescue team get here in due course,' said O'Connell. 'I'd like to be home in time for Christmas.'

'Do you reckon we'll make the papers,' said Cusack, his boyish enthusiasm firing his imagination. 'They might print pictures of us all, along with pictures of the Neppy's.'

'I doubt it,' said Johnson. 'You know how it works. They'll print pictures of the aircrew and the aircraft; the ground crew never gets a mention. No doubt they'll feature the Wing Commander over there, and probably Styles.'

'Yeah, that'd be typical,' said Duckett. 'Which reminds me... I clean forgot! You weren't here, were you?' He was addressing O'Connell, Johnson and Cusack.

'No, what was that?'

'After we got up on the beach, and Varley and me pulled poor old Scotty out of the water, the Sergeant had an all out fight with the Squadron Leader. Called him a fucking incompetent donkey or something, and blamed him for the crash. It came to fisticuffs on the beach.'

'No!' said O'Connell, disbelievingly. 'Don't bullshit.' He started to laugh. 'Are you bullshitting me?'

'No... he's not,' said Varley. 'Fair dinkhum! Styles went for his throat, and Leacock picked him up by the scruff of his neck... no kidding, just one-handed. Then Styles threw a punch and Leacock laid him out. The Warrant Officer put Leacock under open arrest.'

'Well, fuck-a-duck,' said O'Connell. 'I would never have believed it. Styles must have really pissed him off.'

'I'd believe it,' said Cusack. 'The man's an animal. We're going to have to p.put up with that prick for as long as we're here. I feel a bit sorry for the Sergeant, though. He's b.bloody good value.'

'We can go over there in the morning, and express our commiseration's,' said O'Connell, 'let him know whose side we're on.'

'You'd better be careful,' said Varley, quietly. 'Styles is threatening to court martial anyone who goes against him on the island. He reckons he's the senior officer now, because the Wing Commander's not making sense.'

O'Connell looked over to where Styles sat, his back to the cliff.

'As long as we don't antagonize him,' he said. 'We can worry about that bridge when we come to it.' He looked at Varley. 'Anyway, Varley, you haven't told us yet what happened on 286.'

'Did you hear about Morris,' Varley said, guardedly.

O'Connell shook his head.

'No, come to think of it. Where is he?'

Varley nodded out into the bay, where the tail of 286 protruded five or six feet above the water level.

'He's still on the plane, minus the back of his head. Peter Leacock blew his head off with an SLR. Jack brought a gun on board, I think it was a .38. Anyway, he pushed past Duckett and me on his way to the front, and we didn't think anything about it at the time. The next thing, shots are being fired, and he's yelling like a lunatic to turn the plane around and get back to Townsville. He shot out the G2 and the radio.'

'So that's what happened,' said Johnson, whistling. 'It must have scared the shit out of you.'

'You could say that,' said Varley. 'We were on the floor, keeping out of the way. He came out and pointed the gun at me, and I thought I was a goner. But he must have been on some drug or another, I reckon.'

'He was,' said Duckett. 'I was on guard with him at Nadi. I went inside one of the aircraft for a nap, and I could hear him marching up and down, saying left-right-left-right, so I got out to see what he was doing, and he almost shot me with his SLR. He was off his face then!'

'How come you never told anyone before,' said Johnson, annoyed. 'You should have reported the prick. All this might never have happened, and we could have been on our way to Hawaii right now.'

'I didn't want to get him in the shit! You know what it's like – I thought it was just a one-off.'

'It's all got to come out in the end, you know. There'll be a massive enquiry once we get back to Townsville, and we'll be in the middle of it.'

Duckett looked uncomfortable.

'Maybe I shouldn't have said anything. I won't say anything if you don't.'

Johnson looked at him, pityingly.

'Listen LAC… If you think I'm going to lie for you, you've got another think coming. I've still got a career to think about in this Air Force. It's bad enough having Campbell on my back, without covering up for you. You should have reported it.'

Varley and Duckett exchanged glances. This was bad news.

'What about you, LAC Varley. Did you know about this?'

'Well, if I did, I wouldn't tell you now, would I Corporal? From now on we'll tell you fucking nothing!'

'Right!' said Johnson. 'We know where we stand. Don't expect any favours from me.' He turned and swam back towards the shore, leaving Varley, Duckett, Cusack and O'Connell staring after him.

II

They slept on the beach until after ten o'clock. When they woke up it was a different scene facing them than when they'd gone to sleep. There'd been a dodge tide overnight, and 286 was halfway out of the water, standing there like some surreal painting. Beyond the wreck was the curving shape of a reef, which now lay uncovered, a break in the middle of it corresponding to where 286 had skimmed through after the first hit.

'Hey, l.look at that fellas,' yelled Cusack, who was the first to wake up.

They all began to stir at the noise, and sat looking around them, taking stock. O'Connell did a quick count of heads on the beach, then added Styles just stirring over by the cliff-face. There was no sign of Sergeant Leacock.

The Wing Commander suddenly stirred and sat up, looking around him vaguely at the beach and the cliffs. Then he got to his feet and walked down to the water's edge, unsteadily at first, but then quietly staring at the apparition from the deep.

It was as if he'd awoken to a nightmare. His subconscious mind had taken in everything that had been said around him while he'd been lying in a somnambulistic state. An overwhelming sense of guilt had crept into his soul, and he was incapable of shaking it. His natural arrogance refused to accept responsibility for anything that smacked of incompetence, while a deeper voice struggled up from the depths, informing him that as the senior officer, his decisions had caused the loss of two aircraft, and nine human lives. It was almost more than he could bear.

Styles got up and ran over to the group, looking up and down the beach for any sign of Sergeant Leacock.

'All fall in,' he shouted. 'Come on, this is a military parade. I want you all fallen in and accounted for.'

Danny Seaman got to his feet, and looked around him.

'You'd better do as he says, men. Fall in single line abreast. Instead of calling the roll, I'll get you to shout out your rank, name and service number. Corporal Johnson...' He called the sparky over. 'Have you got such a thing as pen and paper on you?'

Johnson searched the pockets of his overalls.

"I've got a biro, Warrant, and my notebook. I always carry it in my top pocket. It got wet last night, but it appears to have just about dried out, now.'

'Good! As they call their names out I want you to list each man. In addition to his rank, name and serial number, just make a note of whether he was on 286 or 292, will you?'

'Yes Warrant.'

'All right, everybody, fall in!'

Johnson wrote slowly and laboriously, first the men who lined up in single file, right-dressed then stood at ease. They each called out their names. Then the officers, who stood off and to the side of this line of four fitters, Corporal Johnson at the front and taking names, and the Warrant Officer, standing behind him. Helen Currier stood with the officers. The list read as follows:

LAC Varley, J. No. R 93122 - 286
LAC Duckett, G. No. R 92007 – 286
LAC O'Connell, W. No. R 92346 – 292
LAC Cusack, P. No. R 93988 – 292
Corporal Johnson, I. No. R 92465 – 292
Warrant Officer Seaman, D. No. R 77895 - 286

Officers:
Wing Commander Fletcher, B. – 286
Squadron Leader Styles, G. – 286
Flight Lieutenant Campbell, E. – 292
Pilot Officer Bishop, S. – 292

Airwoman Currier, H. – 292

As an afterthought, he also wrote:
Sergeant Leacock, P. No. ? - 286

'Where is the Sergeant this morning?' Styles snapped at Danny Seaman.

'Your guess is as good as mine, sir,' Danny replied. 'He must have wandered off while we were asleep.'

'Well, I want him found. He's under open arrest, and he is not to wander away from the main group. There's work to be done, and he can do his fair share of it.'

'Yes sir,' said Danny. 'Don't you think it would be a good idea to get out to the aircraft and salvage what we can while it's still uncovered, sir?'

'Not just now, Warrant Officer. I mean to have a word to the men.' He turned back to the assembled fitters. 'You are all aware by now that a fitter, Morris, ran amok on 286 last night and almost brought the aircraft down. He was armed with a handgun. The result was the destruction of essential flight instruments and the navigator's plotter. If anyone has any insight into why Morris did this, he can see me afterwards. But besides this, I want it to be known that we have a traitor among us. Yes, a traitor! Someone interfered with the nose wheel in 292. It has been suggested to me that Morris might have done this. I think that's hardly likely, as his idea was to turn the aircraft for home, not destroy it. What is certain is that, despite what you heard Sergeant Leacock say last night, the officers on these aircraft are blameless for this disaster. It has been brought about by a deliberate attempt to sabotage the aircraft. The only people able to do that are those who work in a technical capacity on them. So one of you is the culprit. My fellow officers and I will be keeping our eyes and ears open, and anything that appears to implicate any one of you will be duly noted. You're not going to get away with this.'

There was a murmur of dissent among the men.

'Silence! I will not brook any deviation from the normal code of discipline whilst on this island. You will salute officers when you see them, you will stand to attention when you are spoken to, and you will follow out their orders without question. Do you understand?'

The Warrant Officer cleared his throat.

'I don't think that's a very helpful line to take, sir. Making wild accusations at this stage won't promote a harmonious working relationship between the officers and the men. There'll be plenty of time for an enquiry when we get back to Australia.'

Styles looked Danny up and down, and walked around him as if he was an unsavoury object, brought in on an officer's boot.

'Is that so, Warrant Officer. I would remind you that as the senior non-commissioned officer with this party, the behaviour of the lower ranks is your responsibility. I understand that you have only eighteen months to go to your pension!'

'That's correct, sir!'

'In that case I would advise you to think very carefully on your own attitude and behaviour, in case you should be found wanting.'

Danny glared at Styles, and was about to make some reply, but Styles turned his back on him and looked out at 286.

'As to your previous request, very well, Warrant Officer. Detail your troops to go out and collect all personal kits and anything they think might be useful for our survival.'

'You heard the Squadron Leader,' Danny snapped, turning back to the fitters. 'Get on with it. If you can find anything that might help us catch a few fish, bring it ashore. Likewise for hunting! I don't know if there are any animals on the island, but we need to eat. The SLR's should be in the gun locker at the rear. Make sure you bring them ashore, with all ammunition and pull-throughs, oil etcetera to stop any rust in the barrels. We're going to need them.' He walked over to O'Connell, and drew him aside.

'That gun that Morris had. See if you can find it... it should be in the cockpit somewhere. Search his body for bullets.' He started to turn away, then remembered. 'Oh, and there should be a flare gun in the cockpit and a few flares. Make sure you bring those back.'

O'Connell nodded, peeled off his overalls and along with the others swam out to the wreck in his jocks.

The tide had dropped about ten feet. The water was two feet deep inside the fuselage, but the fact that the aircraft was standing on its wheels enabled them to swim underneath it and access the interior via the rear hatch. The aircraft was cold and dead, eery in the sunlight that reflected from the open cockpit and along the fuselage. Various items floated in the aisle, and it wasn't long before a stream of kit bags was being shoved out through the star port, and down through the hatch. There was soon a pile of bobbing kit bags in the bay.

Pilot Officer Jason Mitchell's body lay face down in the water, and this was shoved down through the hatch and left floating beside the plane. Morris's body was disentangled from the legs of a workstation, and floated out also. Before he pushed it down and out, however, O'Connell searched the overalls for bullets, and found twelve, wrapped up in a sock. He also found the book with the cutout inside, and the small plastic bag of white powder. He passed this up through the star port so it wouldn't get any wetter than it already was. Cusack swam it back to the Warrant Officer, and handed it over.

'From Morris's pocket, sir,' he said. Danny passed it on to Styles.

O'Connell found the .38 by feeling his way around the cockpit, a foot deep in water. It was lying behind the co-pilot's seat. He also got hold of the flare gun, and entrusted the flares to Johnson. While the others were busy, ferrying goods back to the beach, he went looking for the gun locker. It had already been broken open.

O'Connell stuck his head out of the star port, and saw Johnson close at hand.

'Have you been into the gun locker, Corporal?' he yelled.

Johnson looked up from the water and shook his head.

'Well, could you ask the others as they come back, who's been in the gun locker!'

He went back down below, and opened the locker, feeling around in the water for its contents. There was one SLR still in place, but when he pulled it out, the bolt was missing. He felt around and managed to get hold of 8 bullets, but the majority had already disappeared. There was a pull-through, and a small can of oil but nothing else. One complete SLR and the extra bolt plus bullets had gone walkabout. He shoved the rifle and other items up through the star port, and got Johnson to take them in.

'Where's the rest of it,' said Johnson from the water, indicating the missing bolt.

O'Connell stood on the fuselage and shrugged his shoulders.

'Not there,' he yelled. 'Fuck knows!'

'Well you'd better ask Mister Fuck what he does know,' said Johnson, 'or the shit will hit the fan!'

O'Connell shrugged again, and dropped back into the fuselage. As he did so he felt a movement in the aircraft. For a moment he thought that the undercarriage was going to collapse, and realized then that although they had put the wheels down before it settled, they hadn't put the pins in place. There was no hydraulic pressure, so the undercarriage could collapse at any given moment. It would only take a slight swell to lift and move it, and down it would come.

He made his way up front to where they stowed the pins and chocks on a trip, grabbed three pins and dived out through the open cockpit into the water. He almost landed on Pilot Officer Bishop, who had ditched the sling and stripped to his shirt, to half wade and half swim out to the aircraft.

'Look out where you're diving, LAC,' he spluttered, as O'Connell surfaced, clinging to the pins.

'Sorry sir, I didn't see you there.'

Bishop was still in a lot of pain, and as a result, not in the best of moods.

'Well you ought to look before you jump! Anyway, don't disappear, I need you to get a few things.'

He reached out and latched onto the observer's surround, the top of which was just clear of the water. There was a jagged edge of perspex where the cone had been, and he wedged himself under this with his good arm.

O'Connell shook his head.

'Sorry sir, but I've got to do this first.' He waved the undercarriage pins with their orange tags at him, thinking he'd understand. He didn't! The orange tags seemed to enrage him.

'I'm ordering you, LAC, to stop what you're doing, and listen to my requirements. Now!'

O'Connell trod water, and glared at him in turn.

'What do you want?'

'Sir! Sir! I'm an officer, goddammit! Have you no respect?'

'What do you want... Sir!' shouted O'Donnell, spitting water. He was twice the age of this pipsqueak, and had never been spoken to like this before. It was new to him, and he was not impressed.

'I need the batteries, LAC. The batteries and the radio.'

'The radio's stuffed, sir. That guy Morris put a bullet through it.'

'I might be able to salvage it. I want you to get the radio and...'

O'Connell shook his head repeatedly.

'It's been full of water, overnight – Sir! Sea water! Salt! Corrosive! It's fucked – Sir!'

Bishop was finding it a strain hanging on to the front of the aircraft, and was losing his patience.

'What the... What would you know, LAC? Are you a Radio Technician, huh? Do you know the first thing about radios? I've built my own! I built my first radio when I was 10 years old, LAC...'

O'Connell was in no mood for this. He desperately needed to dive down and secure the undercarriage.

'Oh - wacko, doodley-pip! Well I'm an electronically trained Instrument Fitter, Sir, and I'm telling you that the radio in this wreck is rooted! Shagged! Actually blown to bits. The bullet shattered the circuit board, sir. The seawater blew the fuses. The components are corroded! Sir!'

A sudden swell rolled by them, lifting them in the water. The nose of 286 lifted slightly, then dropped again. There was an ominous creak underneath. O'Connell looked alarmed, and waved the pins at Bishop, as if voicing his fear would make it happen.

'I'm not going to ask you again, LAC! Get the batteries and...'

There was a sudden dip of the nose, which snagged the Pilot Officer's shirt on the jagged edge of the Perspex. O'Connell thrust himself back and away, in alarm. Then the nose of 286 slid inexorably underneath the surface, taking Pilot Officer Bishop with it.

O'Connell trod water and rode over the bow wave in horror. He turned towards the shore and yelled 'Help! Help!' waving madly, the pins still in his hand. The group on the beach looked curiously over at him, but didn't seem to appreciate his sense of urgency.

'Help, for Chrisesake. The Pilot Officer...' he yelled, and pointed downwards.

Varley suddenly realized that the nose had disappeared, and began to run into the water, shouting to the others. Cusack and Johnson followed suit. O'Connell turned back in time to see the back end of the aircraft settling under the water as the main undercarriage also collapsed. He looked at the pins in his hand, and threw them. Then he dived down to find Bishop, who was still struggling to free himself from the ragged Perspex.

O'Connell tried to rip his shirt away, but just got it more tangled. The strips of material that Johnson had bound up Bishop's shattered arm with prevented him from pulling the shirt over his arm. Then the swell that had been caused by the aircraft's sudden drop, flowed back the other way and sucked Bishop back in through the opening, driving his body into the observer's compartment, and jamming him in the crawlway.

O'Connell tried to pull him out, but he was stuck fast. He reached for the oxy mask which was floating by Bishop's head, thrust it into his face, then found the valve and turned the oxy on. A stream of bubbles began to blow out from the side of the mask, and Bishop grabbed for it and held it in place with his free hand. Then he gave O'Connell the thumbs up. By this time, O'Connell had to surface for air, and indicated as such to Bishop. The Pilot Officer just stared at him, and O'Connell pushed out and up to the surface, finding Varley and Johnson just about on top of him.

'The Pilot Officer, caught in the crawlway,' he gasped. 'But it's okay… I got the oxy on, he's breathing through the mask. Just get him untangled, will you?

Varley clutched for the top of the nose cone, now three feet under the water, a look of horror on his face. He and Johnson dived simultaneously, while O'Connell gasped for breath on the surface. But two minutes later the pair surfaced, dragging Bishop behind them, and it was obvious even at that point that the Pilot Officer was dead. O'Connell swam to the shore, fell onto the sand and lay shaking and trembling in shock.

Chapter Sixteen

While the others had been busy salvaging items from 286, Flight Lieutenant Campbell and Danny Seaman had set off along the beach looking for Sergeant Leacock, but also keeping their eyes open for a possible food source. They returned just as Varley and Johnson were re-joining O'Connell on the beach. Bishop was dead, and they'd left his body floating in the shallows. The Squadron Leader was the first to tackle them.

'What the hell happened out there, Corporal? Why didn't you bring Pilot Officer Bishop back in to shore.'

Johnson rolled over and sat up.

'Because we're bloody exhausted, sir. It took all our energy diving down and trying to free him from the nose cone. We thought he was okay, because O'Connell here had got the oxy going, and the Pilot Officer was holding it up against his face. But while we were down there he just seemed to let it go, and by the time we got him up top he was dead, sir!'

'That sounds dammed funny to me, Corporal! How did he come to be down there in the first place?'

O'Connell sat up and faced the Squadron Leader. He described the events that led up to Bishop being caught on the jagged Perspex, and the nose going down.

'It just took him with it, sir. If he'd just let me dive down and pin the undercarriage, none of this would have happened.'

'So you're saying that this was his fault, LAC.' Styles sneered. 'I find this all very hard to believe. I'm beginning to see the seeds of a conspiracy here. Who's next on your list of victims? Strange how it's the officers who are the unfortunate victims of these *'accidents'*, isn't it?'

O'Connell jumped to his feet.

'Just what are you implying, sir? I did my best to save the man.'

'Oh, no doubt, no doubt,' Styles replied, sarcastically. Then, 'just back off, LAC!'

At that moment Campbell and Seaman arrived, and further argument was delayed by their news.

'We've found something for lunch, men,' said Danny, looking pleased with himself. 'But you'll have to go and drag it back, it was a bit big for us.'

'What's th.that sir,' said Cusack, always the chirpy one.

'We found ourselves a turtle,' said Danny, smiling for once. 'But it's huge. It will take about four of you to carry it.'

'Turtle!' Johnson looked at O'Connell and pulled a face. 'I don't know whether I fancy turtle!'

'Well, you'd better start fancying it, Corporal, because it's the only meat we've got,' said Campbell. 'The South Sea Islanders have always eaten it, and I'm sure it won't kill you. You'd better go and collect it before it crawls back into the sea.'

At that moment there was a cry from Helen Currier, who had been sitting at the edge of the water.

'Shark! Look... out there!'

They looked to where she was pointing, and a fin sliced through the water, headed for the body of the Pilot Officer. The water was shallow, only about two feet deep, but Bishop's body suddenly gave a lurch, and then began to shake about in the water as if the shark was trying to separate a part from the body. O'Connell was off and running before anyone had a chance to stop him.

Tucked in his pocket was the .38 that he'd recovered from the floor of the cockpit, with two rounds still in the chambers. He splashed his way out to the body, then appeared to dive onto the remains of Bishop. There was a gunshot, and O'Connell picked himself up then reached down into the water and grabbed hold of a fin.

'Anyone for Tiger Shark, boys?' he yelled, then began to laugh uproariously. He towed the dead shark back to the beach, and the others helped him pull it up onto the sand. He'd shot it behind the eyes.

Styles approached him, looking grim.

'Where did you get that gun, LAC,' he snapped.

Bill looked down at the .38 in his hand.

'It was Morris's, sir. I found it in the cockpit. There were only two bullets left in the gun, but I found another dozen bullets in his pocket, sir.'

'Give it to me,' said Styles, grimly, holding out his hand.

'But sir... I think I should keep it for hunting... for food, sir.'

'Don't argue with me, LAC. Give me the gun!'

O'Connell glowered at him, but handed it over.

'And the bullets!'

He pulled the bullets out of his pocket, and handed them over. As he did so he said, 'It's not as if *you're* going to go hunting, is it, sir?'

Styles glowered at him.

'I've had about all the insubordination I can take over the past twenty-four hours. I would advise you all to watch your tongues. You are members of the Royal Australian Air Force, and I am your Commanding Officer. As there is no civil administration on this island, I intend to take control. I therefore declare Martial Law! Any further instances of insubordination will be dealt with by court martial, to be held in my presence, on this island, and serious breaches may be dealt with by capital punishment. Do you all understand?'

The Warrant Officer made a move towards him, shaking his head.

'Excuse me, sir, but you can't do that. These men are Australian citizens, and may only be tried by a properly constituted authority back in Australia. This is not a properly constituted authority.'

Styles rounded on Danny and pointed the gun in his face.

'I *am* the properly constituted authority here, Warrant Officer, and it is your job to carry out my orders. Don't make me use this thing.'

Danny backed away, putting his hands up in surrender.

'In all my years in the service, sir, I've never heard the like of this before...'

'That's enough, Warrant! Just make sure that your airmen conduct themselves properly, and there won't be any trouble.'

He turned and stalked off, leaving the others standing there in shock. Flight Lieutenant Campbell followed him along the beach, and stood talking to him while Styles busied himself with reloading the revolver. The two appeared to be having a heated exchange, then Helen Currier got up and walked over to join them. For the next ten minutes they talked quietly together, while the fitters and Danny stood around looking grim.

In the meantime, the Wing Commander, who had taken no part in any of the discussions that morning, but who had just wandered around aimlessly, came over and addressed Danny.

'It's morbidly beautiful!' he said, then swayed backwards and forwards on the balls of his feet, smiling. 'I didn't think it could be so beautiful.'

Danny looked at him, warily.

'We're not dead, sir. This is an island, and we're waiting to be rescued.'

'Of course,' said the Wing Commander, 'of course...', as if he was humouring a child. He looked up and along the channel between the cliffs, at the distant crest of the volcano, just visible from where they stood.

'I have to explain... I have to put our case...' said Fletcher, as if to himself. 'I go to face the awful countenance of God's judgement. Wish me luck!'

Danny looked at O'Connell, the only one of the group he could even vaguely identify with, and that because of his age. There was only nine years between them after all, though a gulf of ranks. Bill rolled his eyes upward, towards the heavens, and turned away so that Fletcher wouldn't catch his smile.

'I think it's time we cooked this shark, Warrant. What do you think?'

Danny nodded, and waved them all away. He stayed talking to the Wing Commander.

'You've had a terrible shock, sir. You're not thinking very clearly at the moment. Why don't you lie down and get some sleep. It might help to clear your head, sir.'

Fletcher smiled at him, and nodded.

'I appreciate your concern, Warrant. But I have things that have to be resolved. I must go now.'

Danny watched as he wandered off towards the cutting, and soon the Wing Commander was climbing up and out of sight. Danny went back to join the others as they cleaned and prepared the fish for cooking, on a driftwood fire on a white beach.

II

Peter Leacock had been up early that morning. He'd only slumbered fitfully, and had watched the others in the water when they'd arrived from the other crash site. Then he'd slept again, and awoken at eight, to find the dodge tide in progress, and the aircraft reappearing from the depths as if by magic.

Making sure to be perfectly quiet he'd swum out to the wreck, gained access through the star port, and gone straight to the gun locker. Extracting one complete SLR, he felt around in the water and gathered up as many bullets as he could find. He filled his pockets with these, and also took a pull-through and a can of oil. Then he removed the bolt action from the other SLR and put that in his pocket. He had no intention of letting Styles get hold of a gun.

Remembering Morris's revolver, he spent twenty minutes feeling around for the .38 underneath the water still swirling around the floor of the cockpit, but had to give up. Every minute was a minute closer to someone waking up, and he wanted to be gone before that happened. Slipping out through the rear hatch he swam off to the starboard of the aircraft, and kept well down until he could climb out of the water further down the beach. He made his way along the southeastern side of the cutting, and was soon up on top of the cliffs, and heading inland to the forest.

On the way, he collected a few items of the more familiar fruit, and ate it as he walked. There were mangoes and custard apples, and he picked up a coconut along the way, resolving to open it once he was safely secreted from the others. The island was only about four miles across, and he calculated the height of the crater to be about two hundred feet above sea level. Everything went downhill from there. The forest on the eastern side dropped down into a valley, and Leacock plodded determinedly through the undergrowth, heading in the general direction of the second crash site.

He might have been 38 years old, but Peter Leacock had never allowed himself to become soft. Six foot tall and stocky in build, he was a dedicated bushwalker and fisherman when he got the time, and was blessed in that his wife Julie shared his interests. She always went along with him on his various excursions, and felt quite at home in a tent or campervan, on a bleak peninsula or remote mountain range. He thought of her as he doggedly forged his way through the trees, and smiled to himself at some distant recollection.

A veteran of nineteen years, Leacock had not had an easy passage in the air force. He was far too outspoken for the powers that be, and had been twelve years getting that first boost up from Leading Aircraftsman to Corporal. From Corporal to Sergeant had taken another five years, because his mouth continued to get him into trouble. A great favourite with the men in his section, he could always be counted on to draw attention to what he saw as an unjust situation, and as these situations were usually brought about by the arrogance of the officer class, his chances of a final promotion to Flight Sergeant before retirement had become exceedingly thin. Now it looked as if the end would be a dishonourable discharge, and a possible forgoing of his pension. To say he was angry would be an understatement.

He came upon the crash site where the nose cone had finally ploughed into the ground. There was an eerie stillness about the wreck. It had a more tragic appearance than the one in the bay. The fuselage had broken in half and the two halves lay at right angles, and ten feet apart, from each other. The starboard wing was just visible through the trees, eerily suspended in the air. Leacock shook his head, and picked his way around various pieces of debris to enter the rear part of the fuselage. He went straight to the gun locker, removed the two SLR's and 36 rounds of ammunition, and dumped them on the ground outside. He also stuffed a pull-through into his pocket, then went in search of the flare gun, and the six flares they'd carried with them.

To do that he had to enter the front part of the fuselage, and climb over what appeared to be a jumble of sleeping bags, smeared in blood. As he tried to step over them, he realized he was walking on dead bodies, and he shuddered and stopped, stranded in the middle of this morass of death. The faces of the dead men rose up in front of him, and he suddenly felt like throwing up. Under his feet lay Barry Mackintosh, Don Grainger the radio tech, Kevin Bailey, and the co-pilot, Peter Dawson. Here lay Ron Gray, the pleasant and unassuming navigator. Peter Leacock had no gripe with him.

He managed to stagger into the cockpit, retrieve the flare gun and flares and, rather than return the way he came, climb out through the gaping hole above the instrument panel. Once outside he looked around for a spare kit bag, emptied out the contents on the ground and filled it with the three SLR's the flare gun and flares, then throwing it over his shoulder, he made off towards the volcano.

III

Wing Commander Barton Fletcher was confused. He thought that he was either dead, or hovering about in some intermediate zone between life and death. The extreme clarity of his present situation, in contrast to the fuzzy, almost dreamlike quality of the memories of his previous life, convinced him that he was on the verge of some primal revelation.

Fletcher had spent his entire adult life inured in the privilege of the class system, as an officer in the RAAF. In an egalitarian Australian society, being an officer in the armed forces was the closest one could get to approximating the British aristocracy, and in many ways, the officer caste was more powerful again. Officers, after all, possessed a power over their detractors that the aristocracy lacked... they had the power to charge dissidents and punish them, and the proceedings were always loaded in their favour. The system looked upon officers as a protected elite, and encouraged them to be boorish, arrogant, contemptuous and complacent about the rights of others.

All this had been effected in the cause of discipline, order, and the chain of command. It was expected to produce a united fighting force that followed orders, suppressed individuality, and got results with the minimum loss of life. (What that actually meant, of course, was the minimum loss of officer's lives, as the lower ranks were still regarded as the cannon fodder of the war machine).

The actual results of this age-old policy were quite different, however. What it produced was a dysfunctional unit riddled with divisions, bitter hatreds and resentments, a veritable pressure cooker that could explode at any moment. Unfortunately, due to the fact that the lower ranks were precluded from expressing their frustrations, the Officers were always the last to find out.

Fletcher had never questioned the overall scheme of things. Why should he? He was moving nicely along the pre-ordained path to the realm of the gods. His next move was to Group Captain, and he was moving as quickly along that path as anyone ever did during peacetime. After that, Air Commodore, Air Vice Marshall, and maybe even, one day, Marshall of the Royal Australian Air Force.

But now, he had experienced a sudden *coitus interruptus.* Losing two aircraft on a Navex was the equivalent of severing the umbilical cord to his next promotion. Fletcher might have been muddy in his thinking, but he was aware that when the enquiries commenced, the inevitable recriminations would roll like an erratic coin in his direction, and that where he sat was where the buck stopped.

Cast out into the real world for the first time in his life, the world of accepting responsibility, of being held to account, of being judged… the world of the lower ranks, in fact, he felt in need of an answer to his predicament. For a Wing Commander, the only heights he could turn to for an answer were beyond the reach of man. He needed a private audience with God! With this in mind, he turned his face towards the volcano.

Chapter Seventeen

After disposing of the shark, Styles ordered the lower ranks to concentrate on building a shelter from the weather. By stripping some small trees up on the clifftop and bringing palm fronds down to the beach, and by using cables and pieces of debris, a three sided shelter was constructed within a couple of hours. It was side-on to the beach, with an open front. At the worst it was shelter from the mid-day sun, and at the best, somewhere to keep dry during the storms that they knew were usual for this part of the world.

'Right, this will be the equivalent of Officer's Quarters,' Styles told the troops, once they had finished. 'If you want to go and build yourselves a shelter, you can have the rest of the afternoon and evening off. I suggest you build it up over by the cliff somewhere. But you will report back here at 0800.'

O'Connell looked at the others and shook his head.

'I thought the shelter was for all of us, sir.'

Styles looked at him condescendingly.

'What on earth would give you that impression, LAC? Just because we're stranded on an island doesn't mean that Air Force traditions won't be upheld. You know very well that officers and men don't fraternise. That is still the rule.'

'It's all right for Officers and an airwoman to fuckernise though, isn't it,' muttered Duckett.

Styles spun on his heel to face him.

'I hope that remark wasn't what I thought it was, LAC.'

'I just wanted to point out that Airwoman Currier is not an officer – Sir!'

'It's hardly your place to remark on the Airwoman's situation, LAC. I have agreed to extend the courtesy of the Officer's Mess to Miss Currier, due to the difficult situation we find ourselves in. You men can look after yourselves.'

'She's not exactly helpless, sir. I should know. I lived with her for six months,' said Duckett, sourly.

'And treated her very badly, I believe, LAC,' interjected Flight Lieutenant Campbell, as he wandered up from the beach.

'I treated her very well, sir. She's just a snob for a bit of blue braid.'

'I have no intention of entering into a conversation with you about Miss Currier,' Campbell said, pompously. 'You will remember your place, LAC. Go and build your shelter, before you get yourself into trouble.'

Duckett stomped off towards the cutting, followed by Cusack, Varley and Johnson. O'Connell turned to the Warrant Officer, who had been talking to Campbell down on the beach.

'Are you coming, Warrant>'

Danny looked embarrassed, and shook his head.

'Er, no O'Connell. You go on! I've been invited to share the Officers quarters for the duration. With any luck the rescue party should be here in the next few days, and this will all be over. Go and build that shelter.'

O'Connell gave Danny a meaningful look, shook his head slightly and went off to join the others. So the Warrant Officer was joining the enemy. Typical! A leopard never changed its spots.

'Well that pretty well tells us where we stand, doesn't it,' said Varley, on the way up through the cutting. 'We're to be the new servant class on the island. All the dirty jobs! We're going to be at their beck and call. They're going to sit on their arses, and we'll supply the labour.'

'What if we don't,' said Duckett. 'This isn't the Air Force now. We should be equal, at least until we get back to base.'

'You heard what he said when he took that gun off Bill, here. He's put us under Martial Law,' said Johnson. 'That means that if we don't buckle to, he'll charge us with mutiny… and the punishment for that out in the field is death by firing squad.'

'He wouldn't fucking dare!' O'Connell swore, puffing from the climb.

They turned as they reached the top, and looked back down on the beach. Styles, the Warrant Officer, Campbell and Helen Currier were standing in front of the shelter, talking.

They turned and kept walking, through light vegetation and down a slope, heading for the edge of a forest of pines. They needed to find a place that would act as a windbreak, as the breeze at this height was fairly brisk. They continued for another hundred yards along the edge of the forest, and then found a large boulder, which could act as the front wall.

'I wonder where the Wing Commander went,' said Varley. 'They don't seem to give two stuffs about him. In his present state he could be lying somewhere, injured… maybe even dying.'

'In what present state,' enquired O'Connell?

'You know, brain damaged! He's not capable of looking after himself.'

Johnson rounded on Varley and grabbed him by the collar of his overalls. There was a struggle, and the next minute Johnson had him on his back on the ground.

'How the fuck do you know he's brain damaged? What do you know about it?'

Varley tried to fight him off, but Johnson was bigger and heavier, and held him down.

'Here, leave off,' said Duckett, alarmed.

Johnson looked up and warned him off.

'Don't you fucking interfere, Duckett. You know more about

this than meets the eye.'

Duckett began to turn red, and O'Connell grabbed him by the arm and held him back.

'Why do you say he's brain damaged, Varley?'

'Get off him, Corporal. I can tell you why!'

This new voice came from a thicket of trees, and was very familiar to them. Sergeant Leacock was standing next to a bush, aiming an SLR straight at Johnson's head.

'Fuckin' hell, Sergeant. You scared the shit out of us,' said O'Connell.

Johnson slowly let Varley go, and got up off his chest.

'What's the meaning of this then, Sergeant,' he said.

'Come over here, out of sight of the pigs on the beach, and we'll talk about it,' said Leacock, lowering the rifle.

They did as they were told, sheepishly, and he escorted them into an area where they couldn't be spied on.

'Now! I think Varley can tell you himself, can't you Varley? I know all about it so you might as well come clean. You see, I signed the servicing sheet on that aircraft, and I know who was on the oxy that day.'

Varley's shoulders slumped. He knew that he couldn't fool Leacock.

'Look... it was just a joke. I thought the worst that could happen would be that the pilots would have a fit of the giggles at 12,000 feet. I didn't realize how dangerous it was.'

O'Connell looked at Varley in horror.

'What the fuck was it... laughing gas? Nitrous Oxide – that's the proper term for it, isn't it?

'Yes – nitrous oxide,' said Varley, sullenly. 'I only put it into the back-up system. Look, I'm sorry!'

'You killed Mitchell, and Bishop, you prick! I thought it was something I'd done!' O'Connell went for him, but was restrained by Leacock.

'Enough of that! Varley will have to face the proper authorities when we get back to Australia. If we let this deteriorate into a bunfight between us all, there's no saying where it will end.' He turned to O'Connell. 'What's this about Bishop?'

O'Connell explained about the events of that morning, how Bishop had been dragged down by the nose when it went, and how he had turned the oxy on under water thinking that would save him until they could free him up, and get him to the surface.

'But when they pulled him out, he was dead,' said O'Connell. 'I've been blaming myself. Even Styles intimated that he thought it was my fault – even accused us of a conspiracy to kill the officers. It was this prick all the time.'

Varley looked miserable. O'Connell and he had always been friends.

'I'm sorry, I'm sorry mate! Really, I'm sorry.'

'Don't fucking mate me,' said O'Connell. 'You're no mate of mine!'

'Right, calm down,' said Leacock. 'We're not here to judge, just to find out where all this began to go wrong. What about the nose wheel on 292?'

'I don't know anything about that,' Varley mumbled, darting a glance at Duckett. Johnson's eyes were as sharp as a hawk's.

'Okay, Duckett. What did he look at you like that for?'

'I saw that too,' said Leacock. 'It's down to you, Duckett.'

Duckett hesitated, then put his hands up to defend himself. Johnson grabbed him by the shoulder.

'Don't fuckin' hit me! Okay! I admit it. I cut the pin at Nadi and thought he'd just turn around and land again. I just wanted to put the wind up the prick.'

'Who? Put the wind up who?'

'Campbell! He's off with my woman... Helen! She was living with me. We were going to get married and have kids.'

Leacock nodded.

'I thought as much. Well, you're a right pair, aren't you? Between you two, a deranged lunatic and the natural incompetence of a Wing Commander and a Squadron Leader, nine people are dead.'

'Oh Christ,' Duckett whimpered. 'We never meant this... we never meant it to come to this.'

The others were silent. One by one they all flopped down onto the ground, except Leacock. He paced backwards and forwards a few times, deep in thought.

'Okay. Now we at least know what happened. Well I for one can understand that what the two of you did wasn't done with the idea of bringing the aircraft down.... I know that wasn't your intention. I think it was incredibly stupid and childish, but I accept that you saw it as a prank, one that you'd probably get away with, and with no one hurt. It hasn't worked out like that, but there's nothing that we can do about it now. I for one don't intend to say anything about it to the officers. I think it would be a bad move. What about the rest of you?'

Johnson sat shaking his head.

'I don't like it, Sergeant. Why should we wear the suspicion of the officers and the Warrant Officer because of these two prats?'

'For a very good reason, Corporal! Now that I'm aware of all the facts, several things become clear to me. The most important, I think, is that the Squadron Leader has also suffered brain damage. I think he's become erratic, irrational, a loose cannon. There's no knowing what he might do if he finds out about this.'

O'Connell sat up, and agreed.

'I think you're right. He's declared Martial Law, and he's already threatened us with capital punishment for insubordination. I think he's off his trolley.'

'I'm sure of it,' said the Sergeant. 'I've known Styles, or known of him, for about eight years. He's always come over as a bit of a prick, but he's never overstepped the mark like this. I don't think he's capable of making rational decisions anymore, and given this information there's no saying what he might do. He might just string these two up.'

'He doesn't have to. He's got a gun,' said O'Connell. 'He'll probably shoot them.'

Leacock took notice at this.

'What do you mean, he's got a gun?'

'That gun Morris brought on board, Sarge. I found it this morning in the cockpit, and he confiscated it from me. He even threatened Danny with it.'

'How many bullets has he got?'

'Thirteen all up, I think. There were twelve carried in a sock, and one left in the gun, after I shot the shark.'

'Oh, for Chrisesake! I thought I'd sorted that,' said Leacock.

'So it was you that took the bolt out of the SLR,' said Johnson. 'I thought so at the time. What about the ones on 292?'

'I've got them too, and plenty of ammunition, don't you worry! They're in a safe place. They won't come out unless we need them.'

'So you're going to come back down there with us tomorrow, Sergeant?'

O'Connell hoped he would get the right answer.

'Not just now, O'Connell! From what you've told me I don't think it would be safe. Styles hates my guts! Give him half a chance and he'll shoot me! No, I think I'll just lie low for a while, wait until he's out of bullets at least. It would probably be safer for you lot, too. I'll be there to watch over you, make sure nothing happens.'

'Our f.fairy godmother,' said Cusack in a falsetto voice. They laughed.

'Well, what do you think... keep hush about these two – at least until we get back to Oz?

They all nodded, all but Johnson.

'I won't lie! I won't say anything unless asked, but I won't lie and wreck my career, not for anyone.'

'Fair enough,' said Peter. 'Fair enough! But you do realize, don't you, that if Styles carries out some sort of kangaroo court here on the island, finds these two guilty and attempts to execute them, it will be on your head.'

Johnson scowled, and shrugged his shoulders.

'I'm not the villain here, they are, so don't put your shit onto me, Sergeant. If they cop it, it's because of what *they* did, nobody else!'

'Yes, but then I'll be forced to intervene, and that could mean more bloodshed. Don't forget, I have the rifles.'

'That just puts you as far outside the law as they are! What about you others,' Johnson said, looking specifically at O'Connell and Cusack. 'What do you think? I think we should take that rifle off the Sergeant and escort him back to the beach. He's under arrest, after all. If we don't, it's our careers on the line.'

'That's not an option, Corporal,' said Leacock, taking a step back and raising the rifle to cover him. 'I'm only under arrest on the word of a man who has lost all sense of proportion, due to the long term effects of nitrous oxide. He's exhibiting signs of megalomania, and that condition will only get worse.'

'I'm with the Sergeant,' said Cusack. 'I think Styles is off his loaf.'

'I'll stick with you, Sarge,' said O'Connell. Then he laughed. 'After all, what are they going to do – bust me back to LAC?'

They all grinned at that scenario. Johnson got to his feet, his face grim.

'Then I can have no further dealings with any of you. I'm not going to fuck my career for the sake of a couple of imbeciles.'

'So you're going to go down there and tell them everything that's transpired here,' said Leacock. 'You're going to put everybody's life in jeopardy.'

'I didn't say that. I just said that I'm not going to lie for them. If I'm asked, I'll answer any direct question. If they don't ask me, I'll say nothing.'

'If we can have your word on that, Johnson, you can go.' Leacock still had the rifle on him.

'Yes, you've got my word,' said Johnson, angrily. 'Okay! Do I have to spell it out?'

'Well go then,' said the Sergeant, and the five of them watched the Corporal disappear through the trees.

II

Down on the beach, Helen had decided she needed to be able to go for a swim minus her clothes. Now that the fitters had gone to build their shelter, it seemed as good a time as any. There was only that old Warrant Officer there, and the Squadron Leader. He had been quite nice to her as it turned out. She'd thought he was a bit overbearing with the others, but with her, he was like putty in her hands.

She walked along the beach a way, then stopped, put her regulation towel on the sand and stripped off her skirt, Now that her clothes were at least clean again, and dry, she didn't see any reason to get them wet. She peeled off her jacket and blouse, and stood in her panties and bra, very much aware of the three pairs of eyes that were on her. Stepping into the crystal clear water, she peeled off these final two layers and threw them back onto the beach

Styles stood as if transfixed. His own wife was a rather shapeless, sexless woman with a tongue like a shrew, and an ugly face to go with it. He had never looked at her as he looked at Helen now. He forgot himself as he stood there, and muttered under his breath, 'Helen of Troy!'

The Warrant Officer cleared his throat and said he was going to have a lie down in the shelter. Danny had never been married, and was not good around women. They embarrassed him, no more than now.

Campbell sat on the beach admiring her body, feeling rather privileged that after all that had happened Helen had naturally gravitated to his protection. He was the only man on the island who could guarantee he was not going to get frustrated during his stay. Or so he thought! He might have been surprised, therefore, if he had been privy to Helen's thoughts at the time.

She was more aware of the Squadron Leader than of Campbell while she was on that beach. When she emerged, after ten minutes of splashing around, she made sure that he was still watching, then turned towards him so that he could get a full view of her breasts, and of that tight clutch of hair at her groin. She picked up her towel and made a great play of drying her hair, seemingly oblivious to the fact that her lower half was uncovered and open to his view. The Squadron Leader began to feel himself stir in response to this voyeuristic experience, and suddenly he knew he had to have her. He looked at the Warrant Officer, now beginning to snore in the confines of the shelter, and at Campbell, sitting some twenty yards away on the beach. He wandered over, casually, as if to chat.

'I've been thinking, Flight Lieutenant. I'm very concerned about Sergeant Leacock, and the fact that he hasn't returned. I want you to go and ferret him out for me. He might be on the other side of the island, or he might be at the other wreck. While you're over there I want you to check for any SLR's that might have been on your aircraft, and any ammunition.'

Campbell looked up, disbelievingly.

'What? Now, sir?'

'Yes, Flight Lieutenant... Now! While it's still daylight! That's an order.'

'But what am I supposed to do if he won't come back with me. He's more than a match for me physically.'

'Use your rank. The more he refuses, the more we've got on him once it comes to a court martial.'

'Can I take that gun, sir?' Campbell asked, indicating the .38 Styles had shoved in his belt.

'You certainly may not! Now go, Campbell, get a move on.'

The Flight Lieutenant took one last look at Helen, now sunning herself on her towel, and turned to go. He looked suspiciously at the Squadron Leader as he left, but put that thought right out of his head. Not Styles... he just wasn't up to it.

The moment Campbell's figure disappeared over the top of the escarpment, Styles wandered along the beach to where Helen lay. As he approached, she covered herself with her towel, and smiled up at him.

'Beautiful day, sir.'

'It certainly is, Helen. I'm going for a walk, down to those rocks at the far end of the beach. Perhaps you'd like to accompany me.'

That wasn't a request, it was an order! Helen felt a thrill of anticipation pass through her. A real live Squadron Leader!

'I would love to, sir. I'll just get dressed then follow you down.'

Styles smiled grimly to himself and kept walking. It had been a long time since he had been worked up about a woman's body, but he was now the leading figure in a small community, and if there was to be only one woman, then that woman would have to be his.

Chapter Eighteen

Wing Commander Fletcher had stood at the top of the escarpment, and gazed across at the volcano. He could either head directly towards it, which would eventuate in a steep climb up its southern face, or he could scout around to the west, where the approach to the volcano summit was a much gentler, undulating rise. He opted to go west.

Fletcher was nowhere near as fit as he thought he was. He progressed by strolling a hundred yards at a time, then sitting down to rest. There was a lot of tropical vegetation over on the western side, and he stared at the various fruits and flowers he came across as if with new eyes. He couldn't put a name to most, though he was surprised to see mangoes, passion fruit, kumquats and bananas. One tree he came across bore sour oranges, rather small in size, but refreshing. There were coconuts everywhere, but it wasn't until he had almost traversed the western side of the island and skirted a swamp that he saw his first coconut crab. It scuttled up a tree as he watched, like a huge spider with one purpose in mind. It managed to dislodge a couple of coconuts at the top, then scuttled down again, and to his surprise cracked the nut open with its giant claw.

It was near the marsh that he saw his first snake, a large brown fellow, six feet long, slithering from pool to pool and quite oblivious to his presence. Fletcher saw he would have to retrace his footsteps to avoid being caught in the marshes. He went back and skirted around them, heading now in the general direction of the volcano. By the time it got dark he had arrived at the base, and as there was what appeared to be a small cave protected by several large rocks, he decided to spend the night there, and demolish the rest of the fruit he'd carried along the way.

It was an unsettled night. He dreamt that someone or something was watching him, lying undercover but following his every move. He awoke with a start at about midnight, and lay awhile, trying to work out what it was that had interrupted his sleep. Then he heard it again, a deep rumbling in the earth, and a feeling that the ground itself was shaking. He waited for it to happen again, but it wouldn't oblige, and he eventually fell asleep and slept dreamlessly until morning.

II

When Johnson left the others, and made his way back down to the beach, he would ordinarily have passed Campbell on his way up, but Campbell had headed straight ahead instead of turning east at the top of the escarpment, and so they missed one another.

When the Corporal arrived at the beach, there was no one to be seen. He went across to the shelter to find the Warrant Officer sound asleep, and no sign of the others. Thinking to investigate, he began to walk along the beach, heading towards a jumble of boulders visible at the southeastern end. He strolled along, in no hurry, and scanned the bay in case they were out swimming. When he got to the rocks he stopped and listened. He could hear the sound of voices, but couldn't work out where they were coming from.

Peering warily around a large black boulder, he saw Helen, naked from the waist down, bent over a rock and being laboriously ravished from behind by a perspiring Squadron Leader. She was letting out little squeals of pleasure, and turning every now and then to groan compliments about his prowess.

'I always knew you'd be terrific, sir,' she groaned. 'You're so masterful and virile! I feel like a virgin maiden being taken by a

Greek God, sir.'

'You're magnificent,' he panted in reply. 'My Helen of Troy! No wonder they fought for ten years over you. But I don't need to fight for you, do I Helen?'

Helen looked over her shoulder, and threw him an agonized look.

'Oh, no sir! I'm yours whenever you want me, sir.'

'Are you sure of that, Helen? You will keep yourself only for me.'

'Well, I don't know about that, sir. There's Flight Lieutenant Campbell, Eddie sir. He might order me, and I'm a good girl, I always do what I'm ordered, sir!' She smiled, mischievously.

Styles stopped thrusting for a moment, seized her hair in his left hand and twisted her head sideways. Then with his right hand he thrust the barrel of the .38 in her mouth. Her eyes opened wide in horror.

'No more Eddie Campbell, do you understand. I can't let my position here be undermined by a Flight Lieutenant. You do understand that?'

He cocked the revolver, and pushed it further into her mouth so that her lips were clamped tightly around the barrel as her eyes bulged white with fear. She tried to let out a little squeal. He climaxed, and didn't remove the gun for a further ten seconds. When he withdrew from her she collapsed, weeping on the rock.

'I promise, I promise sir! I won't go with Eddie, or anyone else. God, I thought you were going to shoot me.'

'Just underlining my authority, child. From now on you will make yourself available to me every day. Whether it's here, or up in the woods somewhere. Wherever I go, you will accompany me. Is that understood, airwoman Currier?'

Helen just nodded her head, and burst into tears again.

Johnson pulled back behind his rock in shock. They were right, the man was a megalomaniac, and a rapist if that was anything to go by. He walked rapidly away, back up the beach. With any luck they wouldn't return immediately, and he could make out he'd seen nothing. There was no telling what Styles might do if he thought he'd been seen.

Styles and Helen wandered back twenty minutes later. Johnson was sitting down by the water, looking out at the bay.

'What are you doing here, Corporal? I thought I told you to go off with the others and build a shelter.'

'We had an argument, sir. We don't really see eye to eye on a lot of things, so I came back down.'

'Well, now that you're here, you'd better make yourself useful. Go and catch some fish so we get to eat tonight.'

Johnson looked up at him, and at the revolver in his belt. Helen stood cowed beside him. Her eyes were still red and puffy.

'Very well, sir! What do I use for bait?'

'Use your friend over there,' he said, pointing to the body of Jack Morris, still lying in the shallows. 'It worked yesterday. It should work again today. Make yourself a spear and get one of those reef sharks.'

Johnson got to his feet and went off looking for a suitable sapling to whittle into a spear, wondering all the while how he'd managed to end up the meat in the sandwich.

III

Peter Leacock left the others to their shelter building activities, promising to keep an eye on the situation and to prevent anything getting out of control if things went a little crazy. He wouldn't tell them where he was hiding out, in case one or the other changed their minds and told Styles or the Warrant Officer.

'Don't blame Danny,' was his parting shot, as he prepared to disappear through the trees. 'He's due to retire in 18 months, after about 25 years service. You can't blame him for being worried about his pension. I was a bit harsh on him before. It's just that he's always been such an unbending old prick in the past, that it's hard to feel sympathy for the man. But in this situation, we should attempt, at least, to be understanding.'

He headed off into the trees with the SLR, the others being no wiser about his whereabouts. Heading due north, he skirted the volcano rim on its southeastern side until he found the footholds he'd already established. Then he climbed quickly and easily up to the rim of the crater, slipped across the ridge and down the other side. From there he followed a ledge that ran for a hundred yards or more, heading due west, and this brought him to a small cave on the inside of the volcano's rim.

Inside he had stored the other two SLR's, bullets, flares and flare gun, fruit, some dry firewood and a rather crushed coconut crab that he had intercepted earlier that day, and killed with a large rock. That was to be his supper. Any smoke issuing from his fire would be seen as no different to those other whisps of smoke that they'd all noticed earlier, issuing from the volcano's core.

He settled in, waiting for the approach of dusk. No one would be crazy enough to want to scale the sides of a volcano at night, with no torches. He busied himself with oiling and cleaning the SLR's, a bigger job than he thought, as the salt water had already begun to pit the barrels, and the bolts had to be oiled and worked, over and over again to free them up. Eventually, however, he had three serviceable SLR's, each one loaded and ready to fire, with a clip of eight rounds each in place. That left him another 34 rounds of ammo as back up, which he had managed to collect from the two aircraft.

At dusk, he lit his fire, and was gratified to see that it gave off a minimal amount of smoke. He cooked the crab and found that the meat was far too much for him. He ate about a quarter of it and threw the rest away, knowing that it wouldn't keep. After a couple of sour oranges and a custard apple, he fished in his pocket and pulled out a rather sad packet of cigarettes. They had been a sealed pack when he jumped into the water to swim ashore, so had avoided the worst, that of being saturated. But a slight amount of water had got in and dampened the bottom of the pack. As a result he had to warily open up the packet and slide the silver paper out with the cigarettes, then carefully separate one from its compatriots. He had 38 left out of a packet of 50, and was resolved to smoke only three a day from now on. The first one, an hour after he woke up! One after a midday meal, and one after dinner each night. He reasoned that this would give him 12 days before he had to go cold turkey, and if it took that long for the rescuers to get there, he'd probably have to give it up for life. He sat back now and enjoyed his evening cigarette, lighting it from the embers of his fire so that he could conserve his cigarette lighter for as long as possible.

The fire gradually went out and the only glow was the glow on the end of this last luxury for the night. He took his time smoking it, then put it out halfway along, just in case he woke up in the night craving nicotine.

He felt uneasy! There was something in the air, and it was affecting his nervous system. He suddenly felt himself to be wide-awake and straining for the slightest sound. Something was watching him, he felt sure of it. Something or somebody was aware of his presence, and was sitting back, waiting.

Nervously he picked up one of the SLR's and pointed it

towards the entrance to the cave. He pulled back the bolt and slid a bullet into the breech, then sat there tense and waiting for any eventuality. It was eery and very frightening!

On his various forays across the island he had kept his eyes open for any signs of wild life that might be present, with a view to future hunting expeditions. It appeared to be very sparse. There were fruit bats, he could see that from the evidence they'd left in the mangoes, lying on the ground. There were probably rats, though he hadn't actually seen any. There was a wide variety of birds, but he'd only really seen them down in the marshes on the western side of the island, where there appeared to be some sort of breeding ground. Of large animals, he'd seen none. No pigs, no goats, no sheep or wild dogs. He'd caught a glimpse of what appeared a sort of wild chicken, but it had disappeared through the undergrowth before he could get a good look at it. Nevertheless, he felt that there was something on this island, perhaps an animal that was either too shy or too sly to have allowed itself to be seen at this stage. They had, after all, been there for less than two days.

Leacock moved further back into the cave, feeling grave discomfort. It was a moonlit night, though not as bright as the night before. For some reason he didn't feel that he could relax... his nerves were so on edge that his body literally tingled.

There was a slight sound, outside the cave and to the left. He raised the rifle, peering through the gloom, and suddenly a large shape rushed at the entrance. He caught a momentary glimpse of gaping jaws, with inch long serrated teeth, dripping with an evil saliva, by which time, purely by reflex action, he'd fired two shots at point blank range down its throat. As it slid to a halt and slumped in front of him, he fired six more bullets in quick succession into the skull, and through a cold, reptilian eye. Then he felt the icy sweat on his forehead, the cramps in his stomach, and before he managed to reach for the second rifle, he realized that he'd thrown up.

The body almost blocked the entrance to the cave... it was immense! Peter pushed himself back and away from the jaws, which had come to rest only two feet away, and he carefully fired another three bullets into its neck and body before sitting back and attempting to get his breathing rate under control.

He stared at the intruder with disbelieving eyes, and searched his brain for answers. It was a lizard, obviously, but what sort of lizard? Then his thoughts came into focus, and he realized that what lay before him was a creature that he'd only read about in books on dinosaurs and their modern descendants. He looked at the huge curved claws that could have ripped him apart, and realized that what he was looking at was a Komodo Dragon.

To his understanding, these leftovers from a prehistoric age had only been found in islands off Indonesia. Obviously, they had existed on other pacific islands as well, and this was one of them.

He gathered up his weapons and stores and carefully crawled around the giant's body, only breathing once he managed to get out into the fresh air. From that vantage point he could see that the body was about ten feet long, and weighed approximately 250 pounds. How could something that big hide so effectively?

He retraced his steps along the inner ledge, carrying two of his guns in the kit bag over his shoulder. The other he carried, loaded, in his other hand. He wasn't going to stay there for another moment. He had experienced pure terror in its most atavistic form, and all he wanted now was the comfort and companionship of other human beings. He descended the rim of the crater, and set out for the spot where he had left the lads building their shelter. He just hoped he was in time!

Chapter Nineteen

Flight Lieutenant Campbell cursed the Squadron Leader heartily. Fancy dragging him away from that vision on the beach, to go hunting a recalcitrant Sergeant who wasn't going to cooperate anyway!

It was getting late. Only another hour or so and it would be dark, and he would end up stuck in the woods, unable to see his hand in front of his face. He decided to head for the wreck first.

He headed inland, and then cut across to the forest to check out 292. It took him over an hour, but he finally came across it, lying exactly as he'd left it, and he entered the rear fuselage to check out the gun locker. It was empty!

Campbell swore again. That bloody Sergeant was going to be more trouble than he was worth! He looked around the wrecked interior, and noted that the two inflatable rafts had been shredded by debris. He jumped out of the fuselage and walked around, meaning to check the flares in the cockpit. As he did so he came to a mess of sleeping bags, or the remains of them, lying strewn on the ground. They looked as if they'd been dragged out of the aircraft, ripped apart by a large animal, and in two at least, the contents had been mauled and partly eaten.

Campbell staggered back in disgust. He put his hand over his face, and hurried to put some distance between himself and that dreadful sight. Forgoing all thought of cornering Sergeant Leacock, he decided that it was more important to return to the beach, and report this happening to the Squadron Leader. There were obviously wolves or wild pigs on the island that saw the bodies of their compatriots as a source of food.

When he emerged from the forest, Campbell found himself walking towards the new shelter that had just been completed by the fitters. They were sitting around, enjoying a break when he emerged through the trees.

'God! I thought you were the Sergeant again,' said O'Connell as he approached.

'What do you mean, again? Has he been here?'

O'Connell looked warily at the others, and immediately regretted his impetuous response.

'Yes sir! He was here about an hour ago. We just had a talk and he went off again.'

'Did he say where he was going?' said the Flight Lieutenant, annoyed that he'd missed him.

'No sir, he wouldn't tell us. I think he's hidden out on the other side of the island, sir!' said Cusack.

'Did he have a gun, or guns with him?'

'Yes sir, he had an SLR. We would have jumped him, but he had us covered,' said Varley, 'so there was nothing we could do! He'll probably come back when the heat dies down.'

Campbell snorted, and made an attempt to laugh.

'There's no way the heat will die down for Sergeant Leacock this side of hell. He's for the high jump when we get back to Australia, if not before.'

'What do you mean by that, sir? Is the Squadron leader thinking about taking action here?'

'You'd better believe it, LAC. This island is under Martial Law. That means that dissent can be punished by a firing squad.'

'Except he's got all the g.guns,' Cusack smirked. 'It's a bit hard to hold a f.firing squad, when you haven't g.got any rifles, sir.'

The Flight Lieutenant turned to face him.

'You're Cusack, aren't you? The smart mouth of the squadron! We'll see you laugh on the other side of your face one of these days, LAC. Consider yourself on Squadron Leader's

Report.'

'Now hang on a minute, sir,' O'Connell expostulated. 'He didn't mean anything by that – it was just a joke! What's happened to humour around here lately?'

'There's nothing humorous about insubordination, LAC. I would advise you to be more circumspect in your manner of speech as well, and avoid the wrath of the C.O.'

'I object, sir! If this is how everything we say is going to be received and misconstrued on this island, then I don't want to be part of this Air Force any more. I want a discharge.'

Campbell's face turned a dull red.

'You are signed on to a fixed term in this air force, and you will serve out every day of that term, under the terms and conditions of service. You would do that back in Australia, and you will do that here, is that understood?'

O'Connell stared at him, then shook his head.

'Unless the officers begin to treat us with a little respect, sir, then I'm afraid you'll find yourself catching your own fish, and cooking your own food, and building your own shelters, sir! We've just about had it!'

'So it's mutiny, is it? Is that what you're telling me, LAC?'

O'Connell looked at the others.

'I can't speak for them, sir, but I'm pretty ticked off with your attitude. I think it's about time you dropped the airs and graces, and mucked in like everyone else.'

Campbell turned on his heel and strode away from the group. He turned back to face them thirty yards away, and said, 'You can consider yourself under open arrest. The rest of you, deliver LAC O'Connell down to the beach, right now, to front the Squadron Leader, or you will all be charged with mutiny!'

'Now hang on,' said Cusack.

'Not on your life, sir,' said Varley. 'We're sticking together!'

'And you, LAC Duckett?'

Gordon looked scared out of his wits. He looked at the others, then started walking after the Flight Lieutenant, making signs to the others like he had no choice.

'I'm with you, sir. I don't want to get in any trouble, sir.'

'You fucking prick, Duckett,' said Varley.

'You weak bastard,' said Cusack. 'Go on, l.lick their arses you pathetic p.prick.'

Campbell turned and walked purposefully towards the cutting, with Duckett hurrying after him, his head down.

O'Connell looked at the other two, and smiled grimly.

'Well, the shit *has* hit the fan, hasn't it fellas?'

II

Wing Commander Fletcher woke up the following morning, and began to make his way up towards the rim of the volcano. He felt especially clear-headed with regard to what he intended doing that morning. He was going to enlist the aid of an entity that was beyond the Air Commodores and Air Marshals of this world, the aid of someone who would not be disobeyed. Perhaps, with the aid of this higher being, he could salvage his career?

He took his time and carefully negotiated the steady rise of the volcanic crater, and after an hour and twenty minutes found himself on the outer rim. The view was magnificent from up there, just the sort of place that a god would choose to pontificate from. He looked down into the crater, and saw whisps of white smoke pouring steadily out of fissures in the depths, and felt the awful majesty and grandeur of a history that pre-dated man by millions of years.

How puny mankind was in relation to these primal forces...

forces that had shaped the planet over millennia. How insignificant and insubstantial were the arbitrary divisions of mankind. Wing Commander, Group Captain! What, after all, did it mean? An artificial method by which one man maintained his domination of another! But the man at the bottom of the pile had to agree to the system before it would work. He would at the very least, have to acquiesce. If not, then those in power had to force his acquiescence, giving him no opportunity to topple the system. Fletcher addressed the volcano.

'Oh awful God of Primeval Time, creator of worlds, and disrespecter of man's vanity and meagre accomplishments... Instruct me! Show me by your infinite, powerful and terrible countenance whether or not I have transgressed in your great scheme of things. If I am at all responsible for the deaths of those nine men, show me now! Wreak your vengeance now, or use your overwhelming power to stay every man's hand against me! Give me eternal truth so that I may walk from this place with a clear conscience.'

As he raised his arms to the heavens, the mate of the Komodo Dragon that Leacock had killed the night before rushed out from behind a bush on the volcano's rim, and with one snap of its jaws took the Wing Commander's leg off.

Fletcher, lying on his back, in the agony of his death throes, watched as the lizard crunched its massive jaws around his erstwhile leg. He looked in horror at the great lizard and saw in it an atavistic God, in lizard form, that he had somehow summoned up from beyond time itself.

It seemed at that moment that man would forever be devoured by the system, irrespective of the Gods he worshipped.

III

When Campbell arrived on the beach, with Duckett stumbling after him, Styles could see that he was in an absolute rage. He guiltily pushed Helen behind him as the Flight Lieutenant approached, and waited for an onslaught on his integrity. He needn't have worried.

'We have a mutiny on our hands, sir,' Campbell began. 'A full-scale mutiny, led by that Instrument Fitter, O'Connell! Actually, I don't know whether Leacock put him up to it, but he and Cusack and Varley have refused to follow orders, have been grossly insubordinate, and I have informed O'Connell that he is under arrest pending Squadron Leader's Report.'

'Where are they now, Flight Lieutenant?'

'Up at the new shelter, sir! It's a couple of hundred yards along the cliff and back towards the forest. I ordered Varley and Cusack, and this one here, Duckett, to arrest O'Connell and deliver him here to you, on the beach, and the other two refused. Duckett here could not, of course, force the issue on his own, but he has stuck with us, sir. He is not subject to any charge.'

Styles led Campbell away from the others, and away from the Warrant Officer who was just waking up in the moonlight. They walked along the beach in the dark, while Campbell delivered his complaint in full. After walking along the beach and back, and thrashing out some strategy, they called Corporal Johnson over.

'We have a situation on our hands, Corporal. A mutiny! It could be serious, very serious indeed. The Sergeant is obviously leading these others astray, and provoking them into a mutinous situation. I don't need to tell you that with the possession of three complete SLR's and most of the ammunition they have us at a disadvantage. The way things are progressing, it looks very much as if they intend to murder us one fine night, and dispose of the evidence. I think they know more about the accidents that occurred in flight than they're letting on.'

Johnson looked uncomfortable, and shuffled his feet. The movement wasn't lost on the Squadron Leader.

'Do you know anything that you should have told us, Corporal? If so, now is the time to do it if you wish to avoid future unpleasantness.'

'This is your last chance, Corporal,' Campbell remarked. 'If this mutiny goes any further, you may well be implicated.'

'All right,' said Johnson. 'Okay! I was going to hold my peace until we got back to Australia, then make a statement. But it looks as if events have forced my hand.' He looked along the beach to where Helen, Duckett and the Warrant Officer were watching their every move. 'There's one of your culprits, right there, sir. LAC Duckett. He snapped off the undercarriage nose wheel pin and left half of it in place. He was just trying to get back at you, sir,' he indicated Campbell, 'for going out with his girlfriend. Helen!'

Campbell's mouth dropped in surprise.

'When did you find this out?'

'Last night, sir, when we went off to build the other shelter! Varley said something that I thought was rather suspicious, and I tackled him about it. Then this whole thing about Duckett came out.'

'So there's more,' said Styles. 'You'd better tell us the rest, Corporal.'

'Well, Varley was annoyed with you, sir, after you charged him with insubordination a few weeks ago. He got ten days CB. While he was on that, he substituted a Nitrous Oxide bottle from Dental Section with one of the Oxygen bottles on the Oxy Cart. Then he filled your backup system with nitrous oxide – laughing

- 191 -

gas, sir! Again, I only found out last night. It was because I said I wouldn't lie for them that they turned on me, so I came back to the beach.'

Styles looked at Campbell, and Campbell glowered back. They were both absolutely livid.

'No wonder the Wing Commander's off his head,' said Styles.

'Wait here for us, Johnson. We're going to have to come to some decision about this. Just wait until we get back.'

The two officers walked off down towards the other end of the beach, and Johnson could see in the dim light that they were arguing heatedly between themselves. At one stage Styles stopped, and addressed Campbell as if he was laying down the law, and Campbell snapped to attention and saluted. Not a good sign. They walked back up the beach without saying a word to each other. When they drew abreast with Johnson, Campbell kept going, and Styles stopped, waiting for Campbell to get out of earshot.

'It's like this, Johnson. What you did was a chargeable offence! Withholding information like that... a very serious offence! I've been trying to work out a way in which we can keep you out of it when the rest of them go up for court martial, and it's going to be hard. That's not to say that we don't appreciate you telling us now, even if it is a bit late. But to demonstrate that you're on our side, on the side of the law, that is, we'll need a further demonstration of your good faith. As a result, we've come up with a solution.'

Johnson felt his heart sinking within him. What the hell now!

'Flight Lieutenant Campbell and I have just held an impromptu court session down the beach there, bearing in mind that this island is under Martial Law. Sometimes, due to circumstances, it's necessary to work very quickly to defuse a situation. What we've got is a dangerous situation, and as the prime mover, Sergeant Leacock, is at present beyond our reach, then we have to focus on the ringleader of the mutiny, LAC O'Connell. Remove O'Connell from the equation, and we'll regain control of Varley and Cusack. Then we'll go for Leacock. That's where we're at, in principle anyway.' He looked to Johnson for any sign of acquiescence. Johnson nodded.

'Yes, I understand that, sir.'

'Good! Well, sometimes hard decisions have to be made, Johnson, and the value of a serviceman is often measured by his ability to make those hard decisions in the field.'

Johnson nodded again. What was he getting at?

'We've decided to offer you the opportunity to redeem yourself, Johnson. There may even be a letter of commendation in it for you, and possibly a commission when we get back to Australia. It's a long shot, but we think it will work.'

Johnson looked at him with a mixture of relief and surprise. Maybe things would work out all right after all.

Chapter Twenty

When Styles returned to the shelter, he found Campbell and Helen standing together, engaged in deep conversation. She was shaking her head repeatedly, and once she indicated the Squadron Leader with a sudden glance, which had the effect of Campbell taking a step back, and staring at her incredulously. Then he looked at Styles approaching, and without a word, turned on his heel and walked off towards the cutting. Within minutes he had ascended to the clifftop and had disappeared.

Styles walked up to her, and reached out, seizing her by the arm.

'What was all that about, Helen?'

'He wanted me to go off with him for a walk… to the woods. I said that I couldn't, that I had to stick around here with you. I don't think he's too happy.'

'He'll get used to it,' said the Squadron Leader, thrusting his chin out as if in defiance of social mores.

'What's that, sir,' said Danny, from the darkness of the shelter. He was feeling extremely uncomfortable with this competition over a woman. It wasn't within his range of experience. He'd never been married, never so much as gone out with a woman since before joining the air force in 1944. He'd been 29 when he joined, so was already a confirmed bachelor even then. Styles turned to him, having almost forgotten his presence.

'Nothing to worry you, Warrant. It's just that Campbell has been a little too familiar with Airwoman Currier here. She has made it known to him that his intentions are not welcome, and he's gone off in a bit of a huff. He'll survive!'

Danny stood in the shelter opening, and looked up at the

moon.

'If you don't mind, I think I'll go and have a look for the ground crew, sir! I need to stretch my legs anyway.'

'I'd rather you didn't at the moment, Warrant Officer. We have a bit of a situation going on at the moment that is currently being resolved. Plenty of time later! If you want to stretch your legs, there's plenty of beach.'

Danny knew when he was being warned off. As a Warrant Officer, he didn't necessarily have to blindly accept orders from Officers, especially when they were so vaguely worded.

'Nevertheless, Squadron Leader, I think I'll go and have a word anyway.'

'I'd rather you didn't,' said Styles, warningly.

'That's your prerogative, sir. Nevertheless, I think I will go anyway.'

Styles stared after him with barely concealed hostility. No one knew better than he how untouchable Warrant Officers were. The old saying was that a Pilot Officer was the shit of the Kings, whereas a Warrant Officer was the King of the shits! Danny Seaman was certainly King of the shits!

As he ascended slowly, along the cutting, Danny saw Johnson disappearing up along the track ahead of him, going in the same direction. He hurried his pace, curious as to what was going on in the lower ranks that Styles didn't want him to see.

Johnson approached the shelter, and found O'Connell, Cusack and Varley sitting around, discussing their situation in the gloom. He stopped fifteen yards away, and stood to attention.

'I've been asked to come up here and deliver a message,' he began.

'Oh, this should be good,' said O'Connell, standing up and facing him. 'I suppose it's for me?'

'You could say that! LAC O'Connell, you have been found,

by a military court convened under Martial Law, guilty of the crime of Mutiny. I have been asked to deliver the judgement of the court...'

Bill looked at the other two, still seated, and grinned.

'...and the punishment!' Johnson drew the .38 revolver out of his pocket, took aim, and before anyone could move, put a bullet through O'Connell's forehead.

Cusack and Varley thrust themselves backwards and away as O'Connell dropped to the ground, his legs jerking in a constant rhythm. Suddenly he let out a high-pitched scream, like the whistle on a kettle.

'Oh God, fucking hell,' yelled Varley. 'You've killed him!'

'You fucking bastard Johnson! What the f.fuck did you do that for,' said Cusack, suddenly sobbing in shock.

The whistling sound didn't stop. Obviously O'Connell wasn't dead, and he was in pain.

'For chrisesake finish him off, you bastard. He's in pain. Finish it you prick!'

'I only had one bullet,' said Johnson, shaking now, and as white as a sheet. 'Styles only let me have one bullet.' He turned and ran back the way he'd come, leaving O'Connell still screaming and twitching on the ground. Varley looked at Cusack, and Cusack panicked.

'For fuck's sake, put him out of his misery, Varley,' sobbed Cusack, holding his ears. The sound was piercing.

John Varley picked up a large rock, and dashed it down on O'Connell's skull. It stopped the noise, but he had to do it again before he could be sure that O'Connell was truly dead.

'Oh, mate! Oh, my old mate,' said Varley, bursting into tears. 'Those murdering bastards! Oh, fuck me!'

'What the hell's going on here,' yelled Danny Seaman, as he came running through the undergrowth. No one had ever seen

Danny run before, but he'd heard the shot and the commotion, and Johnson had dashed past him white-faced, going in the other direction.

'They've fucking killed him, they've fucking killed him, sir!' yelled Varley, twisting on the spot in mental agony, and putting his hands over his head as if he could blot out what he'd just seen. Cusack lay on the ground, curled up into a ball. He just sobbed.

'Who ordered this? I don't believe it.' Danny knelt by O'Connell's body and checked, automatically for a pulse. But there was so much blood, and he was under no illusions.

'That fucking Squadron Leader! He put Johnson up to it. Johnson said they'd held a court, and found O'Connell guilty of mutiny. Then he just shot him – no warning or anything - just bang!'

'Calm down men, calm down! We've got to stop and think! He's gone right off his head. He won't stop now.'

'I'll stop the bastard!' The voice came from the trees. Peter Leacock stood there, covered in sweat, and carrying a kit bag over his shoulder. He dropped the bag and walked over to look at the body of O'Connell.

'What in God's name happened here? No, don't tell me! Styles! The man's a bloody psychotic, Warrant! You should have listened to me.'

'Are those the SLR's,' said Danny, grimly.

'Yes! I've got three complete and the bolt from the fourth. Where's the fourth?'

'Styles is holding it in the shelter down there. He hasn't given up on the idea of getting the bolt back, yet. He's also got about eight bullets, not counting the .38 bullets he got from Morris.'

Leacock turned to the Warrant Officer.

'Do you think you could get hold of it, sir, and get it back to us?'

'I could have a try, Sergeant. But I don't know whether I should. What have you been doing the past couple of days?'

'I've been lying low, hoping that things might calm down. But I've thought all along that Styles was affected by that gas – now I know it! I think he's lost the ability to make rational decisions.'

'I sometimes wonder about you, too, Sergeant. Especially after that punch-up on the beach.'

'I've always been a bit of a hothead Warrant. You know that! I let the situation get the better of me, not without reason though. By my reckoning, the officers are still responsible for this disaster. I put it down to incredible folly on the part of the Wing Commander, programming a Navex in the middle of the night, over the greatest ocean on the planet, with an inexperienced navigator and another not even given the base coordinates. Then that stupidity about radio silence... I mean, what genius thought that one up?'

'You can't overlook what Varley and Duckett did though, can you Sergeant?'

Leacock looked at him in surprise.

'You know about that!'

'It's amazing what you can overhear on a clear night, when everyone thinks you're asleep, Sergeant.'

Leacock nodded, grimly.

'Well, all that aside. I've got news for you boys, and it's not good! Last night I was attacked by a Komodo Dragon. It was about ten feet long, and must have weighed 250 pounds. It damn near got me as well. I put about nine bullets into it before I was satisfied it was dead.'

'What the fuck's a Komodo Dragon,' said Varley.

'It's a bit like a prehistoric leftover,' said Danny. 'Usually they're only found on the island of Komodo in Indonesia. But they're very fast when they attack, and their claws will tear you apart. Still, that's strange, Sergeant,' Danny mused. 'From what I've read they only attack during the day, They're a cold-blooded creature, basically a lizard. The normally wait until they've warmed up in the morning before they attack. They're sluggish when they're cold.'

'Well this one bloody wasn't,' said Leacock. 'It scared the bejesus out of me. Mind you, I was up inside the crater of the volcano, so maybe it was getting its body heat from that. Which reminds me – where's the Wing Commander?'

'He went off on his own yesterday, and no one's seen him since. If what you say is correct, and that was a Komodo Dragon, then I wouldn't give you much for his chances,' said Danny.

They all stared at each other as they tried to come to terms with yet another horror in the background of their lives. O'Connell stared directly up at the heavens, and took no part in their conversation. It was as if he had suddenly packed a bag, jumped out of his body and caught a fast train to oblivion.

'I can't believe we've lost O'Connell,' said Varley, looking down at him.

'Well there's nothing you can do now. We're going to have to disarm Styles and, somehow, neutralize him so he can't cause any more trouble. But that leaves Campbell. Do you think he'll side with Styles over this execution?'

'If he does, then he's got to be off his trolley too,' said the Warrant Officer. 'Having said which, I wonder what he's going to do about Duckett, now he knows the truth.'

'He'll probably make a case for shooting him, too.'

Leacock looked at the long shadows, wondering how many of those dragons were on the island.

'Well at least we know why there are no large wild animals roaming around. The dragons have wiped everything out. An island this size couldn't support more that two or three of those things. They'd run out of food.'

At that moment the volcano began to rumble, and there was a definite tremor running through the ground for at least twenty seconds.

'Maybe we won't have to worry about Styles. If that volcano goes up, we're all dead meat,' said the Sergeant. 'Anyway, let's find somewhere else to sleep for the night, otherwise Styles or Johnson may creep up here later on and take the rest of us out.'

The Warrant Officer nodded his agreement.

'I think I'll just go on back down and blend into the background, keep an eye on things. I'm still considered one of the group down there, so I'll keep an eye on them. If I get the chance I'll sneak that rifle out of there and put it on the left hand side of the cutting, halfway up. If one of you gets up early, just come down and have a look for it.'

They nodded and went their separate ways, Danny back towards the beach, and the others along the escarpment to the west.

II

Campbell walked off in disgust once he realized that in his absence, Helen's favours had been annexed by his superior. The fact that Styles was married would have been enough to create a scandal back home, but here, who was there to disapprove? Only the Wing Commander, and he was off in mental whizz-bang country. He sat down at the top of the cliff and stared out across the waters of the pacific. It would all be incredibly beautiful under other circumstances, but who could think of that? There had been no sign of search aircraft, and in reality, even if they had a radio, they didn't know where they were. The only two officers who might have been able to work out an approximate position, McLeish and Gray, were both dead.

Styles was right in a way. It was certainly strange how the officers seemed to be the major casualties every time there was an accident. Bishop's death had been very suspicious. There again, O'Connell thought he was doing the right thing, no doubt, by turning on the oxygen. He couldn't have known about the nitrous oxide at that point.

His mind went back over the conversation he'd held with Styles on the beach. He was all for holding a court then and there, and making an example of Duckett and O'Connell. When he'd asked what the Squadron Leader meant by 'making an example', he'd made it plain that he was thinking along the lines of an execution.

Campbell was horrified.

'I think that's going way over the mark, sir! I mean, I know they've been insubordinate, even mutinous. But we can't just go around executing people. Can you imagine how news like that would go down in Australia?'

'Who said anyone would be hearing about it in Australia, Flight Lieutenant? We could just put a lid on it.'

'And how do you do that, sir, without killing everyone on the island?'

Styles pursed his lips.

'I don't like your tone, Flight Lieutenant. It's that sort of indecision that will get us murdered in our sleep. But if it makes you feel any better, I'll try to keep us out of it. I'll use Johnson to act as the go-between. He can be the messenger boy. That way the problem is confined to the lower ranks, and we can distance ourselves from it.'

'I think that would be better, sir!'

Campbell snapped to attention and saluted. There was really nothing more to be said. Let Johnson sort it out.

Campbell sat for some time gazing out to sea, and was only brought back from his reverie by the sound of a shot. He jumped to his feet, his heart in his mouth. It must be that Sergeant Leacock – probably bagging some game. He began to breathe easier again, then turned and walked slowly back the way he had come.

Chapter Twenty-one

When Johnson had arrived back on the beach, out of breath from running and pale and white from the enormity of his action, Styles stood in the opening of the shelter, waiting for him to report.

'It's done, sir. He's dead! I shot O'Connell.'

'Give me the gun, Corporal.' Styles held his hand out and took the gun from Johnson's nerveless fingers. He said nothing, but began to put bullets into the chambers, then pushed the .38 back in his belt.

Johnson sat down on the sand, shaking.

'It was terrible, sir! He went down and started screaming. It was like no sound I've ever heard before. It was piercing.'

'No doubt you had your reasons,' mused the Squadron Leader. 'I'm sure that will all be taken into account when we get back to Australia.'

Johnson looked up at him, puzzled.

'What do you mean… I had my reasons? I was carrying out orders, sir. Your orders!'

'Oh, I hardly think so, Corporal. I merely asked you to pass on the decision of the court. The idea was for you to use the gun to deliver LAC O'Connell to me, under arrest. I thought you understood that.'

'Why you fucking bastard,' yelled Johnson, leaping to his feet. 'You ordered me! You specifically told me to shoot O'Connell.'

Styles backed away from him, and drew the gun out of his belt.

'I would advise you to keep your distance, Corporal. You're raving! Of course I didn't give you such an instruction. You obviously misinterpreted what I said. But that's all right,' he went on, trying to cool Johnson down. 'Both Flight Lieutenant Campbell and I will both go to bat for you. The situation here was incredibly dangerous... still is, if it comes to that. As long as Sergeant Leacock is on the loose, with three rifles, none of us are safe.'

'I don't fucking believe this,' said Johnson. 'You set me up! You told me that I would get a commission, a commendation for taking the hard decisions.'

'Pull yourself together, Corporal. You're not helping your cause by going on this way. You acted in the only way open to you when threatened by O'Connell, Cusack and Varley. We realize this, and at the worst, it will come down to self-defence.'

'No... you gave me a specific order, sir. You ordered me to shoot O'Connell! I shot O'Connell. There are two witnesses, Cusack and Varley!'

'Witnesses to the shooting, Johnson! There are no witnesses to our conversation.'

Johnson suddenly saw red, and made a lunge for the Squadron Leader. He managed to get his hands around the officer's throat, and the two men tumbled to the ground. Then the gun went off, and Johnson suddenly went slack. Styles pushed him off and scrambled to his feet as Duckett came running up from the beach. There was blood trickling out of the side of Johnson's mouth, and his eyes had glazed over. Duckett knelt down beside him, and saw where the bullet had gone through Johnson's chest. He was dead.

'You saw that, Duckett. You're a witness! He attacked me, tried to kill me. Luckily I managed to get the gun off him, and as we struggled it went off. He must have gone mad, LAC. He just told me that he'd shot O'Connell. This is terrible,' he said, his hands shaking.

Helen Currier had watched the events unfolding from the safety of the shelter, and now ran terrified up towards the cutting in the darkness. She knew she had to get away from this maniac. She thought that if she didn't get away now, she might be next. On the way up she ran straight into the arms of Eddie Campbell, who was coming the other way. He's just heard the second shot, and was wondering what on earth was going on.

'We've got to get out of here, Eddie. He's mad! He's just shot that Corporal. And one of the other airmen has been shot, on his orders. He got Johnson to do it, and then denied ordering it. Now Johnson's dead. I'm scared!'

Campbell took her by the arm and they went back up the way he'd come. At the top they ran into Leacock, Cusack and Varley, heading west. They were each armed with a rifle.

'For God's sake Sergeant, stop! We've got a maniac on our hands. Styles has just shot Johnson.'

'And Johnson has just shot O'Connell,' growled the Sergeant. 'It was on your Squadron Leader's orders. Now do you see sense? This isn't going to stop until everyone's dead.'

He turned to Varley and Cusack, and told them to go on ahead.

'Go and find a spot on top of the cliffs that's fairly open. That way we'll be able to see them coming. I'll follow in a while.'

The two fitters scowled at Campbell, but turned and wandered off with their rifles at the ready.

Campbell ignored them, and approached Leacock.

'I don't know how many bullets he's got left. I don't think you've got any choice, Sergeant. If we can't disarm him, we're going to have to kill him.'

'I've already come to that conclusion myself, sir. But I've never killed anyone in my life, and I don't really want to start now.'

'Well it's going to come down to him or us, Sergeant. What do you suggest we do?'

'I suggest we keep out of sight until the morning, then go and hunt up the Wing Commander. If we can get any sense out of him, he might be able to convince Styles to give up the gun. That way we can avoid any more casualties.'

'What if the Wing Commander's dead?'

'In that case, sir, it's going to be up to you. He trusts you, and you're probably the only one that can get near him now without getting shot at. He's in too deep now... he'll be getting desperate.' Leacock thought for a moment, then added, a slight smile on his face, 'then if you get shot, sir, we'll know he's gone completely off the planet, and we'll take him out with an SLR.'

'Oh, gee! Thanks Sergeant. That's a comforting thought!'

'There's one other thing you should know, sir. I was attacked by a Komodo Dragon last night, a monster. Ten feet long, and must have weighed 250 pounds. Luckily I had the rifle up and at the ready, or I'd have been dead meat right now.'

'What the blazes...'

Leacock explained what a Komodo Dragon was, and Helen began to whimper in horror.

'Oh god! Oh god! There could be one out here now! Nowhere's safe on this island!'

'Not as long as the precious Squadron Leader's around,' said the Sergeant.

A shot rang out, and Leacock started in surprise. Then a stream of blood shot out from a vein in his forehead, and he slowly toppled over and fell on his face. Helen screamed, and Eddie grabbed hold of her and pulled her down with him to the ground.

'Well this is cozy,' said Styles. He'd caught sight of Helen as she took off, followed her up the path and had been able to sneak up on them unobserved. 'Where did you think you were going, Helen? Not off with the good Flight Lieutenant? Do you recall what you promised me there on the beach?'

'Leave me alone, you murderer!,' Helen screamed at him. 'You're a murderer! You're not an officer, and you're not a gentleman,' she cried.

'Did you hear that, Campbell. The little shrew! She's not worthy of you, she's just a common little slut, aren't you Helen?'

Campbell scrambled to his feet, and looked down at Leacock.

'That wasn't necessary, Styles. You've really done it this time! That's three men you've killed in less than an hour.'

'Don't you dare to lecture me, Flight Lieutenant. Just remember your rank, and call me 'Sir' when you address me!'

'Oh, give over you jerk! Don't you think it's time we stopped playing this pathetic little game. This isn't the Air Force now, this is survival! You can't survive on your own, you're not equipped for it. You can't fish, catch game, cook! You're basically useless, Sir!'

Styles levelled the gun, and pointed it at Campbell's head.

'How dare you address a senior officer in that tone, Campbell.'

'Put it away, Styles,' Campbell sneered. 'In about two minutes you're going to have two SLR's pointed at your head, and I don't think they'll have any qualms about shooting a Squadron Leader – Sir!'

'In that case, Helen...' he reached out his hand. 'You're coming with me!'

Helen looked up at Campbell in a mute appeal, but Campbell was helpless to intervene. Styles stooped and wrested the SLR from Leacock's dead grasp, seized Helen by the arm and backed away with her. Then they turned and he began to run, dragging

Helen with him, towards the forest.

II

Danny Seaman had made his way back towards the cutting, intending to go back to the beach and discover what was going on in the Squadron Leader's mind. It was very dark in places, and as he got to the top of the cutting he stumbled over a rock, and fell heavily.

There was a sudden sharp pain in his ankle, and when he went to get back up, he realized his ankle was broken. Danny sat there, cursing in the darkness.

He called out a couple of times, hoping that Leacock and the others were still within earshot, but there was no reply. He was still sitting there when he heard a shot from the beach, and his skin began to crawl. Backing up to a rock, he tried to make himself inconspicuous, and sat quietly, straining his ears in the darkness to see if he could make out what was going on. He couldn't see the beach from where he sat, but he could see to the other side of the cutting, and when Campbell went walking swiftly down the other side, he was tempted to call out. For some reason, he didn't! Seeing O'Connell lying shot had affected him far more deeply than he would admit, and although he had always been testy with his troops, and annoying in the extreme, that didn't mean that Warrant Officer Seaman had no heart. He was just tired and old, and if the truth were known, just waiting for his discharge and pension so he could work out what he was going to do with the rest of his life.

Now he sat in silence, wondering if he was going to get off this island after all. He watched from a distance as Helen came rushing up the other side, turning Campbell around and disappearing with him over the cliffs to the west. Then later he saw Styles, gun in hand, moving purposefully up and along that path, something grim and determined about the way he carried himself. Minutes later he heard another shot. It was a nightmare!

There was no way he was going to appeal to Styles for help after that. He assessed his situation. If he could sit it out overnight, he might be able to get hold of some palm fronds and bind up his ankle. Then if he could work up a crutch out of some fallen wood, he could go in search of the others.

Luckily, it was a balmy night. The air was warm and fluid, and he managed to slumber against the rock. He woke on two occasions after an attempt to move his position had caused his ankle to react with a sharp pang, but soon fell asleep again, and it was after eight o'clock before he finally woke up.

It was a beautiful morning, the sun was well up in the sky and there was a steady breeze blowing over the top of the escarpment. The long grass waved in the breeze, and Danny looked around to see how far he would have to crawl to find a palm tree. Then he froze.

Not fifty yards away was a long, grey shape, sunning itself on a stretch of patchy ground. At first it looked a little like a crocodile, or so Danny thought. But as it turned its head he could see it was more of a lizard in shape, and an immense lizard at that. Danny held his breath. It had obviously not noticed him yet, and was content to lie in the sun.

For twenty minutes Danny managed to keep silent, though the sweat was running down his face, and his complexion was grey. Then it began to move.

At first it moved slowly, not in his general direction but towards the top of the cutting. It was as if it were curious about what lay beyond. No doubt it may have slithered down to the beach to investigate what pickings were there, but it stopped, turned its head, and fixed one large cold eye on the Warrant

Officer.

There was something primeval about that eye. It was cold and dead, disinterested even. It was only interested in food. It began to turn slowly in his direction, and at this Danny could hold back no more. Forgetting his ankle in his blind terror, he leapt to his feet and started to hobble towards the cutting. If only he could outrun it!

The dragon hesitated a moment, then flung itself in pursuit. Danny had only gone four steps before his ankle gave under him, and he fell, letting out a cry of fear as he did so. The last thing he saw was a pair of huge jaws coming at him, the long serrated teeth dripping with saliva. It took his head off in one grinding bite!

Chapter Twenty-two

When Varley and Cusack came back to find out what had happened to the Sergeant, they stood appalled. Campbell was sitting by the body, shaking his head, his hand over his eyes.

'You fucking did this,' said Varley. 'It was you and your fucking insubordination bullshit that did for O'Connell.'

Campbell put his hand up for peace.

'I can assure you, I had no idea that Styles was going to take matters this far. I would have been happy with a few days extra duties.'

'Aah, b.bullshit,' Cusack sneered. 'We were just j.joking around, and you got in a huff. You f.fucking officers are so full of shit! You make our lives miserable, then expect us to keep your fucking planes in the air. You're l.lucky we don't sabotage the fucking things all the time.'

The Flight Lieutenant shook his head in defeat. He was tired and worn out, and it seemed as if he now had all these deaths on his conscience.

'I can understand how you feel. You've lost one of your mates! I lost a mate too when Peter Dawson died. We went through flying school together. Don't you think that I'm just as cut up as you two?'

'No, we fucking don't,' said Varley. 'Because you've always had things your own way, you fucking officers! You've always had the power! If you got out of bed on the wrong side, you always had someone to sling off at. We were the patsy's, all the time. We'd go out in all weathers, fix the U/S's, do the pre-flights, do the after-flights, do all the 'A' and 'C' servicings, and what did we get? Did you ever, once, say 'well done, fellas, you did a good job there? No, you'd more than likely say, 'that's what you're paid for, do your job!'

Cusack broke in.

'Then if we forgot to s.salute you, we'd be on report. Or if we d.didn't say 'yes sir, no sir, three bags full sir', we'd end up on CB. Do you know what it's f.fucking like being confined to base when you've got a w.wife and kid at home? And the k.kid gets sick and the wife doesn't drive, and she can't get the kid to the hospital, because you've been 'insubordinate'? Well, I can f.fucking tell you... I do! And Morris knew as well.'

Campbell got slowly up to his feet.

'Have you finished your tirade, LAC?' he said, 'I think we've got more important matters to worry about than your list of petty grievances.'

'You talk about petty grievances, and you're standing by the body of a Sergeant with nineteen years service. What did he do to deserve this,' said Varley. 'Oh gee, he called the Squadron Leader a donkey... oh no, an incompetent donkey! Oh dear! How dare he? Just because we had to ditch two planes in the middle of the pacific because we were too fucking stupid to travel with the radio on! Oh! We'll have to shoot him for that. He's so insubordinate!'

'Yeah, yeah!' said Campbell, affecting a wry smile. 'I take the point! Of course, it doesn't help if you've got some traitorous little shit filling up the oxy with nitrous oxide, does it, Varley?'

'It serves you fuckers right! You're lucky that it doesn't happen more often,' Varley spat back at him. 'You pricks seem to forget that when we joined the air force, it was with the idea that we'd make it a career too – just the same as you. But you treat us like peasants, so in the end, that's what you get. Treat people badly enough, and in the end they'll go for your throat! Now you can fucking move!'

Varley motioned with his rifle towards the cliffs, less than fifty yards away.

'What are you going to do?'

'Just fucking do it,' said Cusack, motioning with his rifle also.

Campbell put his hands in the air and started walking.

'This isn't going to solve your problems,' said Campbell. 'Anyway, you should be thinking about how you can save your female compatriot. Styles has got her, and will probably do her some harm.'

Cusack began to chortle.

'Our female compatriot,' he laughed. Varley grinned in reply.

'You mean the officers plaything? The stuck-up bitch from the Orderly Room? It's not us that's been fucking her... Sir! She's the town bike for you lot, you've all had a go haven't you? We don't care if Styles fucks her silly, then blows her head off, do we Cusack?'

'Either that, or we'll g.get Styles first, then she'll find she has to p.put out for the l.lower ranks,' said Cusack. 'Either way, we d.don't give a shit about that bitch!'

'You really are the lowest of the low, aren't you,' said Campbell in disgust.

'Just what you've made us – Sir!' said Varley.

They'd come to the top of the cliff at this stage, and Varley prodded Campbell to the edge. Campbell looked down. It was a hell of a long way to those rocks down there.

'Now what,' said the Flight Lieutenant, blanching.

'Jump!' said Cusack. 'Once you've g.gone, we've only got that other m.maniac to worry about.'

'You realise that when the rescue team gets here, you'll probably end up in jail for the rest of your lives.'

'Why,' said Varley, innocently? 'We haven't killed anyone. It's you lot that have killed people. You killed them in the crash, and now you, personally, have been responsible for O'Connell,

Johnson, and now Sergeant Leacock. We're just protecting ourselves against a couple of murdering officers.'

'There's n.not even any honour amongst you lot, is there?' said Cusack. 'You never even bothered to go in s.search of the Wing Commander, even though you knew his head was affected. Neither you n.nor Styles! You just let him wander off! He's p.probably dead by now.'

'He should never have been in charge of this trip,' said Campbell, angrily. 'Styles should have been the overall commander.'

'Well, that's your officer system for you! Sorry to have to curtail this conversation, but bye bye!'

Varley prodded Campbell in the back with his rifle, and Campbell momentarily lost balance.

'This is murder... don't do this,' said Campbell in desperation.

He was just recovering himself when Cusack gave him another prod, and the Flight Lieutenant toppled off the cliff, those black cliffs that they'd first seen by moonlight in what seemed to be an age ago.

II

When Styles took off after Helen with the gun, Duckett was left alone on the beach, wondering what the end of this was going to be. His initial instinct was to follow, but then he changed his mind.

When he heard the shot that indicated the demise of Sergeant Leacock, he began to panic. Johnson was dead, and Duckett had heard him tell the Squadron Leader that he'd shot O'Connell. Now someone else could be dead, and it only seemed a question of time before Varley would put him in for fixing the nose wheel of 292.

He decided that the best policy for him would be to get the hell out, and to this end he grabbed his kit bag, emptied a lot of the extraneous items out, and packed it with leftovers of the food that was lying about. He also grabbed the SLR from the rear of the shelter, just in case he could manage to re-unite it with its bolt, and use it for self-defence. Then he went down the beach to the lower end, picked a hidden space between the rocks and settled down for the night. He knew he'd have to be up early, to avoid running into Styles, so thought it best if he started off fresh in the morning. It didn't turn out that way.

By the time he woke up it was about eleven o'clock. The sun was high in the sky, and it was only when the shadow of the cliff moved off his face that he was woken by the glare of the sun. Looking cautiously out, he tried to detect if there was any movement up the other end of the beach. It looked deserted.

He was too far away from the shelter to tell if anyone was inside, but there was certainly no sign of anyone on the beach, and he gazed out across the sea. It was then that a bobbing shape came to his eye, and as he focussed he realized that there was a body, floating out in the bay, about fifty yards off shore.

He watched it for some time. It was drifting, but only very slowly. The sea was as calm as a millpond, so the body lay motionless in the sunshine. After a while, he deemed it clear enough to show himself, and decided to wade out and discover who it was. By the time he was ten yards away, he could see the two bars on the shoulders of the flying suit, and he knew then that it could only be Flight Lieutenant Campbell.

Campbell was floating face down in the water. How long he'd been there it was impossible to tell. Duckett dragged the body in to shore, laid it on the rocks and turned it over. There was no sign of any bullet wounds, though the skull was fairly well smashed in, and not at all pretty to look at. Duckett felt his heart sink within him. Styles was on his own!

While Campbell had been alive, Duckett thought that he at least was a moderating voice of reason. With Campbell gone, there was no telling what that madman would do. He gathered up his things and made his way along the beach, leaving Campbell to the mercy of the rock crabs. His one thought now was to find Helen.

With Campbell gone, he felt he might now have a show of patching things up with her. She had been such an obsession for so long that he could forgive all her pecadillos as long as she welcomed him back into her arms.

He struggled up the slope along the right hand side of the cutting, and had only gone a few yards along the top when he saw what looked like some blood-soaked rags by a rock. It was the remains of Danny Seaman's flying suit, with his Warrant Officer insignia at the shoulder. There was half a torso and one leg still intact; the rest had gone.

Gordon promptly turned away and threw up. He could feel the cold sweat on his brow as he wondered what on earth had mangled that body so totally. It took some minutes for him to recover, but then he stumbled away, heading for the forest and 292. He had an idea that he could use it as his base, and from there spread out and search the surrounding island for Helen and the others.

It took him almost an hour and a half to get there, twisting and turning through the trees, trying to find the crash site. When he did, he realized by the sounds coming from the clearing, that he was not alone. Styles had Helen tied to an engine cowling, bent over, with her skirt raised at the back. He was busily raping her as she sobbed and cried, but this only seemed to give him greater satisfaction.

'Come on, Helen, my Helen of Troy… Slut! Scream louder,' he yelled. 'No one can hear you! There isn't anybody left to hear you, Helen.'

'Why are you being so nasty to me, I didn't do anything,' she sobbed.

'You tried to run away, Helen. I couldn't have that. You're the only woman on the island, and when there's only one, she goes to the senior ranking officer. You're now the Duty Slut, Helen.'

Styles laughed, an unusual laugh. Duckett had never heard Styles laugh before, and there was something of the hysterical in its tone.

'Tell me you're my slut, Helen. I want to hear you say it.'

Helen continued to sob, and Styles grabbed her by the hair and wrenched her head back, painfully.

'All right, all right! I'm your slut!'

'I'm your slut, Sir!' he yelled.

'Yes… I'm your slut… Sir!' she replied, as he thrust into her and finally climaxed.

He left her tied to the cowling while he recovered himself, and sat looking at her, revealed, for all to see.

'You're very pornographic in that pose, Helen. I think I'll just leave you there like that, so I can take my pleasure whenever I like.'

'These cords are cutting my wrists,' she cried. 'This position is very painful.'

'But how do I know you won't try to run away again,' he said.

'I won't, I promise! I was just upset about what happened to that Corporal.'

'I thought you didn't care about the lower ranks, Helen?'

'I don't,' she replied. 'I hate them! Please let me down.'

'Not until I'm sure,' he said. He went over to her and ran his hand up the inside of her leg.

'What about that LAC you lived with? What about him? You must have loved him.'

'I didn't, I hated him. He said he was going to be an officer... He lied to me.'

'So you'll only open your legs for officers now, Helen,' he said.

'That's right! Only Flying Officers and above.'

'That's setting your sights rather low, isn't it?'

'I've told you I'm yours whenever you want me... isn't that enough?'

'Nothing is ever enough, my sweet slut, except total faithfulness. You must never so much as look at anyone else.'

'I won't, I really won't. Now will you let me down.'

Gordon Duckett turned away, and slunk off through the trees. He wasn't going to risk getting shot for someone who hated him.

Chapter Twenty Three

After Campbell had fallen from the cliff, Varley and Cusack took off in a western direction. They walked quickly, and in silence, each with their own thoughts. They didn't stray too far from the cliff's edge, as they believed that it was safer out in the open. These Dragons usually liked to stay under cover. If one came for them in the night, they would have a better chance if they could see for a reasonable distance.

'We'll never be free again, you know that, don't you,' said Varley. 'The bastards will get us! It won't matter to them what we say, the whole thing will be dumped onto us.'

'But we didn't d.do anything, only Campbell, and he asked for it. If it hadn't b.been for him mouthing off to the Squadron leader, O'Connell would s.still be alive.'

'They don't listen to the troops,' Varley sneered. 'They always support the officers, even if they're raving mad. We're just shit to them.'

They continued walking for a while.

'Well, we'd better get our s.story straight, before this rescue team turns up. We can say that one of those d.dragons rushed out at Campbell, and he fell over the cliff. Who can p.prove any different?'

'What about the nitrous oxide in the tanks?'

'Well, they're n.not going to kn.know about that. We just won't m.mention it.'

Varley stopped, a look of exasperation on his face.

'Styles fucking knows, you Dodo! ... I think the Wing Commander knows, wherever he may be! And fucking Duckett knows!'

'Now there's a problem,' said Cusack. 'Duckett! He was

quick to d.d.desert the sinking ship, wasn't he? He wouldn't think twice about p.putting you in. We'll just have to get rid of him, that's all.'

'And Styles, and that bitch Helen,' said Varley. 'Let's face it, there's only two people that we can allow to survive on this island, and that's you and me.'

'What about the W.Warrant Officer? We can't just g.go knocking old Danny off. I know he's a prick, but he's been surprisingly s.supportive since we've been here.'

'No, we can't! That means we're stuffed anyway. So there's no point in bumping Helen off. If we can get rid of Styles and Duckett, they're the biggest problems. If we don't get Styles first, he'll certainly get us. How many rounds do you think he's got left?'

'I d.don't know – try and work it out. Morris had eighteen rounds to s.start with, then he f.fired off how many in the plane – four? – f.five? You should know, you were there!'

'I was too busy keeping my head down to count,' said Varley. 'But I'd say about five. Then O'Connell shot the shark. That's six. Then Styles got hold of it, and he gave it to Johnson with one round in the chamber for O'Connell. That's seven. Then Johnson bought it, eight, and finally the Sarge, nine. So he's got nine left.'

'He only needs one for each of us,' said Cusack. 'We have to g.get him first!'

Varley thought for a moment.

'Here, what are we talking about? He's got Leacock's SLR. God knows how many bullets are in that clip.'

'Oh, shit, I'd f.forgotten about that! In that case we're going to have to hunt him d.down first.'

'We certainly don't seem to have any choice in the matter,' said Varley. 'First thing in the morning we'll head for the volcano. We might be able to spot them from up there. It's the highest point on the island.'

They took it in turns to watch out for dragons, and slept fitfully overnight. They were off and moving by eight o'clock, and by the time they scaled the volcano, and climbed up on the rim, it was after midday.

'I'm b.bloody stuffed,' said Cusack, sitting down.

'Don't get too comfortable. There's something over there I want to check out.'

Varley led off, and they made their way around the rim of the volcano, heading west. About three hundred yards further on, they came to a pile of what looked like rags, bloodstained and torn. Nearby there lay a hand, with a watch still on the wrist.

'The Wing Commander,' said Varley. 'Oh God, what a mess. He must have come up here that second day. A bloody dragon got him.'

'These d.dragons are more dangerous than S.Styles,' said Cusack, looking rather green. 'Well, that accounts for another of them. So there's only Styles l.left!'

'Yes,' said Varley. 'And if I know Styles, he'll be hiding out in 292. It's the safest place, isn't it, plus you get a bit of shelter from the sun… and rain, when it comes.'

'I'm s.surprised it hasn't rained so far,' said Cusack. 'It's m.monsoon season after all.'

'Give it time, give it time.' Varley was scanning the horizon, looking for any telltale signs of smoke from a fire.

'We m.might as well just go and s.surround 292! Get it over and d.done with. If you go one s.side and I go the other, one of us sh.should be able to get the b.bastard.'

'I think one of us should start a diversion on one side, so that his attention is concentrated in that direction, then the other should be able to sneak up from behind and pick him off. Sound like a good plan?'

'S.Sounds all right to m.me,' said Cusack, and the pair began to descend the rim of the volcano. They were halfway down when they felt it begin to rumble, and the ground shook under their feet.

'Oh God, don't let it erupt,' said Varley, 'not now!'

The rumble gradually died away, and the earth stopped shaking. There was an uneasy silence, and the two fitters half ran and half slid down the remaining slope. Within twenty minutes they were entering the forest.

II

Graham Styles left Helen stretched across the engine cowling while he sat in the rear fuselage and checked the SLR. When he pulled the clip off, he was disappointed to find that there were only two rounds left. The .38 yielded eight bullets, and he carried that in his belt, while arranging the SLR in the opening of the fuselage so it would be close at hand. He was expecting visits from Varley and Cusack, and possibly even Eddie Campbell. He was under no illusions. They would try to kill him!

The only way he was going to survive this island, with Helen attached to him like an umbilical cord, was by disposing of Campbell, Varley and Cusack. He had enough on Duckett, he thought, to use him as a witness to the 'accidental' shooting of Johnson. If there were only two of them left, he was sure that he could cut a deal with Duckett over the nose wheel incident. No one need know!

Helen was exhausted in her hoist position, and still exposed to the world. She was beginning to think that it was all over with her, that she was doomed to be the sex slave of a maniac, who would abuse her constantly until she had become extraneous to his plans, at which time she had no doubt that he would murder her. She had stopped sobbing from pure exhaustion, and lay gazing over the top of the cowling, resting her face on the warm metal.

It was hard to believe that only days ago those twisted, mangled propellers had been slicing through the night sky, twelve thousand feet over the pacific. The aircraft, what was left of it, was like the remains of a giant dinosaur, left to rot in the jungle after letting out its primal scream of death. It was so quiet, so dead.

As she gazed unseeingly into the distance, a movement behind a tree flickered and caught her eye. She tried to focus on the spot, then made out half a face that appeared to be peering out of the bark. It was Cusack. She had seen him before, and thought him a repulsive little man, and here she was with her skirt around her waist, bent over a cowling, and leaving nothing to the imagination. She shivered involuntarily, horrified at her position, and yet unable to do anything about it.

As she watched, he darted from one tree to the next, and she saw he was carrying an SLR. He was obviously hoping to surprise the Squadron Leader, even take him out, but the thought of such an awful little creep seeing her thus displayed overwhelmed any feeling of self-preservation she might have had if the stranger had been, for instance, Eddie Campbell. When he came within twenty feet of her, she screamed.

Styles leapt from the fuselage and looked at her, noting the way she was facing. He leveled the .38 and loosed off four shots in quick succession into the undergrowth, before halting to see if he'd hit anything.

'Where, where,' he yelled.

'Over there!' Helen replied, unable to move or to point except by the direction of her eyes.

Styles crouched in the space between the rear fuselage and the wing, waving the gun from left to right. Varley rose up out of the bushes thirty yards behind him, and placed a bullet straight through the small of his back. Styles went down like a stone, and rolled onto his back. The gun slipped from his fingers, and he lay there, unable to move.

After waiting for a good thirty seconds, just to make sure he didn't move again, Cusack and Varley came in together from different angles. Cusack bent down and picked up the .38, and waved it in the Squadron Leader's face.'

'Game, set and m.match!' he sneered.

Styles stared back up at him, his face perfectly serene.

'Enjoy the moment,' he said, as a thin line of blood trickled from the side of his mouth.. 'They will lock you up, and throw away the key.'

'Don't worry,' said Varley, pushing into his line of vision. 'You won't be around to see it. Campbell's dead, and soon you'll be dead. You've murdered your last fitter!'

He began to walk away, then turned back with an afterthought.

'Oh, and by the way, the Wing Commander's dead, too. It seems he got eaten by a giant lizard! There's a bit of poetic justice for you.' He laughed.

'I'm paralyzed,' said Styles, as if realizing it for the first time. 'You're going to have to help me.'

Cusack began to laugh, and spun around the clearing, choking for breath.

'You d.don't get it, do you. You arrogant prick! We're going to leave you here. One of those big Komodo Dragons should be along shortly to c.clean up the mess. Did you know they can eat eighty percent of their own body weight? True! Sergeant

Leacock told us. They rush you and bite a big ch.chunk off first, so if you're lucky, it'll be your head. Otherwise you'll have to lie here watching yourself being eaten, b.bit by bit.'

'You wouldn't do that. I order you, LAC... I'm your Commanding Officer!'

'Not any more, Styles! We just got ourselves a d.discharge.'

Cusack turned his attention to Helen, now crying again as she realized the hopelessness of her position.

'N.Nice little rump you have, Helen. So g.good of you to put it on display for us.'

He ran his hand up the inside of her leg, and rested it tantalizingly close to her vagina. She screamed.

'Get your hands off me, you disgusting little creep. Let me go!'

'Oh, no! We're n.not going to let you go, Helen, not after all the insults you've given us over the p.past couple of years. What do you reckon, Varley? She's got a great b.backside, hasn't she? Just right for whipping!'

'Take it easy, Cusack,' said Varley, still standing over Styles. 'Female flesh is a rare commodity around here. We'll need it, later.'

'Don't you dare touch her, LAC,' said Styles, from his supine position on the ground.

'Just don't tell us what to do, dead man,' Varley sneered. 'Go for it, Cusack, give her a good whipping. Let her know what she'll get in future if she doesn't do as she's told from now on.'

'Never!' Helen shouted. 'Never! Ever! You repulse me!'

'*And he didn't?*' said Varley angrily, pointing at Styles. He strode over to where she was tied up, and grabbed her by the hair, pulling her head back, painfully. He let her go and stood back as Cusack picked up a strip of aluminium edging from the wreck. He measured it across Helen's bare rump, pulled his arm back and then gave her a stinging swipe with it. She screamed, and began to howl.

'Oh, I l.like that,' said Cusack. 'Have another one.'

He hit her again, then again, and offered the switch to Varley. Varley was reluctant to take it. Helen was screaming and literally fighting for breath.

'Don't you fucking dare, Varley!'

This was a new voice, the voice of Gordon Duckett. He was approaching warily through the trees, having been attracted by the gunshots. He carried an SLR.

'Cut her loose!'

Varley turned towards the voice, SLR in hand, and curled his lip.

'So, the piker finally shows his face. You weak prick! You were going to put me in, weren't you?'

'So what? You were just asking for trouble.'

Varley slid his free hand between Helen's legs.

'Is this your bitch, Duckett? This little slut!'

Cusack had picked up his rifle again, and was covering Duckett, holding him back.

'Yes, she's my woman,' said Duckett. 'Leave her alone.' He raised his own weapon.

Varley ran his hands across Helen's naked buttocks.

'You can put the rifle down, Duckett. There's no bolt in it.'

Duckett looked undecided, then lowered his weapon.

'All right, Duckett! We'll see what Helen has to say. Do you love this prick, Helen? He says he loves you... Do you want him?'

'No...' she cried out. 'How many more times... No! I hate him! Get him away from me.'

Duckett looked distraught.

Cusack raised his rifle.

'Looks like the l.lady doesn't want you, Duckett. And we s.sure don't!'

He aimed at Duckett's chest and pulled the trigger. The force of the bullet threw Duckett backwards, so he was lying almost beside Styles.

'Do you want me to finish him off, Helen?' Varley said, quietly, stroking her leg.

'Do what you like... I don't care what you do,' she sobbed.

Varley walked over and pointed his rifle at Duckett's forehead.

'Sorry, mate. I thought you were a good bloke – once!' Then he fired.

Styles moved his lips as if to say something, but couldn't seem to get it out.

'Animals,' he finally muttered. 'I was right! You are all animals!'

Varley looked down at him, his eyes cold, dead and expressionless. He was silent for a moment, then he muttered one word...

'Dragons!'

Then he walked away and cut Helen free, leaving Cusack to drag her off into the forest by her hair.

Chapter Twenty Four

John Varley stared across the table at the Squadron Leader, and sighed for the third time that day. Parker raised his eyes from his notes, and made a couple of changes with his pen. Then he put it down, very deliberately, and sat back in his chair.

'Nearly over now,' he said. 'It's been a long haul, but I think we're finally getting there. How many sessions has this been now, I've lost count.'

'About twenty-three,' said Varley.

He was looking old and worn, the lines in his face seemed more deeply etched than the first time they'd met. He stirred in his chair as if he was troubled about something.

'Have you heard anything from this expedition they've sent out there? What have they managed to find out?'

Parker looked at him, quizzically.

'I didn't think you were interested. You made it pretty plain right from the beginning that you already knew the facts, and that was enough for you. So you're telling me now that you *are* interested?'

'I might as well be up to date on the greatest event of my life – even if it has come thirty four years too late. How many bodies have they brought back so far?'

'I'm not too sure of that to be quite honest. I haven't been in touch for the last three weeks. I've been too busy on this. But from what I can make out, the skeletons pretty well bear out your story. Of course, the ones who were eaten by the dragons will never be recovered, though they might find fragments of bone here and there, and with DNA matching these days, they can identify anything.'

'They'd better watch out that they don't end up food for the

Komodo's themselves.'

Parker put his pen in his mouth, and bit on the end of it.

'Well, that's the funny thing! There are no dragons on the island, not now, anyway. They've found the skeletal remains of a couple of the big ones, but they must have died out in the meantime. You say that you and Cusack killed a few in the six months you were there alone?'

'Yes… we'd go on hunting expeditions, looking for the big ones. It was only when our ammunition ran out, finally, that we decided to risk it, and salvaged the raft from 286. We had to wait until another dodge tide so we could dive down and get it out, that's why it took us so long. The rafts in 292 were stuffed. We loaded it up with fresh water and as much food as we could, plus warm clothing, and we set off in the May… worst time of the year, as it turned out.'

'You must have hit some pretty heavy seas that time of the year.'

'Yes, it was bloody awful! We were adrift for about 37 days by our calculations, but I don't know whether that's accurate or not. By the time we were picked up, we were both pretty well delerious. Helen died about 20 days out. She was a real mess, and raving. Then one day we woke up and she was dead. We barely had the strength to push her over the side.'

'That must have been a very difficult time for you,' said Parker, sympathetically.

'Yes. The three of us had shared a lot of trials and tribulations all right. We'd had to share everything, the food, the cooking, standing guard against the dragons. We used to take it in turns. What that meant, of course, was that we rarely got a full night's sleep.'

He was quiet for a moment, reliving distant memories.

'Yes,' he went on. 'Helen was a brick all right. We were both very upset when she died.'

Parker took his coat off and hung it on the back of his chair.

'What I want to do today is just go over the main details once more, just to make sure I got it all right. If we do it by rank, it might be easier to follow.'

Varley sat back and smiled, then shook his head.

'You service guys, you can't help yourselves, can you? You've got rank on the brain. That's the one thing I really hated about the Air Force, that whole rank thing. I thought it might have changed by now.'

'Perhaps it has,' said the Squadron Leader. 'I mean, the ranks still exist, but there doesn't seem to be a great deal of friction between officers and other ranks these days. I can't speak for your period, of course. I suppose every generation's different, isn't it?'

'You'll never convince me of that,' said Varley. 'The system itself just invites abuse from those with the power.'

'I think we'll agree to disagree on that one,' Parker smiled. 'Anyway, back to the business in hand. Now the Wing Commander! Let's go over again what happened to him. You said he was taken by one of those Komodo Dragons?'

'Yes, that's right. He was leading an expedition up to the volcano, a food gathering expedition. They were looking for wildlife, and he wanted to see if the volcano was dormant, or still active. There was a bit of a rumble from it the first night. He went on ahead, and the next thing Sergeant Leacock heard him cry out, and went up to find him halfway down this thing's throat. It was very quick!'

'It sounds horrible,' said Parker, chewing his pen. He looked again at his notes.

'And Sergeant Leacock shot that one?'

'Yes, that's right. I think it fell over the ridge and down onto a sort of flat inner ring, where it fell halfway inside this cave. We pulled Fletcher out, what was left of him, and the Squadron Leader decided that we'd bury him at sea, sort of thing. So they took the remains up to the top of the cliff and wrapped him in this rubber sheet, then launched the body over the cliff where the sea meets the bottom of the cliffs. The only problem was it didn't sink. It floated away, and by the next day it had disappeared completely, out at sea somewhere.'

'What day was this?'

'Umm... it would have been about two weeks after we got there, because there was a lot of unpleasantness before that. He charged quite a few of the fitters for minor offences, you know, not saluting, not lining up on time. He was very strict on procedure, and the very fact that we were on this tropical island – Blackrock Island we called it, because of the look of it from the sea. Those tall black cliffs! Anyway, as I said, he was a stickler for procedure, and gave out a lot of extra duties. He wasn't exactly popular.'

'Let's move on to the Squadron Leader, Styles. He was shot, you said!'

'That's right. Jack Morris shot him on the third day. After forcing us to land in the bay, shooting a hole through the screen and shooting out the radio and G2 compass, he made Styles crash land 286 in the water, and was the first to get out. He disappeared into the island, and was loose for five days. In that time he managed to sneak back and shoot Styles – over by the 292 wreck, actually. Styles went over to check if there was anything useful to us on the beach. Morris must have been using it to sleep in, because he was waiting for him. He shot him in the back and left him there. By the time we got over there, a dragon had been munching on him. There wasn't much left.'

Parker ticked off another paragraph.

'These dragons were the very devil, weren't they,' said Parker.

'Well they certainly were before we managed to cull them. The problem was that we were basically unaware of their presence at first, so we were sitting ducks. They hide, you know, then rush out from the bushes at about thirty miles an hour. If they catch you unawares, you've had it.'

'Is that what happened to Campbell?'

'Basically. He was walking along the top of a cliff, when suddenly this thing came at him, and it gave him such a shock that he fell over the cliff. It was about a hundred feet high just there, poor bastard. He didn't have a chance. His body floated around into the bay the next day.'

'What about his co-pilot, Dawson? Oh, that's right, you said he was killed in the crash. 292 wasn't it, the one that put down in the forest. Why was that, do you think?'

Varley shrugged.

'Why did Campbell put it down in the forest? I have no idea. I was only an erk, remember, not privy to the decision making process. Plus the fact that I was in 286, not 292! Cusack might have thrown more light on the matter, but he's dead, of course.'

'Didn't you ever discuss that aspect of it?'

Parker was curious.

'To be honest – No! I don't think he even knew. He was only an M.T. Fitter and Driver, along for the ride.'

'Okay. Next Ron Gray on 292. You said he got thrown out on impact, is that right? Him, and Flight Sergeant Mackintosh.'

'Yes,' said Varley, wearily. 'Them... and Corporal Bailey, LAC Grainger, the Radio Tech., and the Pilot Officer, Jason Mitchell. Of course, he was in 286. He didn't get out fast enough. He drowned, along with McLeish. They both drowned.'

'That just leaves Bishop, the Radio Operator from 286,' said

Parker.

'Yes, well that was different again. He was out by the aircraft on the morning of the dodge tide. O'Connell was just about to dive down to pin the undercarriage so it wouldn't collapse, and Bishop climbed into the nose cone. The nose wheel collapsed, dragging the nose under water, and Bishop couldn't get out. He drowned.'

'Well that's the officers and the crash victims accounted for. What about the Instrument Warrant Officer, your old boss?'

Varley got up to put the kettle on.

'I'm not a hundred percent sure on that one. All I know is that he went for a walk one night, and didn't go back to the shelter. We found what was left of him the next day, another dragon attack.'

'And when was that?'

'Oh, now you're stretching the memory. Probably about a month after we got there.'

'Was he buried?'

'There wasn't enough left to bury, if I remember rightly. Just a mangled piece of flying suit with the Warrant Officer insignia on the shoulder.'

Varley poured the coffee, and asked Parker if he'd join him.

'Tea, thanks! If you've got it! Anti-oxidants, you know!'

Varley shot him a suspicious glance, then fumbled with the tea caddy.

'Now… Johnson and O'Connell! What really happened there? That seems to have been the biggest tragedy of them all.'

'Yes, it certainly was,' said Varley, putting the tea and coffee on the table. 'It was a terrible day, that day. Johnson was on hunting party, and was down in the woods. He saw a bird, a big one he said, that would have been ideal eating. He took a pot-shot at it with Morris's .38, and O'Connell, who was standing about forty yards away through the trees, copped a bullet right through the head. He was killed instantly. Johnson was so upset that, afterwards, he ran off down to the beach, and next thing we knew he'd shot himself – through the heart. It was a terrible day!'

'Tragic!' said Parker. He looked at his notes. 'That takes us down to the Sergeant, Peter Leacock, and the guy who ran amok in 286, Jack Morris.'

'Yes, well that was a bit of a fluke, actually. If I hadn't seen it happen, I wouldn't have believed it myself. After Morris shot the Squadron Leader we went all out to get him. He was off his face most of the time, drugs! Anyway, I was in a party of three with Sergeant Leacock moving along the top of the cliffs, heading west. Suddenly there's this noise behind us, and Leacock spun round and fired. Morris must have fired at the same time, because Leacock got it in the head, and Morris got the back of his head blown off. It was incredible, really.'

'Yes, you wouldn't read about it!' said Parker, musingly.

He passed the pad over to Varley.

'Well, it's all there, just as you have reported it. How would you like to sign along the bottom, just for accuracy's sake.

Varley signed, and flopped back in his seat.

The Squadron Leader began to pack up his paperwork, and then picked up his phone. He dialed a number.

'Just phoning the driver. An old friend! She's going to pick me up today,' he said. 'You don't mind, do you? I'll introduce you.'

'No, no,' said Varley. 'By all means. Bring her in!'

'Thank you! That's very good of you,' said Parker.

Varley remained at the kitchen table when the car arrived, and Parker went to the door.

It was over! Varley leant back and stared at the ceiling.

'Thank god,' he thought. No more questions! Now he could bury the past forever.

Parker re-entered the kitchen bringing a woman in his wake. She was considerably older than the Squadron Leader, more Varley's age, with predominantly grey streaked hair. She was tanned, and her skin was lined and weathered. Varley thought there was something vaguely familiar about her.

Parker ushered her into a seat opposite him, and Varley stared at her with cold, disinterested eyes. She stared at him, and began, haltingly, to speak.

'Long time... Varley! Long, long time!'

Varley looked questioningly at the Squadron leader, who was staring at him now with undisguised hostility.

'I don't believe I've had the pleasure...' he began.

The woman shook her head. She began to laugh, and that laugh sent shivers down Varley's spine.

Then her countenance changed completely.

She glared at him, and then thrust her face across the table.

'My name's Helen... you heartless bastard! Remember me now?

...Helen Currier, from Blackrock Island!'

www.ingramcontent.com/pod-product-compliance
Lightning Source LLC
Chambersburg PA
CBHW070445260626
47161CB00004B/1205